Mickey's Mayhem

An Elder Darrow Mystery

Also by Richard J. Cass:

The Elder Darrow Mysteries:

In Solo Time

Solo Act

Burton's Solo

Last Call at the Esposito

Sweetie Bogan's Sorrow

Short Stories:

Gleam of Bone

Mickey's Mayhem

An Elder Darrow Mystery

Richard J. Cass

Encircle Publications, LLC
Farmington, Maine U.S.A.

Editor: Cynthia Brackett-Vincent
Cover design by Deirdre Wait,
Cover photograph © Getty Images
Author photograph by Philip McCarty

Published by:

Encircle Publications
PO Box 187
Farmington, ME 04938

info@encirclepub.com
http://encirclepub.com

Dedication

For Anne, as always.

For my parents, fading but fierce.

*"Patience is the sister of mystery
and tirelessness the best of roads."*
—Aleksis Rannit

Acknowledgments

For close readings in early stages that made the final product much better, thanks to Anne Cass, Stephen Dorneman, Alice Smith Duncan, and Stephen Lippman.

For general support, encouragement, and connection over the last year plus, the Friday night Sninks and Dracks crowd: Barbara Kelly, Gayle Lynds, John Sheldon, Brenda Buchanan, Diane Kenty, Barbara Ross, and Bill Carito.

Part 1

1

I could not forget that I'd killed someone, even eight months later. Sure, it had been self-defense, but the fierce rage that pushed that knife that last inch into Edward Dare's rib cage had appalled me. I'd bared a vein of atavistic violence that I'd been wrestling with ever since.

"I'm reading you loud and clear," Susan Voisine said. "It's been the better part of a year. You think you can stop beating yourself up?"

The memory was fading, stubbornly, the way winter unwinds itself into spring here in New England. I was counting on that eventually, how the fallibility of memory heals. We remember the good times as richer and more satisfying than they were and do our best to block recall of the bad. In Dan Burton's case, it was going to take him a very long time to forget what had happened. Maybe he never would.

But right now, in the moments before either of us knew what was going to happen, Susan lay on a beach towel at the edge of a small private pond in northern Vermont, the water calm and dark. She wore only a minuscule bikini bottom, small even for her diminutive body, and she gleamed in the light. The midsummer sun was bright and hot, the insects mercifully at bay, and I was considering whether I could convince her to shuck her swimsuit and make love, either on the beach or up on the screened-in porch.

"You're a pretty loud thinker," she said. "I can tell what's on your mind all the way over here."

"I'm no longer thinking what you thought I was thinking. I'm thinking something completely different."

I watched her from a pine Adirondack chair facing the rolling

3

emerald hills on the other side of the valley. Susan and I had found our way back to each other after some years of to-ing and fro-ing across the country. Only this spring, we had finally reached a comfortable agreement about our relationship, and though she still had ties to Oregon, she was living in my apartment in Boston. It always surprised me to think how long I'd known her, the daughter of one of my long-time tenants in the building on Commonwealth Avenue. Henri had been gone a couple of years by now.

She lifted her head, shading her eyes against the sun.

"Oh. That."

"If you know what's on my mind, why are you still all the way over there? I thought we agreed we'd try and meet each other halfway."

She rose to her feet, her four and a half feet of perfectly proportioned female body glistening with sunscreen, walked across the grass to a point precisely halfway between us, and hooked her thumbs into the waistband of her pants.

I levered myself out of the hard chair and walked down slope to meet her.

She skinned the bikini bottom down over her legs, stepped out of it, and tossed it in my direction. Then she started to walk up toward the house.

"Not out here," she said. "I'm not much of a fan of sand in my whatsis."

Which made me wonder how she'd learned that, since we'd never made love on a beach together. But I shoved aside my unruly thought as I followed her up the hill, her small pale buttocks winking as she walked through the shadows of the pines.

* * *

In the evening, after the sun dropped below the line of trees on the opposite ridge and doused the house in dusk, I laid out cheese and crackers, a glassful of Susan's current favorite wine, a Viognier, and a Waterford crystal shot glass into which I poured an exact ounce before hiding the Macallan bottle away in the cupboard above the slate sink.

Susan had donned a plum-colored flannel shirt made for a bigger man than me. She sat cross-legged on the dusty velvet Victorian sofa in the parlor. I wore a sweatshirt and cotton shorts, enjoying the feel of my legs prickling in the cool air. It was the pleasure of being slightly uncomfortable on purpose and knowing you could change that any time you chose.

I handed her the wine glass, picked up my own, and settled into what I believed was an authentic Stickley armchair. She frowned at my whiskey, as she did every night, but I was long past trying to defend the way I kept my demons away.

"It's working," I said.

After a long and difficult couple of decades as a dedicated drinker, I'd found a way to control my apparently limitless craving for booze, through buying and running a bar called the Esposito and allowing myself a daily indulgence of one ounce of scotch.

"It seems to be." She sounded grudging. "Playing with fire."

"It's gotten us this far."

She sipped her wine, still frowning.

"I'll give you that much."

Buying back the Esposito last year, after I'd sold it once, had been no small part of my attempt to survive this addiction. No counselor or twelve-step guru would have advocated running a bar as a cure for alcoholism, but it worked for me. It was, I was convinced, the daily structure that saved me: opening, closing, serving, managing. The times I'd been most vulnerable to relapse were those months when I hadn't owned the bar. With nothing to frame my days, I'd spent all my time fighting with myself.

For our vacation in Vermont—Susan's idea—I'd left the Esposito in the hands of Isaac Belon, a young man I befriended in those months after I sold out and was looking for something to do. He was a bright kid—he'd been granted a full ride to Stanford, but delayed a year to try making some money in the music business around Boston. It hadn't worked out the way he'd hoped, but I'd convinced him to manage the bar for me until he went west to California in the fall.

In fact, when the phone rang in the middle of our cocktail hour,

I assumed it was him. We tried to check in every couple of days, and though Susan and I had another week on the rental of the farmhouse, I had a fiddly need to reassure myself the bar was still standing. I took the call outside on the porch.

"Green Mountain Inn," I answered.

Frigid silence. It wasn't Isaac.

"Hello?"

"This Darrow?"

Isaac had the farmhouse phone number, and no one else was supposed to know where we were. He and I were going to have words about personal privacy when I got home.

"This is Elder Darrow. Who's this? And how did you get this number?"

"It's about Burton," the voice said.

Dan Burton, a senior detective with the Boston Homicide Unit, was the closest thing to a male friend I had, as much through our mutual involvement in a couple of local murders and other people's shenanigans than anything else.

"What about him?"

"He's in trouble. He needs someone to be looking out for him right now."

The thick vowels of working class Boston could have been from any of a half dozen neighborhoods in the city. The familiarity was more in the way of speaking than in my recognizing the voice.

"Who is this? Is this you, Rowdy?"

Any of my longtime customers, if they found out I was on vacation, would find sport in disrupting it, especially since they'd been able to resume their regular stools once I bought the bar back. Baron Loftus, who'd owned the place for only a few months, had sent them all packing in his attempt to turn the Esposito into the twenty-first century equivalent of a fern bar, complete with piped-in soft rock.

The man at the other end coughed.

"If I say a name to you, I wouldn't want to hear it bandied around town."

Susan stuck her head out on the porch and looked at me

quizzically. I raised my shoulders. She drank some wine and went back inside.

"If this is a joke, I don't appreciate it."

But I was starting to feel a leaden sense of doom. What could have happened to Burton?

"I'm not joking with you, Mr. Darrow. If I tell you my name is Mickey Barksdale, does that gainsay me your attention for a bit?"

My stomach hollowed. Barksdale was Boston's current gangster king, the most recent man with the desire, and maybe the power, to unite the criminals in the Balkanized neighborhoods of the city into a coherent whole. No one had attempted this in several decades, which didn't mean people had stopped trying.

More to the point, Mickey and Burton grew up together in Charlestown, though their respective paths forked in opposite directions early, Mickey to the dark side, Burton to the cops. I couldn't imagine why Mickey Barksdale would be worried on Burton's behalf, but I had to take the man seriously.

"You have my attention."

"Took me a little too long to get it." I heard a faint threat, but otherwise, his voice was flat and unhurried, as if now that he had my focus, he had all day to get to his point. "I'd have expected a little more out of Burton's best friend."

The tone warned me not to push back, but I still had no idea why he was calling.

"Burton?" I said.

"He needs your support right now. But if you know him the way I think you do, you know he's not going to ask you for it."

"What happened? Is he injured?"

"I assume so." Barksdale chuckled. "In his head, at least. He doesn't really talk to me."

"Is he able to talk? Conscious?"

Barksdale understood my implication.

"Mr. Darrow, I don't know you well enough to take offense at that. But I'm also sure you don't want me to. I'm not a threat to Daniel, just an old mate trying to help him out."

The balder threat chilled me. They were mates, not friends. And

I couldn't refuse to respond to what he was asking me. Burton had saved my tail more than once, starting with the first time we met, when his bosses were convinced I was the one who stabbed Timmy McGuire on the stage of the old Esposito. There was no question I would help if I could.

On the other hand, Burton was a cop. If half of what I knew about Barksdale was true, Burton wouldn't want to owe him a thing.

"I'll take your word for it, that this is serious enough to interrupt my vacation."

"Friends are friends, Mr. Darrow. Anything else is gravy."

"I'm four or five hours away."

He sounded amused.

"I know that. I can send someone for you, if you want."

"No. Where is he right now?"

Barksdale rattled off a familiar address in the South End, the triple-decker Burton's old girlfriend Marina and her mother owned.

"Will he be there when I get there?"

"He doesn't know I'm sticking my nose in here, Darrow. And I don't want him to. Understood?"

"Understood." I also understood that Barksdale was loading a responsibility on me. I'd have to think about why he'd involved himself in whatever it was. Old neighborhood ties didn't feel sufficient. "I should be back in the city by tonight."

Susan must have been listening. She made a wordless noise.

"Fine. I'm out of this now, then."

"If you say so, Mickey. Am I supposed to thank you?"

"That's not necessary. And only my friends call me that. Elder."

The line cut out. I turned the phone over and looked at it. Susan stood in the doorway.

"That's it, then? Vacation over?"

I stepped into the parlor, picked up the small crystal glass, and instead of sipping, sank the shot in one swallow.

"For now. It sounds like Burton's in trouble."

2

Susan stared out the passenger's side window all the way down Interstate 89 until we reached Concord, New Hampshire, and then she spoke.

"That was all he told you? That Burton needs someone to look out for him? If you talk to Marina, you'd know that's been true as long as you've known him."

But Marina and I hadn't been talking. She and Burton had planned to marry last year, until she'd gotten bride's cold feet and canceled the nuptials. He'd been unhappy as hell, though nothing he'd done had caused her to back away. I'd stopped talking to her because of it.

I concentrated on threading the Volvo through the heavier traffic crisscrossing the cloverleaf. Once we were on the other side, heading down 93 toward southern New Hampshire and Massachusetts, I tried to explain.

"It's not quite as simple as that."

I hadn't told Susan it was Boston's premier gangster who'd called and more or less demanded my presence. When Susan and I committed to trying to live a normal life together, she'd agreed to give up her social work practice in Oregon and I promised to hire a permanent manager for the Esposito and quit working so many nights. She'd also made it clear that she didn't approve of my being swept into some of the violent and criminal encounters my relationship with Burton had caused.

She cocked an eyebrow.

"You sure about that? Because pretty much everything bad

9

that's happened to you in the last five years stems from running with Burton."

Not precisely true—I'd contributed to the craziness all on my own—but it wasn't inaccurate, either. I hoped my continuing friendship with Burton wouldn't cause friction between Susan and me. I'd seen people enter an intimate relationship bent on cementing their own place by severing a partner's pre-existing connections. Susan knew what she was getting into.

"He's been a good friend. Maybe my best one. Let's leave it at that."

Which shut down the conversation until we reached the city.

* * *

It was past one in the morning when I dropped Susan at my apartment building on Commonwealth Avenue. She didn't say anything as she climbed out of the Volvo. As I watched her trudge up the steps, the brown canvas duffel looped over her shoulder, my gut twisted. We'd argued and struggled a great deal to get this far.

Marina's three-decker in the South End had become much too big for one person after she'd placed her mother Carmen into assisted living a year ago. Carmen's dementia came and went, but a series of frightening episodes had forced the decision. Marina had the money my father left Carmen in his will, so at least she could afford a modern and well-run facility in West Roxbury. Burton had mentioned she was thinking about selling the place now, into the hottest real estate market in decades, but she was still going to have to pay for somewhere to live afterward.

Burton's banged-up Jeep was parked in a loading zone half a block up from the building. He'd placed a BPD Official Business placard on the dash, an unusual mistake. According to him, nothing pleased a meter maid more than a chance to ticket a real cop. Several paper tickets rested under the windshield wiper already. He must have been here a while. Either that or an especially bad-tempered meter reader was holding a grudge.

The steel entry door was closed, but unlocked. All of the city's neighborhoods, including this one, had gentrified in the years since Carmen and Marina moved out of Hyde Park, but there still wasn't a part of Boston where I'd leave my front door unlocked, my own childhood locale of Louisburg Square included. It was less because there was so much burglary as it was common sense. If you tempted the thieves, you almost deserved what you got. Or lost.

"Burton?"

I'd only been here a couple of times, but Marina had remodeled since Carmen moved out. The interior had been opened up, the original three separate apartments melded into a three-level townhouse. A formal parlor and a small guest bedroom formed the ground floor, living room and kitchen on the second, and the main bedrooms up on the third.

"Dan?" I tried again. "It's Elder."

Faint salsa music flowed down from the middle floor. I tiptoed up the outside edge of the stairs, so they wouldn't squeak. The music played through a speaker with a buzz. I shook my head at that, as if a mosquito had followed me down from Vermont.

I stepped off the top step and turned left through a small vestibule into the kitchen, a showplace of copper-bottomed pans, stainless steel appliances, and bright white cabinets. Marina had cooked for the Esposito for years, but this was a major upgrade over my kitchen.

Burton sat at a round gray marble-topped table for two, next to a window that spilled darkness into the brightly lit kitchen. The music gave way to a throaty woman speaking Spanish. He paid her no attention, staring at the reflection of the room in the window.

"What is it, Dan?"

I was tense as wire. I'd speculated without success on the drive down what might be wrong. So wrong one of his professional enemies would break all protocol and call me to help.

"Burton. Talk to me."

Had Carmen died? He and Marina had continued, past the broken wedding date, to try and figure out how to be together. Losing her mother might be something that sent Marina even further away from intimacy. Their relationship first started to deteriorate when Carmen went into care. But if that was it, why was he sitting alone in Marina's kitchen?

He turned his head, only now realizing I was there. The pale Irish skin was bright red on his cheekbones where he'd been rubbing his face. His light thinning hair was askew and his eyes were a red-lined map of emotion. Yes, grief.

"She's gone, man."

I shuddered. Carmen's death wouldn't have hit him this way.

"Marina?" My voice rose, soprano.

He nodded as if his head were too heavy to move.

"What happened? How?"

"Heart attack. In the restroom at the cooking school."

Since quitting the Esposito, Marina had been taking culinary courses, training to be a professional chef.

"At Bunker Hill?" The nearest community college campus.

Burton shook his head.

"They killed the program there. The adjuncts went on strike."

"When did she die?"

"Tuesday. During their lunch break."

It was Friday now.

"You've been here all this time?"

He frowned.

"There are things I need to take care of."

No doubt. Carmen was—had been—Marina's only living relative. No one but Burton was close enough to the family to deal with arrangements.

Now I regretted the way I'd left things with her. Months ago, after seeing Burton reeled in and let go way too many times, I'd told her off. Cut communication.

"What can I do?"

Burton walked around the kitchen, touching the hanging pots, the countertops.

"You know. People ask that question all the time. I must have heard it a million times. It usually means, what can I do to make myself feel better?"

That was as philosophical as I'd heard him get about his work, how death abided in everything he did. At the same time, the comment irked me. I was his friend, and I truly didn't know what he needed.

"Has anyone told Carmen?" I said.

He shook his head.

"The lucid periods are getting shorter and less frequent. I talked to the house doc over there, woman named Pottle. She was willing to tell Carmen, the next time she has a rational moment, but I told her to hold off. It won't change anything."

I ached for him, locking his pain behind the rational wall. An official-looking blue folder sat on the table.

"Is that a will? I wouldn't have guessed Marina thought that far ahead."

Burton flared, as if it were possible to insult someone posthumously. At least all his emotions weren't dulled. He knew death as well as anyone, if not from the point of view of a loved one left behind.

"She would have had to take care of things like that." He sat again, touched the folder. "Because of Carmen. Making sure she was taken care of if anything happened. And it did."

His voice broke. I wished we had the kind of friendship that would let me hug him, but we'd never had that closeness, even in the most difficult times.

"You're her executor?"

I could read where some of his worry was coming from.

"Yours truly. I don't mind, really. I've had to do it before. It makes it real."

I knew what he meant, though I wasn't sure I agreed. When I'd wound up my father's complicated estate, I found myself thinking of his death as something less than it had been, as a transaction rather than as an event.

"You can use Markham to bounce things off of, if you want. My treat."

He raised a small smile. Daniel Markham, my attorney, didn't know what *pro bono* meant. The Esposito no longer required the services of a high-powered downtown lawyer, but Markham had worked for my father and I'd sort of inherited him.

"Thanks," Burton said. "But it looks pretty straightforward."

I sat down across the table from him.

"Look. I know we don't talk to each other like this…"

He held up a hand, walled in to the last.

"I'm fine, Elder. I appreciate your being here. Aren't you supposed to be in Vermont?"

The window of closeness, the possibility of intimacy, slammed shut. I didn't want him to ask me how I'd known to come back. And I wondered what it said about how we got along that I sensed there was something he wasn't telling me.

"In fact, yeah. Give me Markham's number. In case it gets complicated."

"How so?"

Aside from the three-decker, which Carmen bought for cash in the Seventies, Marina's estate probably held only the million dollars my father had left Carmen. Knowing how conservative Marina was, it was probably in a savings account.

Burton slammed the folder with his hand.

"Because she also made me her heir." Emotion cracked his voice again.

My eyes widened. My friend, who probably had no assets but his police salary and his pension, now owned a building worth a million and a half dollars and almost that much cash.

"How is that a problem?"

Marina would have known she could trust him to take care of Carmen, regardless of what happened between the two of them.

"Executor and sole heir? Someone's bound to bitch."

"Who's left that might do that?"

"You never know. There's no other family, as far as I know. I have the feeling she was anticipating trouble. She only did this a month ago. And she could have named the attorney to act as trustee." He pointed to the name embossed on the outside of the folder. "She'd be a helluva lot smarter about this than me."

That was when I saw through his bluster to the fear, that he might screw things up somehow, that the legal and financial intricacies were beyond him. That, at least, was something I could help with.

"Burton. Seriously? Call Markham. He'll walk you through everything."

3

Notice I didn't try and tell him it would all be fine.

Isaac Belon, my bar manager *pro tem*, wasn't very much happier to see me later Saturday morning than Burton had been. Maybe less so. When I walked down the steel stairs into the Esposito, the look on his face was a study in quick consternation, followed by such an affected nonchalance I wanted to audit the books to see what he'd been up to.

"Bossss-man." He stretched the word out in a way that was supposed to be cute, but it carried a definite edge. He'd been reading a lot this summer, preparing for college, and his attitude reflected a lot of the writing around race and caste that was top of intellectual mind at the moment. It seemed to have soured him a little on working for me, either because I was white or because I represented a demographic wealthier than the average nineteen-year-old.

"Thought you were still up there in cow country. Everything all right with the missus?"

"Try calling her that and find out."

I pointed a finger at him and looked around the bar. Reclaiming the Esposito last spring had returned my sense of stability and peace. I still wasn't sure why I'd thought selling out was a good idea, except the real estate developers betting on the Olympics coming to Boston had offered me such a stupid amount of money, I'd felt obliged to take it.

But the pictures of Diz and Miles were back up on the walls under the mini-spots, the photos of Larry Bird and Bobby Orr on the far side. The pastel paint job Baron Loftus had inflicted on the place was now a neutral gray.

Chairs were still stacked on the tables from the night before. I started to lift them down and set them on the floor. Isaac sighed and hustled out from behind the bar.

"I was getting there," he said. "We don't open up for another hour."

He was dressed, as usual, as the upscale bartender, starched white cotton shirt and sleeve garters under the long black apron. I'd warned him dressing up like that only meant outrageous dry cleaning bills, but he told me it was how he curated his image. Whatever that meant.

He was a tall young man, over six feet, and weighed no more than a hundred and sixty. He moved with a lithe economy that made me mourn the supple knees and spine of my youth. Even drunk, I'd been able to ski all day, play soccer.

"Needed to come back into the city. Death in the family."

I didn't want to get into the details of Burton's loss. Isaac hadn't known Marina and he owned the baseline suspicion of any young Black man for a middle-aged white cop. And something beyond that infected their attitude toward each other. They weren't enemies, but they were never going to sit down and have a beer together in Burton's back yard.

We worked side by side for a few minutes, prepping for the day's opening. I made sure the grill and fryer were turned on. Marina hadn't wanted to come back to the Esposito—she'd made it clear it would feel like a step down from her plan to become a professional chef. We were still trying out cooks.

"The agency send over anyone decent?" I said.

"One more coming. Around eleven."

"Him or her?"

"Her." He pouted, skittish, as if he hoped I wasn't going to stay. "The last two they sent were terrible."

I frowned.

"You give them a decent chance? More than an hour or two?"

Isaac had backed into his managerial role only because he knew

17

me, which meant he was less secure about the position than if he'd earned it by experience. Like a lot of novice bosses, he ran hot sometimes, made decisions too quickly, on instinct. And he disliked taking responsibility for his mistakes.

I got a surly nod.

"Burgers and fries and chicken pot pies. Nothing too complicated about beeping a microwave."

He retreated behind the bar, where the book he'd been reading was spread open. I lifted the cover to see the title, one of the many *New York Times* bestsellers this year on the perennially hot topic of race. This was an academic study, all data and turgid prose, treating a subject anyone growing up in the city of Boston knew instinctively.

"I'm picking up a vibe here, Isaac. The bar looks OK, so I know you didn't host a fight club. The pipes didn't burst. So tell me what's going on."

He closed the book on his finger to mark the page. His eyes showed anger.

"Griffe," he said. "Marabou. Mulatto. Quadroon."

He'd memorized these terms. I had no idea what he meant. He stared at me.

"Octaroon, septaroon. Mamelouk." His tongue stumbled on that one. "San-mêlé. A disorder in the blood." He looked like he wanted to cry. "That's one sixty-fourth, Elder. A drop of Black blood six generations back is a disorder in the blood."

I held up my hands, not sure what he wanted me to say.

"You know?" he said. "The Nazis couldn't believe how rigid America was about enforcing the one-drop-of-blood idea? That they thought it was too harsh?"

I sat down on one of my bar stools, deeply uncomfortable. Here was a young man with almost every advantage a society could provide: upper middle class parents, a university professor and a patent attorney; an excellent education in private schools; and all the other benefits of growing up in a suburb more or less free of poverty and its problems. He'd had every advantage but one: a certain color of skin.

But it was incredible to me he was only now engaging the issue for himself, having grown up in this city, with its horrible racial history. It was an awakening I would have expected him to have had years ago.

"All of a sudden, Isaac? You know I don't give a rat's ass about the color of your skin. Or your blood."

"I didn't do anything wrong." His jaw set like concrete.

The shift of topic startled me. We weren't talking about race any more.

"I didn't say you did. Now tell me what's going on."

He looked past my shoulder, up into the shadows of the small triangular stage, and dropped his book on the bar with a thump.

"Evvie's back."

* * *

Evangeline O'Mara had returned from New Orleans, then, where she'd made a devil's bargain with a gangster named Frank Vinson, to trade being his arm candy for his access to opportunities to build her career as a jazz singer. The last thing I'd heard, months ago, was that she'd made a weak cry for help via a video of her singing. Isaac, who was enamored of her, had flown down then to reassure himself she was fine, or so she insisted when he got there.

I'd more or less forgotten her. As it turned out, Evvie had only been interested in me to the extent I could further her career in Boston. Though I'd slept with her once, it was well in the past. With Susan and I rebuilding, I didn't want any confusion, and unless Evvie had told Isaac, he didn't know either.

"Make you feel any better, that she's back?"

Isaac had always carried a torch for her, worrying that her stint in the Big Easy wasn't doing her any good personally. I thought she was a user—Frank Vinson traded her gigs in some of the most storied jazz venues in America for her appearance as his girlfriend. She'd sworn nothing else went on between them. Isaac did not want to know otherwise.

"She's in bad shape," he said. "I've been trying to keep her close."

"She's been here? In my bar?"

I made sure he heard my pronoun. Isaac was testing the limit of my trust in him. Burton warned me against getting involved in anything to do with Vinson. Of course that was before I'd killed Edward Dare, Vinson's procurer. There was no profit in my getting involved with these people again.

"Isaac. I don't want any connection with that woman, where she's been, or the people she's been with. Which includes her hanging around here. I hope that's clear."

He stiffened up behind the bar, throwing off all the injured masculinity of a young man who thought he was doing something righteous.

"She needs the attention, Elder. The connection. She's been staying with me since she got back. She's shaky. And it's not like she'd be drinking up your profits. She just needs to be among people she feels safe with."

I felt myself soften to his arguments, a tendency I'd seen in myself lately. I could be plenty tough on people I didn't know, but once I'd allowed someone into my circle, it got harder and harder to say no.

"Are you telling me she's here right now? Where? In my office?"

Isaac tilted his head. He wouldn't meet my eyes.

"Finish getting ready to open," I said. "I need to talk to her."

He was so worried about his friend, he looked about fifteen. Though maybe she was now more than a friend?

"And for god's sake, put the book away. This is a bar, not a library."

His face clouded up and he shoved the volume under the bar with a bang.

I left him to his pout and stepped through to the kitchen. I was suddenly interested to see if she'd gotten what she wanted, how her bargain had advanced her dream, if it had.

The carpet in the hallway was a flat weave industrial gray over concrete. My feet made no noise as I walked up the corridor toward my office. I slowed at the doorway, telling myself the interest I felt was that of one human for another, not any remnant of the lust I'd once felt.

20

Her head was turned, in silhouette, her neck long as a swan, with pale skin and a scattering of freckles high on her cheek. When we first met, she was all multicolored hair and piercings and attitude, playing trumpet in a Brass House band. Now the steel barbells and nose ring were gone, the holes healed over. She wore a pink button-down shirt—one of Isaac's?—and her hair was cut in a bob, either natural brunette or so expertly dyed as to make no difference. The only signs of strain were a too-translucent quality of the skin at her temples and the beginnings of crow's feet at the corners of her eyes. You wouldn't mistake them for laugh lines.

"Evangeline."

Her head spun like a startled cat. Her brown eyes got large. I looked to see if the pupils were dilated. One of the rumors Burton had surfaced was that Vinson liked to drug his conquests, keep them docile. But her pupils were a normal size and the whites clear. She smiled, as if she knew what I'd been thinking.

"Mr. Darrow."

I felt the pang I always did when someone, particularly an attractive woman, reminded me how old I was.

"You seemed to have survived your adventure."

She stiffened at my tone, which made me feel better. A time with Frank Vinson had crushed the spirit of one other young singer from Boston so badly she'd killed herself after coming home. I hadn't known Evvie well enough to guess how tough she'd be, though she'd been tough enough to resist our attempts to talk her out of going.

"Throve on it, Mr. Darrow. Experience of a lifetime." Her eyes glinted under the fluorescents like the shards of a star. She didn't seem anywhere near as depressed as Isaac had said. "Gained some serious experience in the business in the biggest music city in the world. Made myself some contacts. Even made a little money."

I took in what she was saying, hoping she wasn't lying to Isaac so he'd take care of her.

"Isaac said you were down. A little shaken by the whole thing."

She arched an eyebrow, thin as a comma. It seemed completely in character that she was sitting in my chair and I was standing in the hallway like a supplicant.

"Isaac is a very good friend, Mr. Darrow. He enjoys taking care of people. He needs something to worry about."

"So you're just helping him out that way?'

She screwed up the side of her face in an exaggerated wink.

"I always try and help my friends. Don't you?"

4

For a Saturday night, the Esposito wasn't too busy. Isaac and I didn't mesh together as well as we had in the past, so when the serious drinking sputtered out around eleven, I left him to man the bar and walked back to the office. It was near the end of the month and I wanted to get a start on paying the bills. I'd left Isaac cash for the deliveries while I was in Vermont, but that was all gone by now.

And so was Evvie. She must have slipped out the back door. For some reason, she'd left some printed out pages of the *Times Picayune* on my desk. A sweet perfume odor, something like watermelon and jelly beans, lingered in the air.

I unlocked the safe and pulled out the checkbook, added the stack of invoices Isaac had collected out front to the bills on my desk. Finance was my least favorite part of owning a bar, but I'd learned early on that if you let it go or got sloppy, it was almost impossible to catch up later.

I slipped a CD into the boom box I kept back here, thinking how Isaac would make fun of the ancient technology. Gunhild Carling's trumpet brazened through the tiny speakers. She was a Swede, best known for an energetic stage style and tricks like playing three saxophones at once. I'd first seen her on YouTube, playing jazz bagpipes, but despite the gimmicks, the woman could blow. This recording was a live performance from Montreux, where she played soprano sax on "Baby It's Cold Outside." The music was bright and propulsive enough to keep me awake for my task.

A half hour had passed before I heard a raised voice over the music, out front in the bar. A glass shattered. I came up out of my chair, but stopped. This was a good chance to see how Isaac handled things. Even with the gentrified neighborhood and clientele the Esposito boasted now, people still got cranky when they drank.

And before Susan and I left for Vermont, Isaac had hinted about not taking up his pandemic-deferred full ride to Stanford in September. If he stayed around, I'd consider making him the manager permanently, or as permanently as a nineteen-year-old could manage. I'd gotten used to not having to stand behind the bar every day and night.

I didn't hear any more ruckus, so I assumed all was well. I stayed back in the office, not wanting him to think I was checking up on him, stamped the envelopes, and locked the checkbook away. I even thought about leaving early—Susan was waiting at the apartment, probably still irked with me—but I realized I hadn't had my statutory daily glass of whiskey yet. And better to do it here than in front of her at home.

I was headed out front when a dull bang thumped the steel fire door. I turned and headed down the back hall.

One of the useful upgrades Baron Loftus had added to the bar, beyond a better sound system and a dishwasher that didn't die in the middle of a cycle, was a security camera system. On the small black and white monitor mounted by the door, a disheveled Burton stared into the camera, his mouth hanging open like a rube.

I sighed. I'd bet a million dollars he was shit-faced, and as much as I empathized with his grief, he could hurt himself, and others, in this condition. The times I'd seen him knee-walking drunk, he'd assumed such a pugnacious attitude, anyone crossing his path was in jeopardy. One memorable night at Rita's Place in Chelsea, he'd even taken a swing at me when I suggested Jim Rice might not be the best Red Sox left fielder of all time.

I pressed the panic bar and let him in.

"Was that you making all that noise a little while ago?"

"Bassid," he barked. "Snot-nosed kid wouldn't let me come back to talk to you."

Impressive that Isaac had managed that without fisticuffs. He'd done the right thing for the bar, if not for my friendship.

"Clever of you to think of the back door."

I was trying to judge how far gone he was. He proffered a half-empty plastic jug of Seagram's. I shuddered.

"You didn't drink all that tonight, I hope."

"It's a wake, my friend. I'm awake for the wake. Don't you have to be? Awake for the wake?"

"Get in here," I said. "You need something to eat."

"You know you can't cook for shit, pally. And you don't even have a cook any more."

He sobbed, shoved past me to the office, and threw himself into the chair with the bottle cradled in his lap.

I ached for him, even as I knew there was nothing I could do. Losing Susan, now that I'd accepted her as a hostage to my happiness, would have devastated me the same way.

"I know how to make a sandwich, Burton. I'm not a complete numpty."

He shook his head like a dog with a stick.

"Numpty-dumpty. None for me, thanks. Unless you want to be cleaning it up off the floor." He belched.

Even allowing for the load he had on, he seemed much more depressed than when I'd seen him early this morning at Marina's apartment, more shaken.

"Something else happen? You're not usually this sloppy a drunk."

His eyes rounded, owlish. Thinking was clearly difficult in his state, but whatever emotion he'd been trying to drown had survived.

"I've been to autopsies before, you know. Maybe a hundred."

"Ah, shit, Burton. Tell me you're not going to attend her autopsy. Wait a minute. You said she had a heart attack. Why would they do one? And this fast?"

His eyes closed, then opened, laboriously.

"It's always the medical examiner's call. If he thinks there might be something suspicious. But he won't talk to me. I can't tell what he's thinking."

I shook my head. Burton had offered me the chance once, but I'd never attended a post-mortem. He'd described the process to me, the long Y incision down the chest to expose the organs, the snapping of ribs with the long handled pruner, the saw cutting off the top of the skull so the pathologist could remove the brain. Right now, I imagined what he was seeing in his mind, all those images conflated with pictures of Marina in life. My throat got thick.

"Why would there be anything suspicious?"

He threw up his hands and the bottle slid to the floor, bounced once.

"No one will tell me," he said. "They won't say a fucking thing."

His eyes rolled back and he passed out, with the finality of a light bulb popping.

*   *   *

"I wondered if you were planning on coming home tonight," Susan said.

It had taken her nine or ten rings to answer the land line in my apartment, which said she was still a little tentative about living with me. And the tone of voice told me she wasn't too pleased to hear I'd be late, whether because the Vermont trip had been cut short or because it was Burton who needed my help.

"He's in pretty bad shape," I said. "Marina's death really crushed him. He drove here by himself, but I can't let him drive home."

"You sure?"

She was begrudging me. It made me wonder if she'd ever had a friend she had to sacrifice a little for.

"I'll only be an hour or so later than usual. I just need to get him home and make sure he doesn't pass out. I'll be home by three."

"When I will be dead to the world. You wake me up, *amigo*, and you better be ready to rumble."

Her irritation had slipped into sarcasm, my second language.

"Got it. See you then."

*   *   *

26

I wasn't going to carry Burton in my vehicle on the non-zero chance he might throw up in it. And he would need his Jeep tomorrow, when he reentered the world. Isaac wasn't happy about my asking him to follow me to Burton's apartment in my car, but he knew I was still irritated about Evvie. So he agreed, though reluctantly.

"Man lives in Charlestown." He was sullen, but didn't push back too hard. "I'm not walking home through that neighborhood."

"I'll give you a lift." It would add half an hour to my bedtime, but Susan was going to be asleep. And I understood his concern. Even in the twenty-first century, Charlestown was not a place for a young Black man at two in the morning. "Don't worry about it."

He made a sour face and bounded up the stairs, the keys to my car jingling in his hand. The night lights cast an orange glow that shrouded the tables and chairs. It surprised me how good it felt to be back in the bar, even tonight.

Burton was conscious enough to walk, but not so sober he didn't list from side to side as we navigated the back corridor. I didn't have to hold him up, but he kept putting a hand on the wall and, outside, made full use of the steel banister the city egress inspector had insisted I install on the loading dock.

*   *   *

He'd sobered up enough to be churlish by the time we pulled up in front of his building.

"Can climb the fucking stairs," he growled, unfolding himself from the cab of the Jeep. He leaned on the open door.

"Think of it like we're coming home from a date, Burton. I'm going to see you to the door."

He narrowed his gaze, anger turning his face feral in the white light of the street lamps. I hoped the rage was general, not directed at me.

"You're an asshole."

"Be that as it may. Tonight I'm your asshole."

He grunted, sweating in the brightly lit stairwell as I followed him up the stairs. He fumbled the keys until I took them away and unlocked the door myself. That gave him one more reason to be angry at me. He should have been angry at himself.

He parked himself in the doorway, not letting me inside.

"I'm not going to kiss you goodnight. So you can fuck right off now."

I wanted to see him lying on the couch or in bed, in a position where he couldn't vomit and choke on it. But he was past that stage of drunkenness and his anger was more embarrassment than anything else. Nothing helpful would come of my pushing.

"Don't brood, Burton. It won't change a thing."

His face screwed up as if he might cry. That was the last sight I had of him before he slammed the door.

Isaac was silent on the way to his apartment, though when I parked in front of his building, he made no move to climb out.

"That is sad. This was his woman who died?"

I wondered if he was thinking about Evvie, putting himself in Burton's shoes.

"They weren't together any more. And she'd been messing with his head for a while. But, yeah, it hurts. Something sudden like that, someone you know."

He faced me across the front seat.

"I'm sorry about bringing Evvie in. It was like I got to thinking the bar was mine."

The apology surprised me. He wasn't always that sensitive.

"Small mistake. Not irreparable. See you Monday?"

One of the small luxuries I'd awarded myself in the new world order was closing the bar on Sundays.

"Monday." He opened the Volvo's door. "Still. That is really sad."

5

On summer Sundays, Susan and I liked to get out of the apartment, hit a brunch spot, maybe walk up to the Common and wander a little. After spending so much of my time underground in the bar, I'd come to rely on some fresh air and sunshine to start my week. But this Sunday only offered a wave of ferocious thunderstorms, wind blowing the hard rain horizontal, and we weren't going anywhere.

Which was a relaxation of its own. Susan commandeered the Sunday *Times* magazine for the crossword puzzle and sat with her bare feet up on the love seat. Her Sunday best was a pair of peach-colored sweat pants and a blue hoodie from the Berklee School. I felt full when I looked at her, without doubt we were doing the right thing being together, no matter all my decades as a solo act.

She raised her head from the magazine.

"Kimmie-Joy called me yesterday." She looked back down at the puzzle, quickly.

My shoulders knotted up. Why did so many of these people she knew on the West Coast have odd names? And what did her soon-to-be-former—I hoped—boss in the social work practice want out of her now?

She looked up again and pointed the ballpoint at me.

"Don't give me that look. I cannot leave the job until we find placements for all the current clients. It shouldn't take more than a few weeks."

"Weeks?" I suppose I couldn't complain too loudly. I was the one to cut short our vacation.

29

"I told you this was likely."

She'd accused me more than once of not listening to her, so I didn't tell her I didn't remember. Her warning look reinforced my silence.

"I know. I'll miss you, is all. When?"

"Tomorrow morning. Seven a.m. flight. I know it's early, but…"

"Of course I'll take you to the airport." It was hard not to feel this was payback for staying out late helping Burton. "What are friends for?"

But the fact she was leaving me for a while did give our Sunday afternoon lovemaking a frantic quality, a tinge of sadness.

* * *

I dropped Susan off at the United terminal at about five-thirty. We'd done this often enough to know that communicating while she was in Oregon would be spotty and unsatisfying between the difference in time zones and my nighttime schedule against her day. I drove back into the city feeling bereft.

I went back to bed and caught a few more hours' sleep before I had to open up. Isaac had called Sunday night and begged a couple days off, I assumed to spend time with Evvie. Fine. I wasn't up for much company today.

I didn't pretend to understand what was going on between them. She was playing him somehow, but to what end, I had no idea. He was only nineteen, and it was a young nineteen. He didn't have super-rich parents or the prospect of getting rich himself, at least until he graduated from Stanford. And I didn't think their color difference would hold any interest for her after her time in New Orleans with Frank Vinson.

* * *

I turned the house lights all the way up and clucked at the dried streaks from the wet rag I'd left the night before. I was turning into an old lady.

Brubeck the elder was the right prescription for the long day coming. I whistled under my breath along with "Blue Rondo a la Turk" while I filled the beer cases, stocked the mixes, and cut up fruit. Unfamiliar ingredients behind the bar—weird extracts, bitters—made me wonder if Isaac had been experimenting with exotic cocktails. I hoped not. The last thing I needed was for the Esposito to be on-trend.

About ten-thirty, half an hour before opening time, the street door cracked and let in the sun. In the Esposito's before-time, I used to let customers in whenever I was here, for the company as much as the income. Nowadays, I was rigid about the hours. A fourteen or sixteen hour workday was plenty without adding on.

"Not open," I called without looking up. You couldn't see who it was against the lighted doorway.

"Are you Mr. Darrow?"

The woman's voice was high, like a piccolo. It reminded me of Blossom Dearie.

"I'm from the agency? To cook for you?"

Isaac had mentioned another kitchen tryout scheduled for today. I met her at the bottom of the stairs.

"I'm Elder Darrow." I didn't offer to shake her hand, which was still a fraught kind of gesture. "And you are?"

"Syndi." She spelled it out for me, as if she had to all the time. "Rourke."

She surveyed the Esposito suspiciously.

"Have you ever worked in a bar?"

She was tall and fragile-looking, maybe early thirties, her eyes the pale blue of winter ice. Her arms were no thicker than baguettes and I wondered if she could lift a number ten can of tomatoes. Her hair was thin, the color of weak scotch and water, and the white long-sleeved chef's jacket had her name embroidered across the left breast.

I pointed at the coat.

"That won't be necessary. This isn't that formal a place."

My regulars would make a huge joke out of the bar employing an actual chef.

"OK." She shucked it, which wasn't what I intended, revealing a skin tight black T-shirt, also long-sleeved. She had no breasts at all. "Kitchen through here?"

I hoped she was competent. Isaac had complained about the prospects the agency had been sending, but the Esposito needed to get back to serving food, to placate the liquor inspectors as much as to sustain the business. Baron Loftus had squandered most of the custom I'd built.

"Where did you work before this?"

She inspected the contents of the shelves over the sandwich station, turned on the fryer and the grill.

"It'll be tight, time-wise," she said. "But I can probably throw a decent soup together for the lunch rush. If you have one."

I stared at her.

"Where did you come from?"

"West Roxbury."

The reticence irked me.

"Did you bring a resume?"

She took a deep breath.

"I used to cook for a convent. St. Mag's in the Crags?"

I shook my head.

"Never heard of it."

"Saint Margaret of the Mountain?"

The Catholic parishes around Boston represented enough saints that I couldn't keep up with them all. I wasn't sure cooking for a bunch of nuns was the kind of experience I needed. She had to be quick in the kitchen and unflappable when it got busy. This wasn't a contemplative environment.

"Interesting. And why did you leave your last position?"

Her head was buried in the refrigerator, but her back stiffened.

"Not much future in a nunnery," she said. "Besides, they kicked me out."

"You were a nun?"

She turned and nodded, a head of red cabbage in one hand.

"For a month or two. Sister Mary Mary, at your service."

* * *

"This is a paid tryout, right?" She chopped onions with a blurring knife blade that attested to her kitchen skills. "Not like one of those internships?"

That stumped me. I didn't know how Isaac had worked things with the employment agency.

"Wouldn't you get paid through the agency?"

I didn't want to have to call him and betray my ignorance. Nor did I want the agency to know I wasn't sure how they did business.

"Because they take a big bite out of my hourly rate." She stopped chopping and pointed the big blade at me. "Thirty, sometimes forty percent. The nuns used to pay straight cash. After I stopped doing it for the glory of, if you know what I mean."

"I'm sure we can work it out."

"Good." She scooped the chopped onions with the blade of the big knife into a steel vat of tuna fish. "'Cause I need to go in and pay a little something on my rent tonight."

She pulled a giant jar of mayonnaise down off a high shelf, putting the lie to my worry about her arm strength.

"As I said. We'll work something out."

Back behind the bar, I was pleased to see four people straggling down the stairs from outside. Baron Loftus had known nothing about running this business. I was having to advertise for the first time, to bring back the clientele I'd had before. The Esposito began life as a bucket of blood, full of drug deals and fights in the alley, sometimes right in the bar itself. We hadn't slipped back to those days, but worse, Loftus had turned the place into a bland brass and plants bar, with Neil Diamond sound loops on the stereo system. I wouldn't have drunk in the place myself, and I used to drink anywhere.

I got the four-top seated and took drink orders, passed around menus, crossing my fingers we had enough supplies to cook everything. They looked like tourists: baggy jeans, big sneakers, designer shirts, so it wouldn't necessarily be a disaster if Syndi couldn't cook. They did look like the type to post snotty reviews on Yelp, however.

"The cheeseburger." One of the women, a sharp-nosed shrew, pointed to the menu with a bright blue fingernail, as if I might not understand the word. "Is your beef grass-fed?"

Damned if I knew. I nodded. If she could tell the difference under melted cheddar and caramelized onions, she ought to be writing for *Gourmet*.

Neither of the men had questions about the menu. I gathered the cards and headed for the bar, as the street door creaked open again.

6

Burton walked heavily down the stairs. I pointed him to a stool near the end of the bar where we could talk while I put the drinks together. But when I came out of the kitchen after giving Syndi the order, he was behind the bar, pouring himself a tall glass of club soda and lime. He looked apologetic.

"Looked like you were busy. And I'm dry as the Desert of Maine."

I set a round tray on the bar, uncapped two bottles of Maine Beer Company's Lunch, and poured two glasses of Chardonnay from the portion-controlled wine dispenser Loftus had installed. I liked the idea of a precise pour, though I wasn't sure I was in favor of too much consistency. I paused in front of Burton before carrying the tray out.

"All right?"

He had a solemn look, but his hand was steady as he toasted me. "Take your time."

I delivered the drinks, fielded a couple more overly detailed questions about the food's pedigrees that I had to fake answers to, and returned to the bar. I lowered the volume on Herbie Hancock. Burton's glass was almost empty, an infallible sign he was working on a hangover. From Saturday night? Or more recent?

"How are you doing?"

He was clear-eyed, clean-shaven, and dressed in one of his better suits, with a starched yellow cotton shirt and dark green tie underneath. He must not have been working today—that was when he wore the off-the-rack suits from the Basement, in case a crime scene got messy.

He tipped his head and pushed the glass toward me with his fingers. I sighed.

"Still saving up your words?" I refilled the glass, set it down. "Look, I'm sorry."

"Heroin," he said.

"What?"

"Marina died of heroin. An overdose."

I stopped short, making the duck boards squeak.

"No. That makes zero sense."

He hunched over the bar, trained his interrogator gaze on me.

"You never saw it? Anything like that?"

"Of course not. Half the time, she wouldn't even have a drink at the end of her shift."

His menace deflated.

"You got the autopsy results back that fast?" I said.

He shook his head.

"Only partial. But if I didn't have friends in the M. E.'s office after twenty years, I'd be a pretty shitty cop."

"She was using? Steadily? Could they tell?"

"You'd be amazed what they can tell. But no. As far as I heard, there was only the one puncture. More detail coming in the final report, but that's the outline."

There were other ways to ingest heroin than by injection, but it stunned me to think Marina had done it even once. She was the least likely person I knew to try drugs, though I suppose everyone who's lost someone to an overdose thinks something like that.

"I never saw a sign of it." Burton was berating himself.

"It could have been a first time. An experiment. Remember Len Bias?"

Promising young basketball player, drafted by the Celtics, who tried cocaine for the first time and had his heart blow up.

Burton shook his head.

"I never saw a hint she had a desire for anything like that."

"There was Carlos, remember? The guy she was dating when she first came to work here?"

"Years ago," Burton said. "He died. There's nothing there."

I could see him struggle with the thought that he'd had no idea this was possible. The two of them had been together, off and on, for years, and then last year, they were planning to marry. Something had happened late last winter that caused her to break off the engagement.

"I don't see how you could have known, Dan. She pushed you away."

Burton shrugged.

"Maybe I made that too easy for her. Feels like I should have known something was going on."

"How could you, if she wasn't talking to you?"

A bell dinged in the kitchen, a strangely nostalgic note, considering who we were talking about.

"You find a cook?"

"Trying one out." I started for the kitchen. "Stay for lunch. I'll introduce you."

I trayed the four plates out and distributed them. Syndi had done a decent job, even curling some carrot strips and carving radish roses to class up the presentation. If the sandwiches were edible, maybe I'd solved my cook problem. Back behind the bar, I watched my customers tuck in. They seemed satisfied.

"You're handling the arrangements?"

"Who else? Carmen's not up to it."

"I'd like to help out."

He nodded.

"Logistics more than cash. There's plenty of money."

He sounded flat, all the rage and grief of the other night tamped down. I wondered where he'd hidden it.

Someone came up behind me, Syndi smelling like a fry cook already, grease and potatoes. Burton looked past me and raised an eyebrow.

"Burton, this is Syndi. Syndi, my friend Dan Burton. You'll see him in here once in a while."

Which, I realized, made it sound as if I'd decided to hire her, on the basis of four sandwiches. She lifted her chin and smiled at him. She'd put on blue-framed glasses that clashed with her eye shadow. At least she'd had the sense to don a hairnet.

"Pretty nice suit for a cop. Almost too nice."

"You two know each other?" I said.

"Syndi." Burton mused. "With an 'ess' and a 'y'?"

She looked amused. I was lost.

"My reputation precedes me?" she said.

Was I going to have to fire her before I'd really hired her? If Burton knew her, it was possible she was associated with his criminal world.

"And how is your Uncle Mickey?" Burton picked up his glass. "We haven't talked in quite a while. But you probably know that."

There was only the one Mickey in Burton's sphere, the Mickey who'd called me back to Boston to take care of my friend. Who didn't really appear to need taking care of. Having Mickey Barksdale's niece show up for a job at the Esposito was a long leap beyond coincidence.

"We only see each other at holidays," she said. "Thanksgiving. Christmas. His saint's day."

Burton seemed happy to have something to think about besides Marina's death. If Syndi didn't see Mickey much, how had she known who Burton was? He wasn't that notable physically.

"Tell him I was asking about him." He twisted that into a subtle threat, reminding her he was a cop and her uncle a gangster. He wore a quirky smile, waiting to see what she'd say.

I needed to talk to him before I hired her, but I couldn't exactly do that in front of her.

My paying customers were halfway through their meals.

"It doesn't look like your food killed anybody," I said.

Burton winced.

"I guess we could try you again tomorrow."

"That's it, then? I'm done for the day?"

The Esposito hadn't run a dinner hour since I'd bought the bar back. One more night, with time to consult Burton about Syndi, wouldn't sink this ship.

"Good enough." She scratched her forearm. "What I said about a little cash?"

I counted five twenties out of the register, Burton smirking.

"We'll call it an advance. Come in around ten tomorrow and we'll talk about your schedule."

Her face lightened up, but more like relief than joy. I hoped Burton wouldn't tell me something that meant I'd have to rescind the offer.

"Thanks. I call you Elder?"

I nodded. "That's fine. If the kitchen's clean, you can split."

Burton frowned as she sashayed back inside.

"What do you think?" I said.

"As long as she can cook? There are whole branches of that clan who want nothing to do with Mickey."

"She does bring up an interesting point. What's with the suit?"

"Back into court on the Bousquet thing."

"Shit. They will not give up, will they?"

Two years ago, Burton had arrested someone whose cousins were still pressing a suit for damages. It was personal for them—they wanted Burton to quit.

As he shook his head, the woman with the nose like a blade, crooked a finger at me. Crap. Maybe Syndi wasn't that good a cook.

She pointed her blue talon at the empty plate.

"That was certainly not grass-fed beef. You are guilty of false advertising. I don't believe we're going to pay for this."

I could tell which of the men was her companion by the hunch in his shoulders and the way he wouldn't look at me. Plenty of people tried to chew and screw on me, but usually it was smart-ass kids. These people were middle-aged. And their plates were empty, as were their glasses. If they hadn't liked the food, they'd certainly managed to choke it down.

Her face was frozen in outrage, as if I'd kicked a puppy.

"Doesn't look like anything kept you from eating it."

Burton was at my back before she could respond.

"Hello, folks. I'm Dan Burton." He flashed his credentials. "Is there something I can help with?"

7

It was a long slow Monday night. Susan did not call me from Oregon. I could have used the diversion. After I got rid of the scammers, a couple of my old regulars showed up, looking tentative about how the Esposito might have changed. We had a couple of conversations about the bar's olden days, which made me more sad than nostalgic. Mostly, I shuffled through playlists, trying to find a pleasing run of tunes. I hadn't completely returned to a good working rhythm.

I was closing up, locking the change bank and credit card slips into the safe when I heard the street door open. I hustled out front, expecting to tell some wandering tourist or late-night drunk we were closed. Instead, Isaac was walking down the stairs.

"Funny way to take a couple days off," I said.

I'd had nights like that too, when sitting at home didn't feed whatever urge or itchy nature I had.

"Talk?" He sat at the bar.

"Sure." I'd come to like the kid, and trust him enough to let him run the bar. I didn't want to play his uncle, but I thought he looked at me as a mentor. "Something got you sleepless in the South End?"

He frowned, as if he didn't get the reference.

"Evvie wants me to leave Boston, go to school."

"Out west?" Mentally, I shrugged. I hadn't counted on him staying. "Don't they start in a month? You'd have to have had your paperwork in by now."

I was vamping, really, stuck on the fact he was talking about what Evvie wanted, not him.

"I set it up to go back this year a long time ago. Just in case."

He ducked his head, as if he'd betrayed me. But I was fine with the idea he'd kept his options open until he had to close them. And, yeah, a little disappointed that my plan to take more time off wasn't going to work out.

"I wouldn't ever tell anyone to turn down an education in favor of working in a dive bar. Let alone someone with a full ride to a West Coast Ivy."

"Not so much a dive," he said. "How about you have a drink with me?"

I held up my hands.

"I'm done for the day. You want something, come back here and make it yourself. Just don't make a mess."

He liked building complicated cocktails with esoteric ingredients. I wasn't in the mood.

I stepped out to let him pass me and perched myself on the stool he'd vacated. He surprised me by grabbing a bottle of single-malt scotch and two rocks glasses.

"Oban all right?"

I hadn't had my daily potion yet, so I decided it would be all right. There was no one at home for me to drink with.

"Double? Call it happy hour?"

I'd never mentioned my addiction or the non-standard way I dealt with it. I took a long, thoughtful pause and said no.

"Just the one. Thanks."

He poured the drinks, twisting the mouth of the bottle so it didn't drip, and shot some ginger ale into his. I cringed, but didn't say anything. Then he stood in front of me, seemingly unable to start what he wanted to say.

"Evvie wants you to go? Does she want to go with you?"

He dropped an ice cube in the glass, further ruining the whiskey.

"I'd been thinking pretty hard about going anyway. I was upfront with you about that, wasn't I?"

I picked up the glass and inhaled. When my head went woozy, I put it down again. He'd come for some avuncular advice, which made me feel old. I'd met his mother last year, a lovely but ineffectual woman who'd let him do what he wanted after his father left. It was a tribute to the kid's good sense and ambition that he hadn't fallen into a gang or something worse, despite his better-than-average prospects.

"It ought to be your decision, Isaac."

His forehead wrinkled.

"I know that. But yeah. She wants to come."

"To Palo Alto."

That was a terrible idea. At nineteen, he would be trying to balance studying at one of the toughest universities in the country and his love life, too? Because I had no doubt Evvie would expect him to keep looking out for her.

"You don't know how badly she got knocked around in New Orleans."

"By Vinson? Physically, you mean?"

"No. She's too smart to put up with that. But they wore her down. Psychologically."

I tried to match that with the way she'd come across to me Saturday night.

"She seemed pretty steady when I talked to her."

He took a hit of his drink and grimaced. As well he might.

"She's trying not to show it. But they shook her confidence pretty hard."

"She went down there with her eyes open. And she stayed. She had her reasons and I guess she got what she wanted."

Evvie was not the delicate flower he thought she was. Pain darkened his eyes.

"You never did something you regretted later?"

"What's she going to do while you're going to school. Keep house for you?"

He looked astonished.

"We're not going to live together. She just wants to travel with me. Get away from Boston."

She was a taker and I had to wonder what she thought she could take from him that she couldn't get on her own.

"She could grab a flight. Take a train. Buy a car. Why does she need you?"

That sounded harsher than I meant it to, but it seemed clear she was preying on him.

"We get along," he said. "She needs to get away. With a friend."

"You came in here looking for my take?"

He half-nodded.

"Here it is, then. Go to school, if that's what you decide to do. But give yourself the space to do it right, to focus. Evvie's out for Evvie, and you're smart enough to know that."

He stared out past me, into the bar. I wasn't sure anything I said would get through. But I'd said it.

"I'll give you plenty of notice," he said. "I've got almost a month and a half to decide."

I frowned. Now it sounded like he might change his mind.

"Happy to talk. You don't have to decide this tonight."

8

Isaac wasn't any wiser than when he came in, but at least he knew what I was thinking. He had a hard head, but I hoped he'd at least consider my advice. It wasn't like I'd forced it on him. He'd come to me.

I armed the alarm, another of Baron Loftus's improvements, and locked up the bar. Out on Mercy Street, the night air was thick with that late summer humidity that made everyone think about escaping to the Cape or the coast of Maine. Beyond the smell of hot asphalt and exhaust, I sensed the faintest air of fall, which would be a relief for me and for the business. People spent much more time in bars in the cooler months.

My stomach growled. I hadn't eaten since I sent Syndi home after lunch. I thought about heading over to Kelly's Roast Beef in Revere and grabbing a sandwich to take home.

I'd taken to parking out in front of the bar instead of back in the alley behind the building. The Volvo was more anonymous than my old Cougar had been and it fit in fine in the more gentrified neighborhood.

What was out of place was the big muscle car from the Seventies, gleaming plum and chrome under the street light, nuzzled up to my bumper. I was in no way a car buff, but I recognized the Oldsmobile 442. A classmate of mine at prep school kept one off campus, for weekend trips to Hampton Beach and the ski mountains, though his had been a nondescript dark green. The specimen in front of me could have rolled right out of a classic car show.

A shadow sat behind the wheel. Then the driver's side door

opened and the interior light came on. Once or twice in the early days of the bar, I'd been mugged by a thug stupid enough to think I carried all the immense riches I earned pulling draft beers around in my pocket. Even then, the receipts had been more credit card than cash, maybe an occasional check from someone I knew. And I always left it locked in the safe.

"Mr. Darrow. A word?"

The voice had that familiar croak, a faint reminder of Andy Devine, an old character actor who claimed a childhood accident with a curtain rod had given him his gravel voice. It was the voice from the phone call to Vermont—hell, only four days ago?—the working-class intonation, the dead flat calm.

"You would be Mr. Barksdale."

I arranged my keys between my fingers, though I doubted he'd come to mug me.

He didn't walk so much as strut up the sidewalk, as if to impress a larger audience than one. It might have been a case of little-man syndrome; he was several inches shorter than average height. The pressed khakis and short-sleeved lime green shirt made him look innocuous, but his forearms were massive and his wrists thick as baseball bats.

"Call me Mickey," he said. "We're friends now."

A pack of cigarettes pulled down the front pocket of the shirt. He leaned against the Volvo as if it were his own.

"Mickey. You still worried about Burton? Because he seems to be doing all right."

I felt a gut-clench, fear. Mickey was checking up on me? Making sure I was looking out for Burton the way he'd asked? Nothing Burton ever told me about the gangster hinted at that kind of compassion.

He looked at me the way a cat watches a bird, his eyes bloodshot. Whether he'd been drinking or doping, I couldn't tell, but he hadn't been sleeping well.

"I wanted to inform you how much I appreciated your interrupting your vacation like that. Ms. Voisine is a very attractive woman."

I hated to hear her name in his mouth, but I wouldn't show it.

"It must be nice to have a friend who'll do something like that for you."

He didn't seem like the type to whine about his personal life to a near-stranger. But seeing him in front of me only reinforced my desire to stay out of anything between him and Burton.

"He's a good guy. He's had my back any number of times."

"I'm glad to hear you say that."

Was that uncertainty? Mickey looked like he was at a fancy dinner party and didn't know which fork to pick up. I kept my expression flat. He wouldn't want anyone to see that he was weak.

"Burton and I go way back, you know. Third grade."

I was hungry and tired, a little less politic than I might have been.

"You didn't come across town in the middle of the night to take me down memory lane, did you?"

His chest expanded and his head seemed to swell, his nostrils opening. His face flared from annoyance into anger, but cooled before he hit rage. I shivered, as if I'd dodged a literal bullet.

He reached into his shirt and pulled out a pack of Lucky Strikes, the old unfiltered ones with the red ball logo. I hadn't seen them in ages and I wondered where he was getting them.

"It's very important that Burton stays calm over the next couple weeks." He tossed the cardboard match into the gutter. "This thing with his old girlfriend."

I sensed Mickey knew more about Marina's death than I did. But I doubted he would answer a straight question. Was he involved somehow? Worse, was he responsible?

"I'll do what I can," I said. "Since he and I are friends."

I saw that faint look of longing again.

"You'll know what I mean soon enough. But things are going to get weird."

He elongated the word into two syllables. His standing here talking to me was already weird enough for me.

"Appreciate the warning, Mickey. No more detail than that?"

He flicked the half-smoked butt into the street, scattering red sparks.

"You'll see what I mean," he said. "Soon enough."

* * *

I skipped the trip to Kelly's. I was pie-eyed exhausted as I climbed the stairs to my apartment, not a little bit shaken by the encounter with Mickey. It was difficult for me to believe he was looking out for Burton's best interests, and I resented the way he seemed to think he could manipulate me. Maybe it was time to bring Burton into the loop, let him know about what was going on behind his back.

I was also irked I hadn't heard from Susan. Though there was no reason I couldn't call her, was there?

I tossed my keys on the table and looked at the clock on the stove. It was only eleven out there and she stayed up late. I didn't think I would wake her, but then if I did, maybe that was all right, too.

I punched in the number of the phone she kept in the apartment in Southwest Portland. If she'd put the answering machine on, at least I could let her know I was thinking about her.

The ringing at the other end had a buzz, as if the trunk lines were old. Five rings. Six. I waited for the machine to kick in.

Instead, I got a voice, thick with sleep and foggy, unmistakably male. My stomach cramped.

"What the fuck?" the voice said. "Do you know what time it is?"

I hung up and looked at the phone in my hand, as if it was the instrument that had betrayed me.

"Really?" I said.

I'd known she wasn't happy about me helping Burton out, but taking on someone new just three nights later? That seemed like an extreme reaction.

9

I didn't expect to, but I slept deeply and dreamlessly, though when I woke the next morning, a thick headache gave me the distinct feel of a hangover. It happened occasionally, even though I didn't drink enough any more to cause the genuine version.

I moped through my morning routine, feeling like a sack of rocks was slung over my shoulders. When I turned on my phone, a late-night call from a familiar 503 area code showed, but no message. I thought I'd let the situation settle a little bit before I tried to talk to her about it.

Coffee got me out the apartment door around nine and I stopped in at Mr. Giaccobi's coffee shop, a few blocks up from the bar, and picked up an egg sandwich, still feeling beat up from the night before. It usually took a week to get myself back into a night-time working rhythm, so I knew I'd feel a little sloggy until then.

Syndi was waiting at the front door, half an hour before I'd told her to be there, which I found encouraging. She wore a light pair of pale purple cotton pants and a long-sleeved T-shirt. It wasn't that cold out, but the undershirt looked thin.

She caught my look.

"You ever spend eight hours in your kitchen? Your ventilation system is the pits."

Needless to say, I wasn't in the mood for her conversation or her company. Fortunately, the driver from one of the food distributors banged on the back door and she hustled back to check in the delivery and store it.

I ate my sandwich in peace with another cup of coffee and

tried to use the prose of the *Globe* sports page to clear my brain of personal concerns. The paper still boasted the best sportswriters in the country and these days, they had plenty of good material to report on.

After that, I felt more human, ready to face the world. And good smells started to float from the kitchen—garlic, tomatoes, rosemary. Somehow that calmed me. I refolded the paper so someone else could read it and looked up. Syndi slapped an invoice down on the bar.

"You could do better on some of these items," she said. "Atlantic's not the only distributor in town."

I glanced at the invoice, surprised by a Past Due stamp on it in red. Isaac was supposed to have been paying the bills while I was gone.

"So. How well do you really know your Uncle Mickey?"

I was still gnawing on the "coincidence" of her coming to work here, especially after Mickey's late night concern for Burton's state of mind. I didn't need Burton to tell me no criminal, Mickey included, ever had entirely altruistic motives.

"Hey!" She backed away, her hands in the air. "I don't work for him. That's not what I was trying to do."

It took me a second to see what she meant. She thought I was accusing her of trying to get me to use Mickey as a supplier. Among his legitimate businesses, he ran a wholesale produce stall out of the old Haymarket.

"Not what I meant, Syndi. Your uncle has been up on my radar more lately. He's not keeping a low profile, the way I'd expect someone with his, uh, interests to."

She plucked at the strings of her apron.

"He's like his own branch of the family." She sighed. "Honestly? Most of us pretend we don't even know him."

I supposed I had to take her at her word. It's not like I could expect a straight answer from him.

"He's the reason I had to leave the convent." She sketched a cross in the air in front of her, her fingertips together.

"Really?"

"He donated a big chunk of money to the building fund and the nuns didn't know whether to shit or go blind. They got all fussed about where it was coming from."

"Did they take it?"

"You're not Catholic, are you? Of course they did. They talked themselves around."

"Imagine that."

"Yeah—a Catholic clergy without a conscience. But they found a way to take it out on me."

That wasn't a story I needed to hear. Few people are more bitter than a recovering Catholic. But if Mickey had a hidden agenda, it sounded like she didn't know what it was. I didn't push.

"What do you have cooking for lunch?"

Her face relaxed.

"What about a nice cold soup for a hot day? Gazpacho? And maybe a Greek salad?"

I nodded. I couldn't lose sight of the fact she was solving my most pressing problem. It was a relief having a cook I could rely on again.

* * *

Happily, I didn't have much time that day to chew things over: the connections to Mickey and what he wanted from me, Marina's death, what Susan had been doing with the man in her apartment. The lunch rush was about half what it had been in the old days, but encouraging. It also materialized on the dot of noon, which meant working people on their lunch hours.

I kept the music unchallenging—instrumentals from Brubeck, Paul Desmond, Charlie Haden—and found myself rolling contentedly into the rhythm of working. A couple of my old regulars even showed up, Pedey Thomas from the newspaper and a woman whose name I never knew who used to come down from the financial district for lunch. I was too busy to chat with them, but I wanted to remember to ask Isaac how busy it had been while I was gone. For the first time, I was hopeful the old Esposito could revive.

I carried dirty dishes into the kitchen as the rush subsided.

"Nice job," I said. "That cold soup thing went over better than I thought it would."

She was flushed with the heat of the kitchen. Tendrils of blonde hair escaped from the hairnet and she'd sweated through the long-sleeved tee. She gave me a harried look.

"I need to finish this up. You want a sandwich?"

"Sliced turkey, a little mayo? Maybe some tomatoes?"

The farm market vegetables were starting to come in. Summer was the only time I could stand to eat tomatoes. She nodded.

I went out front, finished bussing the tables, and started to sit, but when the street door opened, I stood up and got back behind the bar.

"Isaac not here?" A voice called from the top of the stairs.

I couldn't make out the face of the speaker against the rectangle of bright sun. I had the impression of someone short and bulky, male, with a lift in his voice that made me think of Hawaii.

"Day off," I called up. "He'll be in Thursday."

Assuming he hadn't bolted for the coast.

The shadow disappeared and the door closed.

Syndi carried out my sandwich, set a nicely composed plate on the bar, the sandwich on sourdough toast cut in triangular sections, a sprig of parsley, and a handful of crinkle-cut potato chips. She watched nervously as I took a bite.

"Nice. Something sharp in there. I like it."

She relaxed.

"A little horseradish in the mayonnaise. Brightens it right up."

I felt like a judge on one of those cooking shows.

"Very nice." I carried the plate around the end of the bar and sat. "Grab something and join me?"

She shook her head.

"I nibble all the time while I'm cooking. I only eat one real meal a day. But I do need to smoke. The alley OK?"

I didn't love the idea, but she was starting to make herself indispensable.

"Set up a can or something. I don't want butts all over the place."

She bristled.

"I'm not a slob. You start being mean to me, I'll start saying the Rosary for you."

I frowned. She laughed and disappeared into the kitchen.

In the quiet of the afternoon, I ate my sandwich and considered the thing that was really bothering me, more than Marina's death, more than Mickey getting weird about Burton. Why else would a man be sleeping over in Susan's apartment if she wasn't cheating on me? Maybe there were personal relationships as well as professional ones she needed to resolve out there. She hadn't been angry with me when she left—I didn't think—but she was also a woman who pushed down her feelings until they erupted, under pressure.

Which begged the question of why she'd agreed to move in with me here, if she wasn't that committed. When I looked back, I had to say she was the one edging us toward a tighter connection.

The smell of cigarette smoke drifted into the bar. I was about to go out back and tell Syndi to shut the door when the upstairs door opened again.

"I see your bar is as popular as it ever was." Burton jogged down the stairs.

I didn't rise to his bait, still a little tender about how badly Baron Loftus had squandered the clientele I'd built up over the years.

"Did about forty covers for lunch. Inch by inch, you know. I take it you're working today."

He wore what I thought of as his uniform, a cheap but respectable suit and tie that he didn't mind getting messed up at a crime scene, over a pale blue Sea Island cotton shirt. The button-down probably cost more than the suit and tie together.

"I am working," he said. "Not in the way you're thinking, though."

When he got to the bottom of the stairs, I saw the cast on his left hand, which worried me immediately. In public, he was always guarded in his moods, but that looked like the kind of injury you got from punching a wall. Or a telephone pole, which I'd seen him do once.

"Trying out for the Golden Gloves?" The cast started at the wrist and covered the back of his hand up to the first set of knuckles. An edge of blue peeped out from under the wraps. "I thought you'd be over the age limit by now."

"This is still a bar, right?"

"If you pay for your drinks? Sure."

Maybe we were friends, but I wasn't going to let him be an asshole.

He pulled out his wallet clumsily and laid a twenty on the bar.

"One fifty one. Straight up."

Another thing to worry about. His usual hard-liquor drink was a whiskey sour, and unless he was on one of his infrequent tears, three was his limit. One fifty one proof rum was something you used in small quantities, a topper in a Hurricane or a spoonful to flame a shot. Drinking it straight was like gargling with kerosene. Bacardi had actually quit making it several years ago. I had a half-full bottle on the back bar that hadn't yet spontaneously ignited.

"You want to get that fucked up, maybe you ought to do it at home."

He moved closer into the light. His face looked like someone from the early twentieth century, someone from Ireland fleeing the potato famine to disembark at Ellis Island. He was raw and drawn, his eyes lined with red, and beaten down, as if his own existence was a weight on his shoulders.

"One shot," he said. "While I tell you a very ugly story."

I had to hunt for the bottle. I short-poured him a little, put the glass down, took the twenty. I shoved his change into the tip jar.

He downed the liquor as if it were polio vaccine and looked into the mirror behind the bar.

"Marina?" I guessed.

"Murdered." He pushed the glass back at me and breathed out fumes. "Someone gave her a hot shot."

10

"I don't even know what that means," I said.

"Someone else injected her with the overdose. She wasn't a secret addict and she didn't do it herself."

I gave him a skeptical look. I knew he wanted to believe that. "Evidence?"

"I'll explain on the way. Can you take an hour? It doesn't look that busy."

He never asked me for a favor directly. Whatever it was, he thought it was important.

"Let me talk to Syndi." I untied my apron and went back into the kitchen.

* * *

Burton drove the unmarked like someone who'd never taken public transportation in his life, slipping easily from lane to lane and navigating the back alleys and shortcuts around the city as if he'd been a cab driver in a previous life. I was too tentative to be comfortable driving in a city where people would flip you off if you looked at them funny. I envied him his ease.

"So how is Carmen?" I asked.

We were quite obviously not talking about how he knew, or believed, Marina's death was homicide. I assumed the full autopsy had given him some incontrovertible evidence, but I figured he would tell me eventually. Assuming I wanted to know.

"I saw her a couple of weeks ago. Before." He yanked the car around a parked FedEx truck, zigging at the last second to miss the driver jumping out of his cockpit. A horn blatted off to our left. He ignored it.

"She has her moments. The docs kept trying to tell Marina it was Alzheimer's, but that just seems to be a name they throw around when they need a label. It's definitely dementia, though there are stretches when she seems like the old Carmen. Who, as you know, hates me."

He grinned across the bench seat. "Which is why I asked you to come along."

"How much do you want to tell her?"

My relationship with Marina's mother wasn't much less complicated than his. She'd been my family's cook when I was growing up, and something in her relationship to the family resulted in my father leaving her a chunk of money when he died. He'd never hinted at what the connection was. Carmen always pretended not to know what I was talking about when I brought it up, and now I supposed it would stay a mystery for all time.

"You mean, am I going to tell her her daughter was probably murdered? I don't think so. Besides, with the dementia—maybe because of it—she gets upset easily. It's not going to add anything for her to know."

"But you do think we need to tell her Marina's gone."

Burton pulled into the parking lot of the Western Addition. Marina had started Carmen out in a facility in Newton, but Carmen hadn't liked the food.

"She's going to notice if Marina isn't visiting any more, don't you think?"

The lobby of the place was wide, high, and open, the calming off-white walls relieved by bright splashes of fresh flowers in niches around the space. The effect was of an upscale funeral home, which I assumed was unintended. Most noticeable was the absence of medicinal smells or anything else implying old age or sickness.

Burton signed us into the register at the front desk. The young man with the black bowl haircut and the nose stud smiled, as if he recognized Burton. I followed down the hallway to an elevator.

"You still haven't told me why you're so sure she was killed."

He winced.

"Let's get this done first."

"Your call." Obviously. He was the homicide guy and I had to respect his expertise, even if it annoyed me.

We rode up to the fourth floor and stepped off into a lushly carpeted hallway, gold and white. I heard a baseball game behind one of the doors, number 46, which was ajar a few inches.

Burton tapped the door frame.

"Carmen? It's Daniel. Burton."

His voice was softer and it made me wonder how changeable he had to be in his work, how much of an actor. And I wondered if he wasn't working now, believing Marina had been murdered.

The door flung open the rest of the way and Carmen glared at him. She was short, but blocky in the way old women sometimes get, her tinted black curls tight to her scalp.

"Daniel Burton. You're interrupting the ball game. Not that they're setting the world on fire." Her creased face broke into a grin. "How nice of you to come visit a cranky old woman. And who's this?"

That didn't do much for my ego. Carmen had known me as a little boy, and more recently, when Marina couldn't work, her mother had subbed in the kitchen at the Esposito. The little I knew about dementia patients was they tended to remember the distant past better than the present.

"You remember Elder, Carmen. Marina's old boss."

What a way to be remembered. I hoped I'd been more than that to her.

Carmen's face dropped, maybe at the reminder she didn't remember as well as she had. She turned into the room.

"Of course I do. I never wanted her to work in a bar. It's not something a nice Catholic girl does."

I thought of Syndi.

Carmen picked up the remote and muted Remy and Eckersley. I could never remember the name of the slick-haired dude who'd replaced Don Orsillo. He always talked too much.

"Where's my daughter today?"

She plopped herself into an ugly vinyl chair that exhaled noisily.

"That's why I'm here." Burton was as soft-voiced and gentle as I'd ever seen and I wondered if that was from experience, notifying the families of his victims. That would have to wear on you. "I'm sorry, Carmen. Marina is gone."

So much for my coming along to tell her. It looked like I was more moral support for Burton.

"Gone? Gone where?"

But the way she clutched at her black cardigan told me she understood what he meant.

"Gone from the world, Carmen. I'm sorry."

He spoke with a tenderness I wouldn't have guessed he owned. Carmen shook her head so hard the curls bounced.

"Oh. She'll be back."

My heart hurt for her. Even knowing her faculties didn't run at full power, I could tell she understood. She just didn't want to.

Neither Burton nor I had sat. I felt him edge toward the door, the hard task accomplished.

"I'll be back to visit soon, Carmen. When I have some news. All right?"

I assumed he meant details about services and so on, though I doubted we'd be able to take Carmen out of here for something like that.

"If you have to." She stared at the silent TV screen, where a ballplayer, not one of the Red Sox, ran the bases with his hands in the air.

Burton moved for the door. I followed.

"She'll be back." Carmen picked up the remote. "She will."

* * *

"Well. That didn't go so well," I said as we rode the elevator to the ground floor. "You think she even registered what you were saying?"

Burton stared at the numbers flashing.

"I need a drink."

"Fortunately, I know a place where we can take care of that problem."

We exited through the automatic doors into the steamy day.

Of course, the air conditioning in Burton's unmarked was broken, recirculating the humid outside air in over the hot engine and blowing it in our faces. We rode with all the windows down, which made the interior even less comfortable than the outside. I was sweating like a hard-run horse when we parked in front of the bar.

He didn't move to get out right away.

"Come on inside and cool off for a bit. You still haven't told me why you think Marina was killed."

He turned off the engine.

"Yeah. We need to talk."

The bar was deserted in the middle of the afternoon. I offered him iced coffee, but he shook his head. It was still a little early, even for a dedicated day drinker. I also left the music off. It concerned me to see him retreat so deeply into himself.

"It was still the right thing to do," I said. "Even if she didn't quite get it."

Maybe he was still worried about disturbing the order of Carmen's universe.

"Which hand did Marina do things with?"

"What do you mean?"

"Simple question. What was her dominant hand?"

I thought, then realized I couldn't say with much certainty. It wasn't the sort of thing you noticed about people. Even people you'd known a long time.

"I wouldn't say I was sure. But if she were a lefty, I think I would have noticed."

He nodded.

"She was right handed. All the way." He smiled a small private smile.

"So?"

"That's how I know she didn't kill herself. Didn't inject the shit herself, I mean."

I made a questioning sound. Where was he going?

"Entry point was in the crook of her elbow. Her right elbow."

I saw what he meant, that she was less likely to inject herself with the left hand. But if that was his entire body of evidence? It was weak as herb tea, and not entirely convincing.

"OK," I said. "It would have been clumsy. But not impossible."

He frowned at my skepticism.

"You do know, this is work I've been doing my entire career? A lot of years. And generally, I do know what I'm talking about."

I held up my hands in surrender.

"Not going to argue with you."

The fact he was so defensive meant he saw the flaw in the argument, too. I could dream up a half dozen reasons to use your off hand to do something like that. It was an anomaly, not infallible evidence of anything.

My next question was going to be harder for him to answer.

"What are you going to do about it? Does anyone agree with you?"

His mouth twisted.

"No one's buying it. There was a little bit of bruising around her wrist, the right one. Maybe an indication someone was holding her? But just the one little hole in her arm."

I knew if I probed to see how serious he was, I'd have to be careful. He was holding an element of hope, a bit of wishful thinking, a desire to tell himself he hadn't missed signs that pointed to Marina doing drugs. Even as a one-time experiment.

"It doesn't feel like a lot to build on. You know she had a thing for the bad boys, right? Before you," I added hastily as the flush rose into his face. "Carlos, way back when. Rasmussen Carter."

"No one ever pushed that woman into anything she didn't want to do. Bad boys or not."

Which only reinforced what I'd been thinking, that Marina might have been intrigued by something daring and so far outside her experience she wanted to try it on her own terms, with terrible results. One of the problems she and Burton had had, I believed, was that she wasn't ready to settle down so soon after Carmen moved out and Marina had gained that freedom.

But I wasn't going to get anywhere with that argument right now. I said the only thing I could say.

"I'm with you, Burton. If there's anything I can do."

He stood up abruptly.

"People say that all the time when something happens, you know? You know what I wish? I wish that instead of asking, people would just fucking do something. Not ask, but do. Even if it was wrong."

He turned and strode for the stairway, not before I saw his eyes glisten. At first, I was offended, but he was right about one thing. Often when we don't know how to help, we use those words to absolve ourselves of the effort.

Because the steel door was on a hydraulic arm, he couldn't slam it. But his exit into the street left a vacuum in the bar.

* * *

Syndi came out from the back. I was still sitting at the table, cold coffee in front of me, trying to think of something I could do to help my friend. Even if I was dubious about his evidence, I couldn't tell him that. The best I could do was nod and hope the opportunity to help came somehow.

Maybe from Mickey Barksdale? I didn't know what his motives might be, but maybe he would have an idea. He'd engaged me to help Burton, after all, and I expected to hear from him again soon.

"Looks like heavy thinking for a Wednesday afternoon," she said. "Don't hurt yourself."

She trailed air that smelled of cigarette smoke and an oddly unpleasant scent, like castor oil.

"There are two more bills on your desk. Guys say they haven't got paid."

"Fine."

"I was thinking a Cobb salad for the special tomorrow. What do you think?"

"You're the cook, Syndi. Why don't you cook?"

I wanted nothing more than a tall brown glass of scotch in my hand, not to drink so much as to comfort me with its presence.

She stopped short in the doorway, as if I'd thrown something at her.

"Sure thing, boss man. Let me just get my white ass into the kitchen. And cook."

11

I felt bad for snapping at her, but didn't have the chance to say so until later that evening. We were trying a dinner service and the response was enough to keep me on my toes for a solid two hours. Some of the crowd were tourists and people from out in the suburbs—the urge to get out of the house and go places had been pent up for some time—but more importantly, I was starting to see faces I recognized, even an occasional customer from before who greeted me by name. All I'd ever wanted was a decent neighborhood joint. Maybe if this kept up for a month or two, I could start thinking about bringing live music in again.

"Sorry if I was sharp with you," I said, the next time she came out front. "Got some things on my mind."

"Your old cook." She nodded. "I heard."

I wondered where, though in many ways, Boston was a very small town.

The crowd winnowed itself down to two young guys in business suits—who wore suits to work any more?—drinking beer as if neither of them planned to go into work tomorrow morning. An older woman with a chair full of bags from Newbury Street finished up a chicken sandwich and her third glass of Chardonnay.

Syndi smelled like cigarettes. If she hadn't been a smoker, she would have been close to perfect. Even in the heat of the rush, she never dropped into the weeds, never mixed up an order or got flustered.

She rolled her shoulders as if my irritation was something she was used to. I hadn't been raised a Catholic, but my impression of nuns was that they were long on rigidity and discipline and short on the milk of human kindness, reserving that for their priests and their God. Which may have accounted for why Syndi always seemed ready to wince, as if she could minimize the pain by anticipating the blow.

"No big deal. I got a lot worse from the nuns, believe me."

"Still. Whatever I have on my mind shouldn't spill over on you. I don't have to be a jerk."

I used a different word than the one I meant, out of deference to her. I needn't have bothered.

"Don't worry about it. You start acting too much like an asshole, I'll let you know."

"Oh-kay."

"But we did good, right?" She waved a hand at the tables. "This is working out?"

She was looking for approval, not my strongest suit as a boss.

"You're doing fine. The food has been good, you handled the rush without panicking. If it isn't clear, you are officially the Esposito's new cook."

She slapped her hands together.

"Goodie. I was hoping." She looked around the walls, the jazz photos, the iconic Boston sports shot that gave the place its name. "One thing."

"What?"

"Do you mind paying me in cash?"

I walked the length of the bar and ran a glass of club soda, surveying my remaining three customers. I'd heard rumors the Liquor Licensing Board, concerned about untaxed income in cash businesses, was mounting sting operations, trying to cut down on a skimming practice that was as old as metal coins.

"I don't have any problem with that." I sipped, watching her face. "But you need to understand I'm going to 1099 you at the end of the year. I can't afford to screw with the IRS."

She nodded.

"I get it. It's just my expenses run close to the bone. I can't afford all those deductions every week."

"You'll still have to pay the taxes, you know."

She nodded, reached into the pocket of her blouse.

"By the way. I didn't need this."

She handed me a hundred dollar bill.

"That was supposed to be an advance."

"I'd rather wait until regular payday. Which is?"

"Saturday night. After we close." The register would be at its fullest then.

She pushed the bill at me. She was going to be insulted if I didn't take it. I made sure she saw me put it back in the register.

"Are we going to run a full dinner the rest of the week? I have some ideas to try out."

The business hadn't rebounded to pre-Loftus levels, but it wouldn't get better until I took some chances.

"Let's go on a regular dinner schedule starting next week. Tuesday through Saturday."

Her face fell.

"I will pay you for the rest of the week. Maybe we'll do a soft open Friday night. You're going to have to plan the menus. Get the kitchen organized the way you want it. Stock up."

"Aces." She pointed at me. "You probably ought to clean up those past due bills, too. Or they'll start making you pay on delivery."

I had to ask Isaac about that—I'd thought I left him enough cash to pay everything while I was gone.

The matron with the shopping bags wobbled up the stairs. I hoped she wasn't driving herself back to Chestnut Hill or wherever all her purchases were bound. I went to bus her table and saw she'd tipped well and I waved two fingers at her back as she navigated around someone in the doorway.

I was going to have to install a stronger bulb up there. I didn't see it was Isaac until he was halfway down the stairs. The two beer drinkers, both white, took one look at him, threw some bills on the bar, and got up to go.

Isaac limped across the floor toward the bar, moving at the pace of a geriatric. Syndi gasped at the sight of his face. Bruising darkened the skin up around his left temple and the eye on that side was swollen. Dried blood rimmed his nostrils.

"Old woman called me the N word." His words were muffled by the swollen lips. "Nice to live in a city that never changes its mind."

Syndi put a hand over her mouth.

"What the hell happened to you?" I said.

"That's what I need to talk to you about."

* * *

Isaac was not a ghetto-tough kid, someone who'd grown up fighting. His parents were professionals and he'd attended a suburban high school, where any harassment would probably have been more psychological than physical: words, attitudes, social isolation. More damaging, maybe, but nothing like trying to protect your literal ass and get an education in an inner city public school.

I sat him at the bar, gave him a wet towel to dab at the dried blood. His hands shook and he kept swiveling his head to look behind him, as if to make sure no one was sneaking up. His eyes were dull with pain and fear.

Syndi slipped away into the kitchen. I broke one of my own rules and poured him a small glass of coffee brandy. He leaned both hands on the bar, as if he didn't trust his balance, and shook his head.

"You know I don't like to drink."

Since when? We'd drunk together.

"Even mouthwash has alcohol in it. This will slow you down."

The fight or flight instinct still had him jazzed. He closed his eyes, then grunted, as if a pain had gone through him. He pulled the glass toward him, fingers trembling.

"So what happened?"

He tossed back the drink, exhaled. Syndi came out of the kitchen with an ice pack wrapped in a towel. He looked at her.

"Thank you."

He pressed the ice against the swollen side of his face, which calmed him somewhat.

"I got mugged. Just a while ago."

That seemed obvious, but I'd have to let him tell it his own way. Syndi retreated to the kitchen.

"It still happens," I said. "This isn't the shiny New Boston all the politicians would like you to believe in."

Especially for a young Black man out at night, which is what I assumed his story was a version of.

Isaac shook his head.

"This was not random. I was a target." Anger shuddered his chest. "You know how I know that? Besides hearing that word in my head over and over?"

He stood up, wobbling, as if his knees wouldn't lock. I stepped out from behind the bar and took his arm.

"Sit down. You eat anything today?"

I put him at a table close to the bar. Syndi carried out a bowl of soup, left over from lunch, a chunk of bread. I nodded thanks.

"They told me it was because I was helping Burton. For driving over there the other night? Shit. I don't even like the man."

That sounded strange. He'd only driven my Volvo so I could leave Burton's Jeep at his building. And Burton didn't have enemies in the criminal world in Boston, at least ones who would try and punish him for something or target his friends. His successful cases usually resulted in someone going to prison for life, and in the unsuccessful ones, the defendants were usually shy about stirring things up.

"I wonder why they thought the two of you were friends. It doesn't make sense."

He snorted and picked up the spoon to dip into the soup.

"They talked about me being in Charlestown. Besides, it's the only time I've been near the man or had anything to do with him. You know we're chalk and cheese."

He was reminding me of the first time they met, in the warehouse where Isaac was hosting a rave. It hadn't been smooth.

"Where did this happen?"

He shied a little.

"What?"

"Mattapan Square. Off the Avenue. It was barely dark, for God's sake."

Right off of Blue Hill Avenue wasn't a place someone like Isaac would normally hang out.

"What were you trying to buy?"

I was disappointed. I thought I knew him well enough to say he wouldn't be tempted into any of the usual stupid teenage tricks, but the only reason for him to be in that neighborhood at any time of day was to buy drugs. I doubted he'd been peddling his ass.

"They weren't for me!"

Then he put his head down and spooned soup into his mouth, tore off a piece of the bread. I read what he didn't want to say.

"For Evvie."

He nodded miserably.

"What was it?" It wouldn't make a difference, but I wanted to know. "Heroin?"

His face flashed, as if the thought horrified him.

"God, no. Just coke. She's trying to taper off."

Just.

"You know better than to hang down there." His look was way too suburban to fool anyone. "White guys or Black?"

"Two of them. White. That thick accent."

By which I took it he meant the tones of a neighborhood like, say, Charlestown. I wondered if Mickey had been behind it, though I couldn't see how that fit with his trying to protect Burton.

"They mentioned Burton's name?"

He dropped the spoon into the bowl with an angry clatter.

"They made one solid fucking point of it. All right? Kept repeating the name."

"I'm on your side, Isaac. Don't yell at me. You report it to the police?"

"Me? In Mattapan? They would have laughed me off and given me an aspirin. They don't stick their noses in the business down there."

If it wasn't Mickey, he could probably trace who'd done it, especially if I could convince him the thugs were a threat to Burton. It sounded like they'd been told to scare off anyone who tried to help him.

Isaac half-lurched out of his chair and headed for the men's room. Before he could make it, he vomited the soup he'd been eating, bent over, and wrapped his arms around his belly. He groaned. I worried that he might have internal injuries, too.

"Call 911," I yelled to Syndi.

"It gets worse." His voice strained. "Evvie? She's gone."

12

Isaac protested the whole way against the 911 attention, though one of the paramedics, a red-haired woman, whistled when she inspected the cut over his eye. She made him sit and let her check his pupils.

"No sign of a concussion." She grinned. "But someone's going to be sore. Rest, ice, sleep." She looked around the bar. "No alcohol. He should go home and rest. Nothing you can do if the ribs are broken except tape them up."

I felt better about his condition when he asked for her phone number.

"I'll call him a cab."

With Isaac ferried back to his apartment and the bar empty, I was surprised to see it was only about ten-thirty. Probably time to face the domestic chore I'd been ducking.

Susan had left a message on my cell, knowing I wouldn't pick up the Esposito's house phone unless there was no one else in the place. Her "Call me" was brusque, though I heard a tinge of desperation. I'd already ignored two of her calls.

It was seven-thirty on the West Coast, early enough she should still be around. If she was home. My mouth tasted like ash when I thought about her going out.

But, no way out but through. I punched in the number and didn't have to wait. Her phone didn't ring twice.

"Elder." She sounded out of breath. "Where have you been? You had me worried."

No doubt.

"Hey. How's everything out in the wild, wild west?"

She paused. I felt her trying to read my mood.

"Fine. Except for the part where my lover doesn't call me back for two days."

"Shit. Has it been that long? The bar's been really busy."

More silence. Then:

"Well, that's a good thing, right? Something to be pleased about? The place is coming back?"

"In fact, it's kind of busy right now."

I looked out over the empty floor, only slightly embarrassed by the lie.

"You called me," she said.

"Just checking in. I thought it would be polite."

A half-laugh at the other end.

"Well, I'm glad you finally did. Did you call here the other night? Late?"

Here we were. Was she going to lie to me? Or tell the truth and have it be a prelude to a kiss-off?

"It's fine, Susan. We're both grownups. You're on the West Coast and I'm here. No harm, no foul."

"It's not what you seem to be assuming."

"It never is, is it? Sorry if I'm being unclear—it's fine. Consider it your free pass."

I was goading her and I knew it, but I couldn't seem to quit.

"My what?" Her voice dripped sarcasm. "How utterly generous of you, to grant me permission."

Now she was white-hot. We were one tiny push from one of us saying something irrevocable.

"I didn't mean to step on your toes. Do you have any idea when you'll be through with whatever you're doing there?"

Because, no matter how angry I might be about the other night, I wasn't ready to blow us up.

"No. I don't." Her voice was cold as January, her anger building now that mine seemed to ebb. "There's a shit ton of work here to do. It could be months. I'm kind of busy."

I heard the mockery.

"This is getting us nowhere."

"That much is true. But you don't get to whip up a fight, then pretend to step away. You've already made up your mind what happened."

Again I had the sense that the wrong word would tip us into a void. I was suddenly tired of the sparring.

"I miss you, is all."

"Funny. I don't get that feeling at all."

The high whistle of rage returned. My ears felt clogged.

"Is this doing us any good, Susan? Or is it just making it easier to say fuck it and move on?"

I should have known better than to push her up against any kind of wall. Her reply was hard as a chip of granite.

"Better think about what you're saying, Mr. Darrow. What you really want."

"What does anyone want?" I said. "Besides loyalty. To be able to trust."

The next sound I heard was no sound, the faint hiss of an open line. She'd hung up on me. I closed my eyes and cradled the phone.

"That sounded like fun." Syndi stepped out of the kitchen with a pad in her hand, a pencil tucked behind her ear like a carpenter. She'd been just in time to catch the last few lines. "Two beat-downs in one day. I hope it's not a trend."

The comment yanked me out of my mood. Susan would do what Susan would do. But Isaac getting beaten up reminded me too much of the Esposito's bad old days. I hoped we weren't sliding back.

"What?"

She flinched as if I'd thrown something at her.

"Menus? For next week? I thought I could tell you some ideas I had."

I took a couple deep breaths and stowed the phone under the bar. Taking my problems out on her wouldn't do either of us any good. I looked at her, suddenly aware her nipples stuck out through the thin cotton blouse.

"Are you cold?" I handed her the cotton bar jacket I kept on a hook by the door. "You look cold."

She looked down, blushed, and handed me the pad while she shrugged on the coat.

"Colder out here. The A/C. I was thinking chicken pot pies," she said. "Like comfort food. Make them ahead and heat them to order."

My mind was not on what she was saying. Had Susan and I just called it quits? Almost before we'd gotten started?

"Sounds good. Order whatever you need and we'll go for it."

But instead of looking pleased, she acted hurt, as if I weren't taking her seriously enough. I shrugged. Today's score currently? Women two, Elder zero.

13

Burton took a couple days off after he got the news about Marina. She wasn't technically family, so he didn't qualify for bereavement leave, but Lieutenant Martines, his nominal superior in Homicide, had been decent about it. There was only one case on the board at the moment, a drug-related shooting in Dorchester, and Liam MacDonald, the newest detective on the squad, was assigned to that.

When Marina had postponed their wedding last year, he'd believed the two of them were finally done with each other. He'd been relieved, though there was no way to tell her that. It was clear she had neither the self-confidence nor the desire to go through with it and it was better for her to bail out, even at the last minute. He was well-lapsed from his childhood Catholicism, but enough of its influence remained that he hadn't been going to walk into a marriage thinking about his exit strategy.

Now that he was back on the job, the current lull in murder cases was doing him no good. He'd never wish for someone to die, but in the absence of work, he thought he might be perseverating a little too much over how Marina had died. It wouldn't be out of the question for someone to inject herself with the off hand—who could guess what an addict might do?—but it was the kind of detail that would have snagged his thinking even if the victim hadn't been a woman he loved.

At the cough from the entrance to his cubicle, he looked up. Liam MacDonald stood there with his arms crossed. He was slender and very tall, six four at least, and dressed casually, as if he were going on a stakeout. Burton hadn't had much to do with him yet, except for the occasional all-hands meeting, but he seemed competent enough, if early reports from the field were accurate.

"Burton. This Antonelli thing. Anything weird there?"

Burton couldn't help stiffening up. He wasn't giving up his interest in the case unless someone wrestled it away.

"What's the matter, Liam? Not enough to do?"

"It's all junkies killing junkies. Not much meat there."

One thing Burton had heard about MacDonald was that he wasn't inclined to treat every unexplained death equally, that he liked to pass judgment on the victims, slot them into some personal hierarchy of worth. Burton didn't know if that meant his effort level got tailored to a victim's status, but it was a slippery slope from judgments of that kind to a compromise in how seriously you treated a case.

"Waiting for the full report from the ME. But it looks like what it looked like."

"More fucking junkies." MacDonald growled. "Never did understand that mode of self-abuse. I like a drink as much as anyone, but the drugs? That's just suicide, fast or slow."

"Yeah, well." He didn't know the man well enough to tell him what he really thought, what a couple of decades of dealing with people had taught him. You never knew what a human would do when he or she lost their hope. However that happened.

"You knew the vic, the loo said."

"Yes." And leave it at that, Burton thought. He didn't like the idea Martines was talking about his personal life behind his back. Probably thought he was promoting team building.

"Well, if it turns out to be anything, think about this poor rookie. Wait. You wouldn't be handling the case anyway, right? Unwritten rule."

Unwritten rule said that people didn't work on cases they had a personal stake in. He'd postponed thinking about that, mainly because he didn't know what the final autopsy report would say. If he continued to be convinced Marina had been murdered, which was what his gut told him, he was working the case, regardless. But he'd wait for that report before declaring.

"Don't know about that." He wished MacDonald would leave—the ambition rolled off him in waves, a stink. "Might go the other way, too."

"But you'd put in a word for me? Senior man on the squad, your recommendation would mean a lot."

Burton doubted his stock was high enough with Martines that the lieutenant would listen to anything he said.

"We could even work it together. Even if you didn't get assigned. I could learn from you."

Though MacDonald didn't sound convinced of that.

Burton recalled his own eager attitude from his early career. It hadn't survived a full year—a year of senseless deaths, frigid stinking autopsies, and endless paperwork. He tried to generate empathy for where MacDonald was and couldn't. The best he could do was not bring him up short over his eagerness for people to die to serve his career.

"I'm not too concerned," Burton said. "I've seen the preliminary and it looks straightforward. Accidental OD."

His stomach hurt as he said that. He was half-convinced he was lying. But if there was something here for him to investigate, the last man he wanted on the case was a raw-assed rookie with preconceptions.

"Whatever," MacDonald said. "Any luck at all, we'll get a bunch of cases all at once. Nothing I hate more than being bored, not having anything to do."

Burton was trying not to judge the detective on this little interaction, but he was less impressed than he'd been before the conversation started.

"I'll make sure you get a copy of the final when it comes in. Since you're interested."

MacDonald didn't seem like the type to read paper. He put a finger alongside his nose.

"Be a fine thing if you did." He buttoned his suit coat. "Talk soon."

He was already ahead of MacDonald on one score—he knew the autopsy wasn't going to tell them definitively whether Marina had been murdered. That was the investigation's job. The report could say she'd died of a shot of heroin, whether it was too strong or adulterated with something poisonous, but not whether she'd injected it herself.

MacDonald should have known that. It made Burton wonder about his background, what police force he'd come into BPD from. Whatever else, he had no intention of partnering with the man, not if his attitude was that some people deserved dying more than others.

He swiveled the chair to reach his computer. Nothing to do right now but wait, wait for the autopsy report, wait for someone else in the city to be killed and give him work to do. Some days, he wondered about the professional choices he'd made, tying his work life to something so generally tragic. He envied Elder the simplicity of owning the bar sometimes, the pleasure of non-criminal companionship. Here was something he could do for him.

He clicked over to a search engine and dropped in Evangeline's full name. Something Elder had said about her return to Boston was raising questions.

* * *

He tapped the manila interoffice envelope on its edge. He hadn't expected the final autopsy so soon, but Robbes, the diener he'd befriended in the Medical Examiner's office, sent it along as soon as the ME was through. He wondered, since it happened so quickly, if Marina's autopsy had been moved to the head of the line, and whether someone somewhere was trying to do him a favor.

The actual official version lay in the digital bowels of the state's computer systems. The paper version was his own fetish—paper was permanent and tangible. An electronic file could be manipulated.

Impatient with his own impatience, he tore the flap on the envelope as he unwound the string from the fastener.

"B," a note clipped to the top sheet read. "Final. n.b., pages 3 & 7." It was signed with two capital T's, Robbes's nickname.

He folded the note and tucked it in his pocket. Not a good idea to leave around evidence of his unofficial request. One of the first lessons you learned was to protect your sources.

He leafed through the report, not greatly different from the preliminary version he'd had about a couple days ago. He had remembered correctly that she'd been injected in the right arm.

He flipped past the dry listing of weights and measures of organs and fluids with a lurch in his throat. He found himself on the first page Tee-Tee had highlighted, wondering if it supported his theory about her death.

Page 3, Other Markings. In addition to some mild bruising around the wrist, "small areas of hematoma around the upper triceps" of the right arm. A rough diagram of what might have been fingertip splotches. On the injected arm. He frowned.

And page 7, after he'd waded through more numbers and technical terminology, it appeared that the heroin that killed her was nearly pure, unadulterated by any of the dilution ingredients commonly used, baking soda or powdered milk.

He slid the report back into its envelope and locked it in the one secure drawer of his desk, sat back in the chair, and put his feet up. He wasn't quite ready to share this with MacDonald. It would arrive through official channels eventually.

The worst temptation for an investigator, one he admitted falling into occasionally, was to construct a story describing a crime and its motives ahead of time, then whittle and sand all the available scraps of evidence to make them fit. This tendency was encouraged by the fact that most murders were simple and straightforward narratives: someone's temporary loss of control, a reaction to greed.

He'd learned about Occam's Razor at Middlebury in a philosophy class. Commonly, it was rendered as the simplest explanation of something being the right one. Technically, it was the explanation that required the fewest number of assumptions: hoofbeats generally mean horses, not zebras.

But the autopsy report tempted him to assume he was correct, that the bruising was evidence of a strong hand immobilizing Marina's arm while the other hand shot her up with heroin so pure that her heart slammed to a stop almost immediately. He turned the assumption this way and that, trying to see it in the coldest light possible. Try as he might, he couldn't think of an alternative explanation as compelling as that. Marina had been murdered.

The question was why? A woman taking cooking classes to become a chef, no connections to anything criminal, even sketchy? What made her a threat to anyone, enough of a threat that she had to die?

14

The Esposito was finding its rhythm again. I didn't know what business had been like while I was in Vermont with Susan, but Isaac must have had something to do with the bar business coming back. And Syndi was showing she could handle the kitchen. We'd agreed to try out a dinner service tonight before starting in full scale next week, and it was working. I'd never wanted to worry too much about the food anyway—the jazz and the drinks were what I was in the business for—and Marina had always handled the rest. But Syndi turned out to be an excellent successor.

So I worried a little about the new equilibrium when Isaac called me Thursday night and told me he'd be in to work on Friday. I wondered how his injuries had healed and whether the three of us would mesh. I'd pretty much assumed from our last conversation he was going to leave for school in September, so I was more concerned about keeping Syndi happy than him.

When he showed up on Friday afternoon, he didn't say anything about Evvie, so I assumed that situation was under control. I hoped for his sake she was gone for good. It might be an ego blow now, but better in the long run.

An old acquaintance from Berklee, back from the days when Cyrus Nance was a friend and sending me student musicians to play at the Esposito, dropped by after a gig at Sculler's. He asked if I minded him playing for tips. I was glad to have him. The next step in resurrecting the Esposito was starting up live music again. This would be a good test. The pandemic year had been so hard on everyone, I was hoping there was a demand for good live jazz.

Reston carried the Marshall Mini amp and his guitar case up onto the tiny stage and started plugging in. I sat on a stool outside the bar, content to let Isaac serve unless the crowd got too busy. I liked watching him work: he had an ease with people and he moved economically, as if he'd been dispensing drinks for decades.

Reston nodded at me from the stage. I stood up. I'd agreed to quiet the crowd long enough to introduce him, but he was on his own after that. He'd set up a black top hat, brim up, on the edge of the stage, a small hand lettered sign that read "Fear Change? Leave it Here." I dropped a five in the hat to prime it and grabbed the microphone.

"Ladies and gentlemen. A little extra treat tonight, no cover charge. From the Berklee School of Music, right down the street. Reston Prentiss."

Reston hit a chord, I stepped away, and returned to my seat at the bar. He kicked off with a Wes Montgomery tune near and dear to me, "Bumping on Sunset." My chest swelled with pleasure. The Esposito was back.

Isaac walked down to where I sat, shaking his head.

"Old man music," he said. "That's awful close to elevator."

To the extent I'd thought about it, I knew twenty year olds and forty-five year olds were never going to love the same music. Most of us were stuck for life with the music we heard in our teens and twenties, imprinted with memories of those formative times. Taste tended to calcify, if you didn't work at it. It was difficult for me to open myself to new artists and modes. It was like challenging yourself to read a new author against re-reading a book you loved.

"Take a look at your crowd," I said. "Not exactly cutting edge."

"This place is like a boomer cocktail lounge." His voice was bitter.

"Who peed in your ginger ale?"

He huffed and walked back down the bar to put clean glasses away. I shook my head.

Reston was a sad story. I wasn't supposed to know it, but another friend at Berklee told me he'd been diagnosed with Parkinson's. You couldn't tell anything tonight from the way his educated fingers flicked through an intricate instrumental bridge off of "Stars Fell on Alabama," but the notion of a guitarist losing muscle control was about the saddest thing I could think of. And incrementally, so he could feel it happening, not all at once. As if he felt me thinking about him, Reston lifted his chin and smiled.

Which put me in mind of other sad things happening right now. Marina's death stuck in my consciousness with the presence of a thick splinter, painful, but a wound without blood. She and I had parted ways after she dumped Burton again, and I wondered what he planned in the way of a remembrance. I also worried whether his certainty that she hadn't died accidentally would haunt him or if he'd be able to resolve it. No one ever knew the depths of someone else's unhappiness.

Isaac swept past me into the kitchen, I assumed to pick up a food order for someone at the bar. I was drawing a pint for Marian Stoner, a librarian neighbor who dropped in once in a while, when I heard angry voices out in the kitchen, then a crash, as if a pot had fallen on the floor.

I cocked my ear as the beer finished pouring, hoping it was an accident. Then Syndi rushed out through the kitchen door, shedding her apron and shoving it into my chest.

"If that's the kind of bar you're running, I don't want a bit of it." Her anger released the brogue in her voice. "I may not have been good enough for the convent, but I'm not going to stay around in an atmosphere like this."

She ran noisily up the stairs. Reston, his eyes closed, never missed a note. Marian questioned me with a look. I shrugged, as Syndi went out the door.

Isaac came back out of the kitchen carrying plates with an innocent air, as if nothing had happened, and even if it had, it wasn't his fault.

"Want to tell me what that was all about?"

He ignored the question and delivered the food, got very busy down at the far end of the bar checking the beer coolers, the cabinets for napkins and other supplies.

Reston finished the tune with a run of musical kisses, running down the scale into silence. Polite applause ensued. Several people got up to drop something in the hat, which pleased me. He tipped his fedora and started to noodle around on the guitar some more.

A party of four, two couples dressed up for a night out, beckoned me over and asked for menus. I dropped them on the table and came back behind the bar.

"I sincerely hope you know how to cook," I said to the volatile boy. "You chase my cook away, you're going to have to do her job."

He started to shake his head. He only liked working the bar for the chance to be out in public, exercising his charm and social skills. If I put him back in the kitchen, he'd probably feel like he was working at the 7-Eleven.

But he didn't argue, stalked past me, and reached a long apron down off the hook inside the kitchen doorway. I hoped he'd be able to fake it well enough to cover it the rest of the night and that no one got sick.

I seriously considered picking up my mood with a shot of scotch, then discarded the idea with an ease that warmed me. The bar business had plenty of unexpected wrinkles: drunks, short deliveries, bounced checks, and drink scammers. What I was sure Isaac didn't know was that Syndi, in a week, had become more important to the Esposito's future than he was. If one of them had to go to keep the bar running smoothly, Isaac was in for a surprise.

He pulled such a piss-poor attitude the rest of the night that I closed the kitchen early and sent him home around eleven-thirty. The music scene and the bar business in the city hadn't rebounded completely from the downturn. By this time of night, I was down to three solitary and dedicated drinkers at the bar, none of whom was drinking anything complicated enough to tax my bartending skills.

Which was all right. It gave me time to finish the cleanup, fill the supplies and the beer coolers that Isaac, despite his momentary focus on them, hadn't restocked.

When the door opened at the top of the stairs, I was leaning against the back bar, listening to Jaco Pastorius play "Donna Lee" and wondering how he got that eloquent sound and syncopation out into the world in a way I'd never heard another musician do. I was checked out for the night and I almost didn't want to see another customer.

I wanted one even less when I saw Mickey Barksdale stepping down the Esposito's steel stairs with a weird jaunty air, as if arriving on stage in a Broadway musical, chest out, a strut in his gait.

He hit bottom, unbuttoned a pinkish linen sport coat that clashed badly with his complexion, and seated himself at the two-top in the farthest back corner. He'd probably picked that table because it was the farthest from the bar, so I'd have to come to him.

He didn't even look at me, as if he knew his presence brought the message he wanted to talk to me. My last drinker must have recognized him. He left in such a hurry, he forgot his change from the twenty lying on the bar. Nice tip. Thanks, pal.

Mickey watched the guy go, a touch unhappily, but he must have been used to people being leery of him. I ambled to the table.

"Mickey."

He nodded, smiling at the sound of his name.

"Working late. Got a little peckish, as my mother used to say. Thought I might talk you into making me a sandwich."

He was as insouciant as a boulevardier in a bistro, with his Palm Beach-meets-Vegas outfit, but underlying the sprawling attitude, something dark vibrated, something I wanted no part of.

"Kitchen's closed."

He nodded agreeably. "Sandwich sounds pretty easy."

I looked up the stairs.

"I was thinking of closing up early."

He nodded again, as if that were all right with him. My worry warred with curiosity. What did he want from me now? Because Mickey always wanted something.

I untied my apron.

"Let me go lock the door," I said.

"Excellent idea. Then we can talk."

I had no trouble guessing what the topic was going to be. We had no mutual interests beyond Burton. He looked around the kitchen as he followed me back, as if interested in the layout.

Isaac had forgotten to turn off the grill. I twisted the knobs.

"I thought you'd hired a new cook."

Syndi insisted she didn't talk to Mickey much, but he was obviously keeping track of her. I wondered if he'd had anything to do with her applying here for work.

I could have reminded him it was none of his business how I ran my business, but dealing with Mickey was a delicate dance. If you rolled over too easily, he wouldn't respect you. But if you pushed back too hard, you triggered a predatory response, found yourself flat on your back with him at your throat, figuratively and maybe literally.

"Night off. What do you like?"

"Ham and cheese. A little mayo?"

"Tomatoes? From the market. It's prime season."

He considered, nodded, and leaned against the door frame to watch me work.

I took bread out of the steel crisper, pulled a half-carved Serrano ham on the bone out of the fridge.

"Swiss or American?"

"Muenster. You know why I'm here."

"Burton."

I concentrated on my fingers as I shaved the hock. I'd had all the knives sharpened last week and they were honed like razors.

"My old friend Daniel," he said almost wistfully, as if it were true.

I didn't know the ins and outs of their relationship, though I knew they'd grown up together in what, at the time, was one of the more contentious and bluest of blue-collar neighborhoods in Boston. And, not incidentally, what was rumored to be the bank-robbing capital of Massachusetts. Burton was too serious about his work to cut corners or make deals, but I knew he wasn't above using his connection with Mickey on behalf of murder victims. And Mickey had saved his life at least once that I knew of.

"He's my friend, too, Mickey. Which makes me worry what you want out of him. Out of me."

Mickey certainly knew my history with Burton was knotted, dating from the day Timmy McGuire's dead body showed up on the stage of the Esposito.

"Good, good. That means we both want the best for him, right? Our mutual friend?"

I'd stopped building his sandwich while we talked. He jerked his chin at it, urging me back to work. With a cheese slicer, I skimmed some thin leaves off a block of Muenster.

Mickey's look bore on me, a weight.

"Burton's girl—that was in no way accidental. She did not kill herself, no matter what the coroner's telling him."

I dropped the knife. The tip dug into the wood floor and snapped off.

"You sound pretty certain of that. Shouldn't you be telling Burton this?"

I picked up the knife, thinking hard. Burton should have been here right now, to ask the questions I didn't know to ask, to learn how Mickey knew what he'd said.

"Let's just say I have some inside information. And no, he doesn't need to know this."

He plucked a scrap of cheese off the cutting board and popped it in his mouth. His tongue was pale gray, his teeth even and white as breath mints.

"Why not?"

He shook his head.

"Other people are taking care of it. Look, I know he suspects it. But we can't let him think that that was what happened."

"We."

He nodded.

"You know what happened, because I just told you. He doesn't need to. I'm taking care of it."

"Why freeze him out? It's his job." And because it was Marina, a passion too.

Why had Mickey come to me tonight? What was this sack of bricks he was handing me?

"You two are friends." He said it as if it were the most obvious reason in the world. "You can save him some *agita*. You have an influence on him."

I frowned. What was it he wasn't saying? That he wanted me to tell Burton not to do his job?

"That he and I are friends? I'll agree to that. But I have almost no effect on anything he thinks or does. You know how guys are."

His face clouded, anger and a touch of pain. I realized that, no, he didn't know the way male friends danced around telling each other what to do. His status as boss of all gangsters meant he could not trust anyone, ever, male or female, not to want something from him. Or take.

"Whatever. I'm asking you for your help here. Which is a positive for you."

That straightened me right up. Mickey Barksdale asking me for a favor was high on my top ten list of things I didn't want to carry. I had no desire to help, even if I knew what he wanted from me.

"You know what that means?" he said. "I'm asking you to do something for me."

"I can't make him think something different from what he's already thinking. As you said, he already suspects she was killed."

My mind was processing what Mickey was saying without saying, that Marina's death was connected to his business somehow. I could see why he wouldn't want Burton to know.

He nodded.

"I know. I'm not an idiot. And I've known Burton long enough to know he has a brick skull. All I want you to do is slow him down while I take care of this. Make him doubt what he thinks. If he gets involved in it, he'll just muddy up the waters. He'll be a loose cannon."

I hadn't heard so many clichés since the last time I watched TV. I concentrated on laying the tomato slices on top of the cheese, then the top slice of bread.

"Pickle? Chips?"

Mickey shook his head, solemn as the cross.

"Just wrap it up. I'll eat it later."

As I cut the sandwich in half, I nicked my finger.

"Shit."

I held it away from the food.

"Easy." Mickey stepped to the small first aid kit on the wall, took out a bandage, and wrapped it over the cut gently. "I want to be sure we understand each other. We work together on this, it could redound to your benefit."

I finished wrapping his sandwich and fastened it with a piece of butcher tape. Regardless of what I actually did, there was only one right answer.

"I'll do what I can, Mickey. That's all I can promise."

"Good man." He tucked the package into the pocket of his sport coat. I hoped the paper wouldn't leak. "Don't worry. There'll be something in it for you."

15

The encounter with Mickey gave me more to think about than I wanted on my way home. The idea I could convince Burton not to do something was laughable, especially if it had anything to do with his work. He gained his energy from pushing back against something: his command structure, people's perceptions of cops. He'd blow up whatever friendship we had before he'd allow me to tell him what to do, especially if it involved Marina. He might have made mistakes in their relationship, but he would be the first to tell you they were his mistakes and he owned them.

And I had to wonder about the link between Mickey and Marina's death. I couldn't imagine what the connection between them was, but I wasn't sure I wanted to propose the question to Burton, either. Mickey had to know I didn't control my friend. Better to forget the whole conversation.

Someone had left me a very tight parking space, two doors down from the front door of my building on Commonwealth Ave. I backed and filled a few times to shoehorn the Volvo in, finally tapping the bumper of the pickup truck behind hard enough to chirp the alarm. Living in the city.

I walked up the sidewalk. Early morning in the city here was peaceful and silent, almost soothing. The day's heat was backed down into a pleasant warmth on the skin. I felt oddly relaxed, wanting nothing more than a shower to clean the work of the night off my skin and then drink my nightly ounce of Macallan. Until I saw the light in the front bay window of my apartment.

Both of my parents, despite the wealth they'd grown up with, were as stingy about electricity as a Vermont farmer. I'd inherited the trait. I never left lights on.

My heart rate kicked up as I climbed the outside stairs. The door hadn't been jimmied, so whoever had been in my apartment had keys. Which was actually a very small set of people.

The door to the apartment was slightly ajar. Instrumental music played through my bookshelf speakers so quietly I couldn't identify it until I stepped inside and recognized Hiromi Uehara playing the old Lovin' Spoonful tune "Rain on the Roof." My intruder hummed along. I smelled lemon herb tea.

"Susan."

I suppose I shouldn't have been surprised, given the way we'd left the conversation hanging on the phone. She would never let anything rest unaddressed for long, argument or compliment. I did wish she'd stayed in Oregon, though. This additional business with Mickey and Marina and Burton now occupied a huge swath of my forebrain, and I wasn't sure I had the mental energy for a relationship talk right now.

"Elder." She looked up from a copy of the *Atlantic* she'd been leafing through, then burst into tears.

I closed the apartment door and locked it, walked into the kitchen to feel the tea kettle, seeing if there was enough hot water for another cup. This was not the kind of night where I was going to break out the Macallan bottle and have my peaceful measure, let alone shower and sleep. Especially since our conversation had started out so well the other night.

She wiped her eyes with a tissue.

"It was my brother," she said. "He needed a place to stay for a couple of nights."

I fought with myself whether to believe her, this being the first time she'd admitted to having any living family. When I'd asked her early on, she waved her hands and said only that her parents were long gone. She made it sound as if she'd never had any familial support at all.

"First I've heard about you having any sibs."

We'd moved to the kitchen table, which was less comfortable

and more suited for a heavy conversation. I squeezed the tea bag dry between my fingers, ignoring the scald, and dropped it on the table. She went to the cupboard, pulled down a saucer, and put the bag on top. I felt admonished.

Her gaze held on me.

"If I called him a black sheep, it might make him sound cuddlier than he is. He's been in and out of jail in Seattle, where he's living. He showed up in Portland right after I got there…" She cradled the mug in her hands. "I think he was kind of on the run."

"Kind of. What's his preferred mode of crime?"

Could I believe her? I wanted to, but why bring in the past now? Had I trusted too much to press her for details?

"Mostly little stuff. He's younger than I am. He had a hard time getting himself established. And he attracts the wrong kind of friend."

"If he was on the run, he must have done something fairly serious."

"He sells a little pot. To get by. He has learning challenges, Elder. He never did finish high school."

That seemed like an excessive amount of detail to make up about someone who didn't exist. Maybe I needed to ease up, take what she said at face value. Believe her.

"What's his name?"

She hesitated.

"Ronald. Ronald Marque. We had different fathers."

"You never mentioned him before."

She sipped at what must have been cold dregs of tea.

"I was afraid it would cause friction with us. Me taking care of him. You probably would have had Burton run a search on him, find out what he's done."

Good idea even now, if it was a somewhat personal favor to ask. Burton wasn't a fan of Susan's.

"I wouldn't have done that."

She shook her head and we let the lie sit between us on the table.

"So. Can I stay the night?"

I was stunned that she felt she had to ask. Couldn't she read that I was believing her, provisionally at least? Or was she hoping the argument might pull us apart?

"Of course you can. Nothing's changed for me."

She rose from the table and rinsed out her cup in the sink and left for the bedroom without another word.

We shared the bed, though we did not rest equally well. Annoyingly, she slept soundly enough that I could tell the argument hadn't bothered her as much as it had me. I flipped back and forth between a restless dream-ridden unconsciousness to that half-aware state that convinces you you're awake when you're really asleep.

Our morning conversation was no more comfortable than the night before. I was relieved, after a tense dance around coffee and access to the shower, when I got a text from Burton inviting me to breakfast.

16

My taste in restaurants had improved while I wasn't running the bar and had more time to eat out, but Burton was fond of a hole-in-the-wall on the edge of Chinatown, run by a Greek ex-wrestler he'd known for decades.

I hustled along the sidewalk on Kneeland Street, already late. The morning was warm, but without the usual August humidity, one of those rare late summer days when you could actually enjoy being outside, even in the city. Not only was I late to the meeting, I was late to any serious consideration of how to fulfill Mickey Barksdale's request to dissuade Burton from looking too hard into Marina's death. I told myself it was a good idea to keep Burton from making himself crazy over it, but I had to acknowledge it was partly my fear of Mickey that drove the decision.

He looked up from his omelet and nodded when the little bell over the diner's door announced my entry. It was long past any breakfast rush and the Greek's was too much of a working-class joint to attract the brunch crowd. Burton and I were the only customers.

The waitress, who'd been sitting on a stool at the end of the counter smoking a cigarette and reading the *Herald*, grabbed a menu and stood up. I waved her back.

"Coffee and a toasted muffin. Corn if you have it."

I sat down at the wobbly Formica-topped table. Burton ate mechanically, as if feeding a coal fire. He put down his fork and rubbed his mouth with a napkin.

"Thanks for coming out early. I know you're back working nights."

He wasn't usually so formal with me, and it made me wonder if he wanted something. Our friendship sometimes had the prickly quality of porcupines negotiating, but he'd helped me through enough situations that I wanted to reciprocate.

"Something important?" I said.

I nodded to the waitress, a radically skinny older woman with hair she'd colored so often it was thin and brittle and betrayed her scalp. The coffee was surprisingly good.

"Marina."

Was this going to be my worst fear? I'd pushed off Mickey's pressure so far, but was I now going to have to lie to Burton to keep Mickey happy? Caught between the proverbials, and not sure why I didn't just tell Burton about Mickey.

"They determined it was an accident?"

I must have sounded hopeful. He frowned at me, then picked up his fork with his uncasted hand and started pushing the oozing remains of his omelet around the plate. The Greek, a massive man with a soccer-ball belly and a shiny bald head, turned up the volume on the plastic radio above the grill. Klezmer music poured out. There was no accounting for musical taste.

"They don't determine anything, Elder. Homicide says if there's been a murder." He turned his head to look out the grimy front window.

I started to sweat. Was this the last lunch counter in Boston that wasn't air-conditioned? The second-hand smoke tickled my nose.

"So. What did Homicide decide?"

"I say it's a murder."

I didn't like the shock I felt.

"You're investigating?"

He shook his head and I saw his misery.

"Not me. Martines took me off it."

His boss. I felt relieved. Maybe the hard place wasn't as hard as I'd thought.

"That's it, then. It will get solved."

He frowned at me again, as if reading my relief and not understanding it.

"No. That's definitely not it. It just means I have to work behind the scenes, around the edges of it. Behind his back."

My relief skimmed off somewhere. I peeled the paper wrapper off the bottom of my muffin and split it with a knife.

"What is there to work? I can't imagine where you'd start."

He drank the last of his orange juice.

"Which is why I'm a homicide detective and you're a bartender. Excuse me, a bar owner."

"So what am I doing here? You don't need my permission." I was concerned about the precariousness of my position. I had no idea how I was supposed to encourage Burton not to do the job he'd done all his professional life.

"Well, all of a sudden I'm rich," he said. "No, check that. You, of all people, know what rich is. But Marina left me pretty much everything. Which is not inconsiderable for a boy from the projects."

I always laughed when he poor-mouthed his background. His parents had brought him up in a small neat house on a leafy side street in Charlestown, not anything like a project.

"But it's not something I'm used to thinking about. Especially since I have more important things to figure out."

Investigating Marina's death put us both in more jeopardy from Mickey. Part of me wanted to tell him what Mickey demanded, but part of me believed I could work my way through this without getting him involved. He'd already passed the decision point whether to investigate, clearly.

"Radical," I said. "So, I repeat. Why am I here?"

"I know fuck-all about having money." He sounded abashed.

"You want me to be your investment advisor?"

"Don't be an asshole. She left it all to me. Including what Carmen's going to need. I don't want to fuck it up."

"I gave you Daniel Markham's number, didn't I?"

"He's got no skin in the game." He sounded embarrassed at putting this weight on what we tried to maintain as a frictionless friendship. Or at least as frictionless as it had been up to now. "I need someone I trust to look over my shoulder, especially if

I'm going to be focused on finding out what happened. I can't multitask with either one."

He was saying, "what happened," as opposed to "who killed Marina." Maybe there was a hope he would convince himself it was an accidental overdose and Mickey wouldn't be on either of our asses. And how hard could it be to help wind up the estate of a woman whose last full-time job was as a cook in my bar?

"I'm in." I felt a little greasy saying it, since it would also keep me close enough to see where he was going with his investigation. If necessary, maybe I could manufacture a financial issue to divert his attention. "I'll do my best to cover it. What's the immediate concern?"

17

"When were you going to tell me the woman left you like a million dollars?"

Burton and MacDonald were sitting in a little-used conference room on the second floor of the precinct, at MacDonald's request. Burton understood the younger homicide detective was trying to disarm him, make the conversation feel less like an interrogation, though they both knew that's what it was. MacDonald hadn't been able to hide his satisfaction that Lieutenant Martines had assigned him the case.

Burton shook his head. The kid's technique, if you could call it that, was clumsy as a preacher's kiss.

"We were engaged to be married at one time. Last year. It's not like she's some old lady I scammed out of her life savings."

MacDonald had arranged a yellow pad in front of him with a bullet-pointed list of questions in a handwriting so cramped and tiny Burton couldn't read it upside down.

"She broke off the engagement, huh?" MacDonald inked a minuscule note at the bottom of the page. "Bet that pissed you off."

So he'd learned somehow that Marina was the one who cut off the relationship. MacDonald was making the cardinal rookie mistake, fastening on an explanation before he'd gathered all the evidence and seen where it might fit. And might not. He probably didn't believe Burton had killed her, but the blinders a hypothesis laid on you could make it easy to miss evidence.

"MacDonald. I didn't kill the woman. For money or love. Find a better story to tell."

MacDonald spread his palms, all sweet reasonableness.

"I'm not seeing any other story, Burton. The woman led an exceptionally boring life: cooking school, visiting Mom. Not much in the way of a social life. You're the only connection to the criminal world she had."

Burton flexed his fingers to keep from clenching his fists.

"'The criminal world?' What is this, Movie of the Week?"

"Then give me something else to go on," MacDonald said. "Other than you, I've got nothing."

Which was bullshit. It wasn't so much that MacDonald had no other evidence than that he wasn't sure how to develop it. He'd shoved his way past Burton to get assigned the case, but hadn't a clue where to start. Too much theory, not enough practice.

"Get out on the goddamned street," Burton said. "Knock on doors, talk to people. That's usually how it gets done. What about the cooking school?"

"Don't pull the 'tude with me. Just because you've been around here longer than anyone else. Seniority doesn't buy you shit, with Dennis or me."

Dennis? Now he was on a first name basis with Martines? What a suck-up.

"Detective. I knew the woman. Very well, in the past. As I said, I've had no contact with her in months. Six at least. You need to start looking in a different direction."

"Who were her friends, then? Who did she hang with?" MacDonald threw a leer Burton wanted to slap off his face. "Was she doing the horizontal mambo with someone else? That piss you off?"

The what? Did this yoyo think he was in a P.I. novel?

He laced his hands together, resisting temptation.

"I told you. I don't know what she was doing. Or with whom. We broke up." He felt renewed pain, remembering the finality of the way she'd done it.

MacDonald hunched up his shoulders for another run.

"You made it sound like—before the autopsy came out—you suspected she'd been killed. What was that all about?"

So Martines had been talking to MacDonald. At least they were acknowledging now that Marina had been murdered. But MacDonald didn't have anywhere near the desire to solve this as he did.

"I told you once before. I knew her. Well enough to know she wasn't the type to experiment with heroin. Tell me something—is there anything other than the fact that she was injected with her off hand? And the bruises on her wrist and upper arm?"

He sensed other evidence might be in the mix, something MacDonald wasn't telling him.

And, yeah. MacDonald practically shied from the question. Not much of a poker face. But when he shook his head with a phony sadness, that was the moment Burton realized MacDonald seriously believed Burton had done it. He was dead tired of the dancing. If this was the best work MacDonald was capable of, he was in over his head. And if he and Martines didn't know Burton was going to investigate the murder on his own, they were either stupid or kidding themselves.

The young detective shook his head.

"You know we don't discuss investigative pathways."

With suspects, Burton heard. He shook his head.

"The reason I don't want you chasing down some rat-hole is because whoever did this gets that much more time to cover his tracks. Or hers. Do what you need to do, but don't feed me chicken shit and tell me it's chicken salad. You can't razzle-dazzle your way past me."

MacDonald appeared unfazed by Burton's burst of temper, which gave him the feeling maybe his own stock with his boss might have slipped, that Martines trusted MacDonald more right now than he did Burton.

"I'm not trying to bullshit anyone, Dan. You'd be following these same paths, presented with the same information."

"Not something as flimsy as this."

He was frustrated. The cooking school where Marina had been studying was a building full of suspects all by itself, people who needed to be interviewed immediately. It was a far more fruitful place to start than an ex-boyfriend who hadn't seen the victim in months.

"Not so flimsy as that, Dan."

MacDonald smirked. Burton read his cheap theatrics from a mile away. He was about to make a reveal, give up some dramatic bit that was designed to shock Burton into confessing, or at least admitting MacDonald wasn't just spit-balling. Burton was annoyed the kid didn't think he could see this coming.

"Spit it out."

"We have a witness who places you hanging around the cooking school. Recently."

Burton scoffed. He didn't even know where it was.

"First? Not possible. And witnesses? We both know what they're worth."

MacDonald leaned across the table, serious now.

"Someone she spoke to about it, Dan. She told them an ex-boyfriend was stalking her."

* * *

Burton was certain that once MacDonald was done "interrogating" him, he was going to be frozen out of anything MacDonald did as far as an investigation. He'd have to decide how hard he wanted to push things. Talking big to Elder about leaving the force was one thing, but he wasn't sure he was ready to give up his job over this. And if he did quit or get fired, he'd have far fewer tools to work with.

"Come on outside and get some air," MacDonald said. "I need to smoke. And we can talk somewhere else, away from the room."

Which was, Burton assumed, wired for recording. Did MacDonald think he'd confess, off the books?

And of course the punk was a smoker, another young buck who thought nothing could ever kill him. Or he'd taken up the habit to suck up to Martines better, the lieutenant notoriously an on-again, off-again smoker.

"Sure," he said. If they talked off the record, maybe he could get MacDonald to see that Burton could help, even if he wasn't assigned to the case. He couldn't have been more wrong.

MacDonald lit up as soon as they cleared the back door, and shot a long plume of bitter smoke out into the humid air.

"You're not fooling me, Dan. I want you to know that. I know you know something."

Burton's nose twitched as he smelled the cigarette. His grandfather used to smoke a pipe he never cleaned and he enjoyed that stench about as much. One of the best days of his working life had been when Boston passed a no-smoking ordinance and he could walk into a bar or a restaurant—or a crime scene—without smelling burning tobacco.

"I'm not trying to put anything over on anyone, Liam." He leaned on the man's name, reminding him they were supposed to be colleagues, not combatants. "Look, the woman meant something to me at one time. I know her background, her friends. I can help with this."

He disliked pleading, but he couldn't not offer. Finding Marina's killer was the most important case he was ever going to have, solving it maybe a requirement for his continued sanity.

MacDonald scoffed.

"I'm sure you could. And then I'd never get to arrest the man who actually did the deed."

He flicked the half-smoked butt toward the sidewalk, where it smoldered in the bark mulch under an arbor vitae bush. Then he chested up and poked Burton with a forefinger. "You, old man. I'm talking about you."

Burton resisted the urge to slap the finger away. He'd have to swallow his pride if it meant he could stay somewhere close to the inside.

"I would never have hurt Marina. We were engaged to be married, for god's sake."

"And we both know too much about domestics to believe that argument."

Why was he so adamant about Burton as a suspect?

"This isn't so much about you as a murderer, anyway," MacDonald said. "Even if it turns out you didn't do it. You could have. It's about being a drunk and someone who doesn't work for the team. Not to mention someone with ties to the biggest gangster in town. You think no one knows you're best friends with Mickey Barksdale?"

The ice of fear shocked Burton. How had MacDonald found that out? He'd never implied Mickey was a source, even when some information he'd supplied had helped solve a case.

"I'm not best friends with Barksdale." Burton knew the protest was weak, but he had to make it. "We grew up in the same neighborhood is all."

"Not that hometown ties ever overrode a man's commitment to the law."

MacDonald's sneer was as toxic as the smoke smelled. But both of them remembered the Boston FBI agent who'd been compromised by a local criminal kingpin in the Seventies.

"Fine." Burton was done with the phony interrogation. He turned to go back inside. "Let me know down the line if you think I can help."

MacDonald grabbed him by the arm.

"Hang on there. We're not done until I say we're done."

Burton pulled away as MacDonald tried to grab his other arm and pin him back against the wall. Burton set his feet. As the younger man scrabbled, trying to put some kind of wrestling hold on him, Burton said fuck it and drove a hard short jab into the approximate location of MacDonald's liver.

MacDonald groaned, his hands fell away, and he dropped into a deep crouch, grabbing at his side. Burton jabbed him in the nose, then restrained himself from throwing another punch, though his adrenaline was up. He walked back into the building, not bothering to speak.

The meeting with Martines, later that morning, was short and predictable. Having guessed that MacDonald was enough of a wuss to make a formal complaint, Burton had already cleared the file and his copy of the autopsy report out of his desk to take home.

"Jesus H. Christ, Daniel." Martines had adopted the avuncular habit of using his detectives' first names. Burton thought it betrayed managerial uncertainty. "This is a nice position you put me in."

It was entirely typical that Martines would see this as an affront to his political and bureaucratic status, not as a disturbance in the effort to provide justice for the victim of a murder.

He considered pointing out that MacDonald had laid hands on him first, but that smacked of schoolyard whining.

"Sorry, Loo. You have to admit, he's an abrasive little prick."

"And you're Rebecca of Sunnybrook Farm. I know. Be that as it may. If it's an official complaint, I have to take action."

Burton was unsurprised. Martines was always going to cover his own ass first.

"Fine. I'll disappear for a few days." He clenched his jaw tight enough for Martines to see. "But don't ask me to apologize to the little shit."

"One week out of the office, Daniel. Out of the rotation. Fortunately, it's been quiet. I can afford to go down a man. And you'll still get paid." He played with the unopened pack of Marlboros on his desk. "We'll call it a suspension, but I'll keep it out of your file."

Because a written report might foul the Lieutenant's nest.

"Just between us boys, Loo."

Burton gave him a thumbs-up and walked out.

18

Susan and I spent a quiet Sunday, though we stepped so lightly around each other it was clear things were not back to normal. It was a relief when the work week started and there was somewhere I had to be besides the apartment.

When Syndi ran out of the bar after arguing with Isaac, I wasn't sure I'd see her again. I hadn't planned a dinner service for Saturday, so I didn't miss her then, though I did have to turn down some lunch orders. And since she wasn't there, I had no way of finding out what had triggered her. Isaac had said nothing.

So, come Monday morning, I was surprised to see her leaning against the brick wall by the front door of the Esposito, her shoulders hunched as if expecting a beating, watching me approach up Mercy Street.

"Morning." I didn't want her to see how relieved I was not to have to go find another cook.

"I'm sorry," she said. "I shouldn't let some things bother me, but sometimes you can't help it. You know?"

Which begged the question all over again. What had Isaac done that set her off?

"You want to talk about it?" I wouldn't push if it made her uncomfortable.

Her lips stretched tight. Determination? Stubbornness? She shook her head.

"It took me by surprise is all. It won't happen again."

I unlocked the door and let her precede me down the stairs, flipped on the main lights at the bottom.

"Can the two of you work together? I can't have you at each other's throats."

"No, no. I'll be OK. He seems like a decent kid. He just has a fresh mouth."

It was an adjective my mother might have used. I held in a smile. Syndi obviously hadn't realized a reliable cook was more important to me than a flighty teenage boy who might not even be in town a month from now.

"Well, the two of you work it out. If there is anything to work out."

"We will. I promise." And she fled for the kitchen.

I frowned. Was this something I needed more detail about? Or a minor friction that would work itself out? Isaac had been the boss while I was gone. Maybe he'd been flexing his own version of managerial muscles on her.

I worked through the Monday morning prep, poured myself a mug of coffee and stood behind the bar, listening to the sounds from the kitchen and the syncopated piano of Scott Joplin and the "Maple Leaf Rag." Other than the tiff, things felt right, for the first time in a while. The bar was returning to the version I hoped for, and I felt like I was where I needed to be, too. Susan and I were dancing around each other, but I thought we would survive. She was headed back to Oregon tomorrow and promised to be back in a week. I hadn't challenged the story of her brother again.

So I did feel content, until Burton blew in the door and rattled down the stairs with a face like the start of a thunderstorm.

"Any more of that one fifty one?"

Truth to tell, I'd poured the rest of the rum down the sink the other night. The liquor frightened me. When it first came out, the Bacardi people fitted the bottle with a flame arrestor on the cap, partly as a marketing gimmick, but partly because the liquor was as volatile as gasoline. We were long past the decade of flaming shots—it made no sense to keep it around.

"Christ, Burton. It's eleven in the morning. Have something with fruit in it. Some vitamins."

He was in no mood for jokes, and I wondered why I bothered. Sometimes my existence as a bartender rested on tamping down my own moods to accommodate everyone else's.

He sat down and nodded, as if I'd said something intelligent.

"Build me a Bloody, then."

A breakfast drink, for him. Which meant he wasn't working today, because as much of a functioning drunk as he was, he never drank on the job. That I knew of, anyway.

I pulled the tomato juice out of the cooler, trimmed a scraggly stalk of celery. The Esposito didn't host a lot of brunch drinkers, especially on a Monday.

"Gin or vodka?"

He stared as if I'd cursed.

"Vodka. And double it."

"Rough weekend?" He wouldn't talk about it unless he wanted to, but I offered him the opening. If he was anything like me, pre-Susan of course, Sunday afternoon was a dark deserted plain no number of baseball games or newspapers bridged.

He took the pint glass, tossed the celery on the bar, and swallowed a third of the drink so fast the ice clattered against his teeth.

"Suspended."

Fuck. Or maybe for the best. He couldn't investigate Marina easily if he wasn't on the job. Which would make Mickey happy.

"Again?" I tried for lightness. He hated sympathy.

He glared at me, which meant he knew whatever he'd done was wrong.

"What? You bought the wrong flavor doughnuts for the break room? Failed to wash out the coffee pot?"

Something pulled the corner of his mouth. Whatever it had been amused him.

"Nothing that bad."

I poured my cold coffee into the sink and refilled the mug.

"I know you're dying to tell me. So spill it."

He drank another swallow of the Bloody Mary, wiped his mouth with a napkin.

"Uh, happened to smack someone."

Huh. His temper was touchy, but he wasn't prone to expressing it that way.

"Suspect? Department brass?"

He sniffed.

"No such luck. Another detective."

"Ah, a colleague. Well done, Burton. That ought to make the Labor Day picnic interesting."

I looked at his expression and quit the joking. Whatever pleasure he'd had in the act or the telling was long gone.

"This asshole thinks I killed Marina myself. For her money." He drained the glass and shoved it across the bar at me, his wordless ask for a refill. "You've got to help me do this, Elder. I'm not going to be able to find out what happened without help."

Exactly what I didn't want to hear. Part of my ongoing tension with Susan was being involved in Burton's world. And then there was Mickey.

"I'm here," I said. "I just don't know what I can do. These things never seem to come out the way they're planned. And someone's always getting hurt."

He stared at me, those ice-blue eyes as focused as if he were reading my brain.

"What's going on with you?"

"What do you mean?"

"You're acting like you don't want me to do this. Find out who killed her."

I held up my hands.

"Not true. You just grab hold of things sometimes and bite down too hard. Not the best thing in the world for your psyche."

"Fuck my psyche." He stood up. "You can't be bothered, that's fine. Stay down here in your little black cave, doling out the booze and pretending not to drink. I just assumed you might give a shit about Marina, too."

What he really meant was give a shit about *him*.

"I'm sorry you feel that way."

Trying to discourage him had not kept him calm. Maybe I was fooling myself. Maybe I'd done this more to placate Mickey than

I wanted to admit.

"Later," he said, and dropped a twenty on the bar.

I watched him leave with the heft of stone in my gut. I'd failed him, and probably Mickey, too.

19

But I didn't spend a lot of time worrying about Burton after he took his morose self off into the day. We'd had our differences before and he'd always come around. What did start to worry me was that I hadn't heard from Isaac since Friday night. I figured he might still be embarrassed about the argument with Syndi and was avoiding the place. I had to remember he was only nineteen, still prone to act like a kid. Of course, he might be recuperating from the beating he'd taken.

Another unexpected thing happened later that day. Evvie, looking for Isaac.

She stomped down the stairs in the dead part of early evening, her boot heels ringing on the risers. No one in the place noticed her come in except me, which was probably a disappointment for her.

For some reason, she carried a hard-sided saxophone case. It banged against the front of the bar when she set it down.

"Where is he?" she said.

I'd only seen her the once since she returned from New Orleans, the night she'd sat in my office. She'd come back to Boston voluntarily, or at least that was how she was telling it. Her decision to be Frank Vinson's arm candy in exchange for access to the jazz scene down there had been cold and calculated. I still thought less of her for it.

Her face had hardened in a not-quite-definable way, and she'd lost weight she hadn't needed to. She carried herself with an air of mild desperation, as if preparing herself to avoid something she didn't want to see.

"Who? Isaac?"

Though I knew that was the only 'he' she cared about.

"Yes, Elder. Isaac." Her voice was curt and cold and vibrated with fear. "Your bartender? Your manager?"

I had no answer for her, though I'd read his ambivalence about staying around Boston versus going out to Stanford and suspected he'd made his decision. The choice might have been eased by Evvie's desire to escape with him, or not.

"I thought the two of you were living together."

She gave me the look that said I was being stupid.

"Don't believe everything you hear. And why would I be bothering you if I knew the answer to my own question? He's missing."

Her fingers jittered, rapping out a paradiddle on the bar top. Her mouth twitched, nothing close to a smile.

"I expected him in to work Saturday night. He didn't show. And tonight."

She looked at her fingers as if she could will them still. Fear peeked out from under the bluster.

"It's Vinson." The one word chilled me to the core. "Can we turn this shit off?"

Not exactly shit—Coltrane blowing on "All of You" on an early Miles album. Though this wasn't his most melodic, I was surprised an erstwhile sax player wouldn't recognize or appreciate one of the masters. I thumbed the remote.

"Frank Vinson." A weight compressed my chest. "Are you saying Isaac got crosswise with him?"

She looked at her hands, which were shaking then.

"You know how to make a French 75?"

I hated to open a bottle of champagne to make one drink, but there was a split one of the distributors had given me somewhere.

"In a minute. I want to hear about Frank Vinson. And Isaac."

She pouted, not prettily, and ripped off another drum solo on the bar.

"Story goes better with a little lubrication."

I surveyed her face, the way she licked her lips, and recognized another inhabitant of Planet Drunk, though maybe a new arrival. She hadn't been much of a drinker before she went South.

I rooted in the cooler until I found the champagne—Korbel, not Veuve Clicquot or anything fancy—and popped the cork. I muddled together the gin, the lemon juice, and the syrup with ice, shook it up, and poured it into a cocktail glass, floating the champagne on top. She drank it like a glass of lemonade on a hot day, and wiped her mouth with the back of her hand.

"Isaac," I said, not letting her put me off any longer.

"My deal with Frank Vinson," she said. "I never slept with him, you know. He had prostate cancer. Soft as a noodle."

I'd forgotten how cruel she could be.

"Your deal with him."

"Supposed to last a full year." She tapped her fingers on the base of the glass, as if contemplating ordering one more. She looked as if she wanted my approval. "But you know how things change when you get what you want. Am I right?"

I didn't like the implication she and I had any attitudes in common. My failure to nod seemed to stall her.

"I left him early. And I can tell you that Mr. Vinson was not, as the Brits say, well pleased."

I was both appalled and impressed she'd had the chutzpah to disrespect a gangster kingpin, the New Orleans equivalent of Mickey Barksdale. It was the arrogance of youth, the certainty nothing bad could happen that she wouldn't survive.

"You pulled a skip on Frank Vinson?"

My tone must have conveyed what I thought about the idea.

"I know. I know." She pushed the glass forward. "Is there enough in the bottle for another?"

Whatever she needed to tell me the rest of the story. I mixed another and gave her the rest of the champagne, too. She took this one a little slower.

"Isaac," I said.

"He came down to visit me a couple times, you know?"

"Once, I thought."

She smiled.

"He was worried about me." She looked at my face. "I didn't ask him to come and rescue me. I didn't lead him on. He was being a nice guy."

Nineteen-year-old males didn't fly to New Orleans to check on a woman to be nice. If she didn't recognize he had a thing for her, she was lying to herself. And to me.

"He and Frank meet while he was down there?"

She stared into the mirror behind the bar.

"They did. It went OK, except for the part where Frank called him a jumped up little… well, you know."

I appreciated her not saying the word. I'd been around people all my life who tossed that epithet as loosely as hell. Still didn't mean I liked to hear it.

"Isaac got beaten up last week. You think something's going on there? That it was Frank?"

Her face strained, making her look almost as young as she was.

"I don't know. Frank told me it was OK to change my mind. He didn't mind me leaving. He said."

"Frank told you that?"

She didn't understand male ego if she believed that. Especially the ego of someone who'd invested time and money in her career.

"Look. Evvie. You know Isaac can be unreliable. Maybe this has nothing to do with Frank. Maybe you don't go looking for trouble. He'll show up."

Though that did leave open the question of how he'd gotten himself beaten up.

She bit her lower lip.

"Hey, I know I'm selfish. Sometimes. But trying to do what I've been doing?" She took in a ragged breath. "You don't know how much harder I've had to work, just to get to this stage. All the extra bullshit. Does every woman you ever meet wonder whether she could fuck you?"

I did not want to argue gender politics with her. I'd witnessed people getting into it at the bar on occasion, and like every other argument these days, it seemed that there was nothing left people could discuss rationally, without engaging high dudgeon.

Nowadays, you raised your flag and defended against all comers, even if your position was absurd.

"It's always been a tough business. But I'm trying to focus on Isaac here. Do we need to worry about him? I'd say no. He didn't leave a note? Or an abandoned pet? No mail piling up on his doorstep? He'll probably show up and be surprised anyone was worried."

My reassurance wasn't helping.

"Something you're not telling me?" I said.

She shook her head as if avoiding a fly. Her skin was chalky and sweat gleamed on her temples.

"Look at this, what happened." She bent over behind the bar.

I walked around to see what she wanted to show me, and got a whiff of stale body odor, as if her clothes hadn't seen a laundry in some time.

Someone had painted an intricate multicolored portrait on the flat side of the sax case. I thought at first it was a mandala, but the longer I looked, the more it resolved into a slightly abstract cat's head, the horizontal whiskers like white feathers against the light purple of the face. The feline bore a knowing smile and a single fang sticking whitely down from the corner of its mouth. The effect made me shiver.

"This is voodoo," she said.

"Oh, please." The image was sinister enough without invoking that.

The detail and precision made it look more like a stenciled piece than an original, like one of those Banksy pieces people kept finding on walls. Whoever rendered it had talent, though. The cat's grin had a queasy life.

"Frank has a houseboy who paints like that. I used to see his pictures all over the house."

I grabbed my phone and took a picture of the cat. Everything I knew about voodoo, about religion for that matter, said its power relied on belief. Hard for me to think Evangeline was that gullible.

"So?"

"I'm being warned," she said.

"To do what? It doesn't mean Isaac is in trouble."

Her temper sparked. "So you're not going to worry about me? Or your favorite little bartender buddy?"

"What would you like me to do?"

"You think I don't know why you like keeping him around? There's plenty of that down where I just came from, you know."

Her rage spun wild, thrashing as if I were the source of her problems.

"First of all, I don't swing that way. As you know. And second of all…"

"Second of all, if you did, it wouldn't be with a Black man, right? Except there's a couple hundred years of American history saying otherwise."

How had her worrying about Isaac degenerated into this?

"Evvie. I hired Isaac because I liked him. He's competent, he's good with customers, and we both like music. What's racist about that?"

She shook her head sadly.

"Other than the fact you get to decide all that?"

It would have been easier to listen to all this if I thought she really gave a shit about Isaac and not just what he could do for her. I felt my own temper rise and flick its tongue.

"So what? Because you're woke? This doesn't affect you?"

"You don't get it, do you? Isaac wants to be *you*."

That was so bizarre it made me snort. A nineteen-year-old man with his future ahead wanted to be a middle-aged alcoholic who owned a dive bar and didn't know if his girlfriend was cheating on him three thousand miles away?

"Come on."

"But he can't be, can he? Because you have the one thing he can never have."

"I get it. And I understand there's not a thing I can do about that. If you're really worried about him, though, let's focus on where he could be."

Probably reacting to the rising voices, Syndi emerged from the kitchen, holding a cleaver down by her side. I was bushwhacked with the memory of Marina throwing a knife at a thug who'd threatened me in the bar one day.

Evvie's eyebrows went up, as if she recognized Syndi from somewhere else.

"Ask her." She nodded at my cook. "She probably knows."

Part 2

20

The Blue Sash, which Burton understood as a playful translation of the French *Cordon Bleu*, occupied a long low building of grimy white-painted concrete block on East Street, not too far from South Station. The windows were opaque, that milky breeze block glass you see all over Florida. As he walked toward the entrance, which sat under a robin's egg blue canopy, he had to pardon-me his way through a pack of smokers. He must have hit the place right at a between-classes break.

The school catered to a diverse population, obviously, though the commonalities were mainly extensive tattooing and inventive piercing arrangements. He had to wonder how Marina, a nice conservative Italian Catholic girl in her thirties, had fit in with the crowd. As he grasped the door handle, he was taken with a wash of regret over how badly things had gone between them, and yes, some guilt. He owned a piece of their failure.

"Couldn't you wait and come back later this afternoon? We're in the middle of classes for the day. After four, say?"

The chief administrator—or chef administrator, Burton joked to himself—was one Pierre Macaron, as unlikely a name for even a French chef as Burton could imagine. He was a tall spare man in his late fifties with a slight hunch to his shoulders and a magnificent swept-back thatch of silver hair. But when he opened his mouth, it was clear that he was about as French as French fries. The accent was old-school Boston, broad diphthongs and flat vowels, hard consonants.

"I'm sorry to have to disturb your operation. But one of your students has been murdered. Time is, as we say, of the essence."

He had no idea why he was making himself sound snooty, except that Macaron was such a phony he felt like poking him.

The chef made a moue of shock at the M word, but a shrewd look belied his insouciance. He did not want anything to interrupt the operations of his kingdom, least of all official attention.

Burton wondered what he might find in the way of fiddles and cheats the school undertook to survive. All the well-known and well-respected culinary programs, at places like Johnson & Wales and the Culinary Institute of America, were close enough to Boston to draw off the cream of the students, at least ones who could afford to pay. The Blue Sash was likely the equivalent of a community college: a decent enough practical education that paid its teachers shit and attracted students on price.

Pierre swerved his ergonomic chair to a side table and moved a mouse to activate the display, tapped and scrolled.

"I don't remember Ms. Antonelli specifically. We do train a very large number of students here and I'm in the kitchens less and less as we grow. I do see she was a full-paying student, which is unusual."

Given the small crowd outside, the idea of growth seemed more aspirational than actual, but for now, he had no reason to antagonize Macaron. If the school was running scams, he only cared insofar as it had anything to do with Marina's death.

"I'll need a list of her teachers. And class lists. Any students she might have been close to."

Including anyone who might be shooting heroin. Judging by the dark look of some of the aspiring chefs outside, edginess was part of the persona. The question, as always, was how far people were willing to take the pose.

Macaron shook his head doubtfully.

"I'm not sure I can provide you with student data, Detective Barton."

"Burton."

Macaron smiled drily.

"Of course. My apologies. But there are fairly stringent laws against my disclosing student information."

It never failed to amuse Burton that people willingly stored their credit card numbers online, filled out surveys, and daily used social media that harvested their personal data to resell to other businesses, all so they could be researching light bulbs at nine a.m., and then at ten, receive a coupon for them in the email. Yet they still cried privacy issues when a duly constituted authority needed the information for an actual purpose.

"This is a murder, Pierre. If you make me jump through a lot of legal hoops to get there—and I will if you force me to—I might be inspired to wonder what you might be hiding. It might be something our Business Division is interested in."

Macaron's face went red as fresh beef. He turned away, pounded some keys on his keyboard. A printer behind Burton's shoulder started to make angry clashing noises.

"There's no need to be offensive, Detective. This school provides valuable vocational education for people with a passion for the food world. I'm sure your career as a policeman has conditioned you to see crime everywhere, but I assure you, there is none here."

But he would say that, wouldn't he?

"You can take that page on your way out." Macaron's white jacket strained against his offended breathing. Burton made him nervous, which was interesting. "The list is Ms. Antonelli's instructors. They should be able to tell you if she palled around with any of the other students."

Neatly done, shoving the responsibility off on his staff. Burton suspected Macaron was shifty enough to put on a French accent when he was in the classroom kitchen. He stood, letting the chef have his small victory over student names.

"I understand you're not out in the kitchen much." Burton saw him flinch and wondered why. "But if anything comes to mind."

He handed him a card with his private cell number. It wouldn't do any good for Martines to learn he was working the case this soon.

"You will call me, Pierre. Yes?"

Macaron seemed to relax at the knowledge Burton was leaving. But it might be instructive to mention the Blue Sash to a cop he knew over in the fraud squad. Maybe get someone to look into the ownership, vet the books.

"Of course. Now. If nothing else, I would ask you to please not disturb the classes." He smiled greasily. "Some of our instructors have quite the temper. And of course everyone has knives."

Burton stared. It was a veiled threat, but a threat nonetheless. What made this lightweight think he could get away with that?

"I hope you're not finding this funny, professor. A woman was killed. Nobody turns that into a joke while I'm around."

Macaron threw himself back in his chair, an overdramatic response to the words.

"Of course. Of course. I had no intention…"

He did not meet Burton's glare.

Burton plucked the sheet of paper from the printer and left the office, almost happy in the feeling of forward motion, of being on the hunt. Until he recognized one of the names on the list of instructors. What in the hell was Antoinette Bordaine doing in Boston?

21

Evvie stomped off up the stairs, her worry over Isaac lost in rage. I wasn't sure what she expected me to do about him, or even if she expected me to do anything. Her experiences with Frank Vinson might have spoiled her for dealing with people in any way that wasn't transactional. How else could you react but with suspicion when you're being paid for something you are in turn paying for?

I looked down at the knife in Syndi's hand.

"Appreciate the thought. Thanks. Though it would have made a hell of a mess."

She blushed, as if she'd forgotten she was holding it, and turned back to the kitchen.

"Wait. What did Evvie mean? About you knowing something?"

"My stock is boiling," she said. "Hang on a minute."

But while I waited for her to come back, a pack of young women in yellow satin bowling shirts clattered into the bar, chirping and laughing. My Tuesday night was off to a banging start.

In fact, it was the busiest weeknight since I'd come back from Vermont. I found it soothing to wash all the questions and mystery out of my mind, as well as the sadness and complications of the last week: Marina's death, Burton's grief, the way Mickey Barksdale had insinuated himself into all of it. I'd skated out to the edge of my capacity to absorb it, but tonight I could lose myself in the work.

The energy reminded me of the Esposito's first year, when deadly empty weeknights blossomed into wild weekends: crowds, live music, and the entirely fulfilling sense I had created something worth having in the community.

I was happy to see Burton come in, late, even after the way we'd snapped at each other. The crowded version of the Esposito was not his favorite. He preferred a quiet sit at the bar. But he nodded at me, accepted the offer of a beer, and parked himself at the pass-through end of the bar. Since I had no help tonight, no one was passing through.

He didn't seem very happy—did he ever?—but he wasn't obviously morose, which was an improvement. Because of his work, I assumed death, even murder, was familiar to him, that it didn't affect him the way it did civilians. But he ran so deep, I wasn't confident of that.

It was past midnight before there was enough of a lull for me to stand and talk a bit. I switched the music over to a playlist of ballads and slow blues numbers that would eventually calm the boisterous crowd and prepare them for last call.

I ran myself a glass of club soda and walked down to his end of the bar with a fresh beer, glad to see he wasn't pounding down his drinks, for once.

"Slow night," he cracked, nodding thanks for the beer.

I shoved a five from his change into the tip jar.

"Don't be a smart-ass. This is as good as it's been."

"Since Baron Loftus? You can say his name. He's not coming back."

"Don't remind me. You cruising for company tonight?"

It was a running joke. Burton was about as easeful chatting strangers up in a bar as I would have been at a murder scene. Which was odd, considering that a good part of his job was interviewing people, using conversation to get information from them, even encouraging them to confess.

"Came by to warn you," he said.

"Oh. What now?" I tensed.

"Your cook. The new one?" He tipped his head toward the kitchen. "She has an interesting history."

"More interesting than being Mickey Barksdale's niece? She

told me all about the convent. She wanted to be a nun, but they said she couldn't cut it. Then she worked for them as a cook for a while."

"No. My kind of history." He picked up the bottle. "She tell you they kicked her out because she was stealing?"

"Huh. No, that wasn't mentioned."

"Apparently she went into the convent with a small opioid habit, hoping to kick. Got into the petty cash to buy."

"Huh."

"That's all you've got to say? Then this. I'm out at the cooking school this morning. Where Marina was studying? Trying to trace her activities."

"I thought you'd been suspended. Again."

He waved that away, not unexpectedly. He spent more time on suspension than any other homicide cop in the city, by his own admission. I should have known he wouldn't let Marina's death go, regardless.

"Marina didn't have a lot of friends at that school."

"That doesn't surprise me. She always kept herself close."

Burton's eyes clouded for an instant, the pain of talking about someone gone.

"Most of these wannabe chefs are like fifteen years younger. The piercings, the tatts, rainbow hair. You know the type. But Syndi was a student there, too."

"And she would have stood out the way Marina did."

Syndi was waifish and pale, without skin art. And she looked her age.

Burton nodded.

"I gather they kind of stuck together. One of the instructors insisted they were a couple."

"Hold on."

I walked down the bar and popped a half-dozen more bottles of beer for the bowling team, mixed a Gibson for a solo female sitting at the bar, her clutch purse an exact match for her candy-apple red nails.

Burton lowered his bottle as I returned.

"So they hung out together," I said.

"Until Syndi got her ass tossed out of the school."

I remembered the casually feral way she looked when she came out of the kitchen with the cleaver in her hand.

"For?"

"Attacking another student. Apparently some of the males think the food business is like what they see on TV with all these mad chefs screaming at people. There's a lot of grab-ass, propositions, occasionally what a reasonable person would call sexual assault."

His voice was tight and angry, as he thought about Marina putting up with that.

"Attacking?" There must be something more to it.

Burton loosed a grudging smile.

"With a bread knife. Rapped the serrated blade across the asshole's knuckles."

"And they threw her out for defending herself."

"Kid's mommy is a corporate lawyer, threatened to sue. And Syndi did sever some tendons. With surgery and therapy, he'll be OK. In a year or so."

"Guess I'd better not piss her off, then."

"Which is the favor I need from you."

"You want to talk to her? About Marina?"

"And I'd like you to be there."

"I doubt she would take a blade to you."

He gave me the look that said he wasn't joking.

"I want her to know the conversation isn't official."

22

Burton knew it was only a matter of time before the homicide board started to fill up again and his unofficial suspension strained the division, so he wasn't surprised to have a voice mail message early Wednesday morning from Martines telling him to report for the eight to four shift forthwith.

He jogged up the stairs to the office area, weirdly happy to be back. God forgive him, he loved his work, even if doing it meant someone else in the city had died an unnatural death.

MacDonald was standing inside the break room, poking at the innards of the coffeemaker with a knife. Burton saw a flash of electric blue on the man's face and smiled. He didn't remember hitting him in the face as well as the gut, but it looked like he'd broken the man's nose.

"Burton!"

Lieutenant Martines bellowed at him from the door of his office, the only door in the place that would close. MacDonald turned his head at the noise, saw Burton standing in the hall, and turned away. Good. MacDonald could mount all the whacko theories he wanted, as long as he left Burton out of it. If anyone was going to find out the truth of what happened to Marina, it was going to be Dan Burton.

"I do not want to hear the tiniest whiff of a whisper you're trying to work the Antonelli case," Martines said. "I assigned it to MacDonald and that's where it's staying. Am I clear?"

So he could fuck it up, most likely.

Martines fondled a pack of nicotine gum, which meant he wasn't smoking this week. Burton nodded. Also good. No more intimate parking lot smoke sessions where MacDonald could pour bullshit into Martines's ear.

"Don't just nod at me, for crissakes. Say it out loud. You understand what I'm telling you. Use your goddamn words."

Burton frowned. Was Martines paranoid enough to record their conversations?

"I hear you, Loo. I'm not assigned to the Antonelli investigation."

Burton knew his boss recognized the prevarication—Martines looked like he'd bit into a mealy apple. But Burton tried not to lie.

"I am serious." Martines popped a piece of the tooth-shaped gum out of the blister pack and cracked it between his teeth. "I had to talk MacDonald out of filing a formal grievance against you."

Burton would bet it hadn't been a hard sell. Homicide—hell, most of the cop world—was macho. No one wanted to admit in public he'd lost a fistfight. Or worse, get a reputation as a whiner. Burton softened his attitude.

"I appreciate that, Loo. Really. Now what came up so hot you had to un-suspend me?"

Martines shook his head and frowned.

"A weird one. Torture/murder in a house over in Hyde Park. At first it looked like thug on thug, but the victim's a woman."

Burton couldn't help that jolt of anticipation he always felt at the start of a case.

"I guess I better not hang around until the coffee gets made, then."

Martines's face darkened.

"No joke, Daniel. I'm as serious as cancer. You're walking on eggshells here. In golf shoes. Stay the fuck away from MacDonald."

Burton checked that he had everything he needed in his pockets, including evidence bags and nitrile gloves.

"I don't think that's going to be a problem, Loo. In fact, I don't care if I ever see the cocksucker again. You might want to warn him to stay away from me."

Martines smirked.

"Watching him right now? I don't think that's going to be a problem, either."

* * *

He pushed the unmarked through heavy traffic until he picked up Blue Hill Ave., then took it straight into Mattapan Square and followed River Street up into Cleary Square. The address was in Fairmount, on the other side of Truman Highway. When he was a kid, the highway ran through a quiet residential area, but now it was a sprawl of light industrial warehouses, car dealerships, and big box stores, almost as ugly as Route 1 in Saugus.

He navigated up a narrow, winding hill that would be a bitch in the wintertime. The clutch of vehicles parked outside a slumping bungalow made his destination obvious. He nudged the car in, half up on the cracked sidewalk, and got ready to do his work.

"Glad you could make it," the man in the white Tyvek suit said. He was younger than Burton by a dozen years, with rimless glasses and a mustard-yellow bow tie peeking out from the neck of the jumpsuit. His shaved head beaded with sweat. Burton didn't know him, but he had heard the ME's office was hiring. Increase in business.

"Sorry. You caught me in the middle of my pedicure and I had to wait for the polish to dry. Is there a body in there? Or did you get dressed up on my account?"

The ME gave off a sound halfway between a sigh and a hiss. The uniform behind Burton muttered to someone else.

"Yup. That's Burton."

Burton turned, grinned at him, took the clipboard to sign in.

He followed the ME in onto a long sunporch on the street side of the house, three-season at best because of the thin drywall and the cheap aluminum windows. A wooden bench ran the length of it, piled with a jumble of electronics and components: circuit boards, switches, light bulbs and sockets, as well as cardboard boxes of transistors, resistors, and capacitors.

"The owner?"

"City owns the property," the ME said sulkily. "Or so the database says."

Burton turned on him.

"You guys been doing detective work? That might be a violation of the union rules."

"Came up when we plugged in the address to the GPS. Abandoned property." He mopped his bald head with a blue cowboy bandana. "Oh, shit. You're *that* Burton?"

Burton ignored that, except for an inward smirk, and stepped into the living room. The sight of the body stopped him. Unusually, his stomach cramped.

"Whoa."

The ME at his shoulder swallowed, hard.

"Not something you see every day."

The woman whose body was strapped to the wooden Windsor chair wore a black cotton hood, tied tightly around her neck. She'd been secured to the seat by red nylon movers' straps, with the ratchets that let you tighten them mechanically. The bands had cut deeply into the purpled flesh around her ankles and upper arms, binding them to the uprights of the chair back. She wore a black "Boston—Cradle of Liberty" T-shirt and beige linen shorts, badly soiled now. The dark red hole where the bullet had entered her chest had been a mercy. The top joints of her first three fingers had been snipped off clean, the meat-colored stubs raw.

"Tortured," the ME said unnecessarily.

"And they got what they wanted fairly quickly. Can we look under the hood?"

The ME untied the knot with trembling fingers and pulled off the black cotton cloth.

"Ah, fuck me," Burton said. "I know this woman."

23

There was peace in the hours before the bar opened, the time of day when I felt most clear about what I was doing here, creating a neighborhood place with an atmosphere where anyone felt welcome and I could play the music I wanted to play. It hadn't started out that way and it may not have been what I dreamed about doing as a child, but who remembers that far back?

I'd signed a dozen or so checks and left some cash for Isaac to use to pay for liquor and beer deliveries while I was in Vermont. He'd thrown the invoices onto my desk with all the junk mail and flyers for the fall elections, as well as the shopper newspapers that were the only places I could afford to advertise. Susan was back on the West Coast, not calling me, and Isaac was somewhere in the wind. I suppose I was feeling lonesome.

I cued up a Paul Desmond/Brubeck playlist, something smooth and familiar that wouldn't make me think too hard. It was music I knew well enough to put in the background. I settled into my office chair to separate out the piles of paper.

Throwing out the junk mail was the easiest. Isaac hadn't bothered to mark any of the invoices paid, so I had to try and match the amounts to entries in the checkbook, not all of which were filled in.

It took about thirty seconds of doing this to spot the inconsistencies. Some of the amounts didn't match the invoices, which could have been just sloppy bookkeeping, but a number of checks, backed only by handwritten receipts, had been written to my meat and produce vendors. Isaac had written each of them a hefty check each of the two weeks we were gone, but the problem was this: except for the one-lunch tryouts for a new cook, the Esposito's kitchen had been closed for the duration. Where had all those meats and vegetables gone?

I felt gut-punched. It had never occurred to me that I couldn't trust the kid. But now I remembered Syndi saying some of the invoices she'd been receiving were marked Past Due. There were safeguards out front in the bar, where Baron Loftus had upgraded systems so a dishonest bartender couldn't give away too many drinks or slip cash in his pocket, but out here in the office? Giving Isaac access to the checkbook was my way of showing him I trusted him.

The safe.

I spun the dial on the box the original owners had cemented into the wall, an artifact of when the Esposito was as frightening a place to work as it would have been to drink. I kept it locked, but the combination was inked inside the back page of the checkbook, along with the Wi-Fi password. The sequence of digits would be obvious.

My head hurt and I wanted to throw up. I'd trusted the kid's values, seeing him operate those musical pop-ups and pay his musicians fairly and on-time. And when I'd asked him to manage the place for me while I was gone, I'd raised his pay by a third.

I turned the heavy metal handle and yanked the safe open. My heart slowed down when I saw the half dozen stacks of bills were still there. I didn't remember how much cash I had in there. I tended to throw together the twenties and fifties and band them together when I had a couple dozen.

I reached past the folder of legal papers I kept in there, the title to the building, which I'd bought when I was flush with cash a couple years ago. Maybe I'd jumped too quickly. Maybe there was a reason for the anomalies in the checkbooks I wasn't seeing.

I picked up one of the stacks of cash and felt something off, as if the bills were too stiff. Riffling the edge, I saw what he'd done, slipped pieces of paper in between to maintain the thickness of the stacks. At first glance, they looked fine, until you actually touched one. I felt my way through each stack. Same story. A real bill on either end, carefully cut bond paper slipped between.

"Shit."

I slammed the stacks back into the safe, slammed the door, and slammed the handle around so hard my wrist twinged. This had not been a spur of the moment theft. It required planning, forethought, extra work. And he'd taken the time to conceal what he'd done. To put off my discovery? Or because he thought he might replace it eventually? He could have taken the money and left a big blank place in the safe.

Had he disappeared for good, then? If so, why all the finesse of phony invoices and fake bills? He had to know it wouldn't hold up for long. So if this had been a last fuck-you before he took off for Stanford, why try and delay my finding out? I wasn't going to call in the police.

I heard noise out front in the bar, slapped the checkbook closed, and shoved all the invoices into the drawer. I could total up what my trust had cost me later. Right now I was too angry and disappointed to want to know. Here I thought I'd been doing the kid a favor. I'd been fooling myself.

"Elder?" Syndi stuck her head into my office and read my face. "What's the matter?"

In the background behind her, I heard Brubeck playing "Let's Get Away from It All."

"Nothing," I said. "I'm fine. Let's get to work."

24

Martines was waiting for him in the precinct when Burton got back from the scene late that afternoon, almost evening. Martines must have been concerned, because nothing would normally keep him in the building after five o'clock.

"What?" Burton slipped past him and sat in the chair in his cubicle, feeling a kind of exhaustion that was not physical. He was still processing the notion that this murder somehow connected back to what had happened last spring, with the young women being recruited to New Orleans.

"Your vic is a cop?"

"Was," Burton said.

He wanted a drink badly, though he had never allowed himself to become the cop with a bottle in his bottom desk drawer. Too much of a cliché.

"I don't have all the details yet, but she was carrying a retired New Orleans PD card." He wasn't sure how much detail he wanted to burden Martines with, especially his thought that she might have been working for Frank Vinson.

The lieutenant rubbed both hands back over his military-short black hair.

"You do have a positive talent for getting shit on your shoes, don't you?"

Martines's worry amused Burton more than it pissed him off. It was characteristic of all bureaucrats to want things to run smoothly, but Martines was in the wrong job for that. You got to the truth of things not by jamming them into neat boundaries and preconceptions, but by wading into the chaos, welcoming it, using its energy against itself.

"These things are always complicated, Loo. Even the ones that look like they should be simple."

Because whatever else you had, you were dealing with people: unpredictable, unreliable, and sometimes unfathomable.

"What do you know?"

"Antoinette Bordaine. Thirty-two. Black hair, brown eyes. White female. Resident of New Orleans."

He didn't recognize the address on her driver's license, but it would be easy to find out what quarter it was in. If it made a difference.

"You knew her."

"You remember I went to New Orleans on that extradition thing a couple years ago? I met her then."

He'd brought back a material witness on a warrant, a favor for another detective who wanted to attend his daughter's high school graduation. What he remembered most vividly was Antoinette taking him out on the town to eat and drink in as many of the tourist traps as they could manage in thirty-six hours. She called it the Tour Grandée and said it meant he'd never have to come back. He also remembered the killing hangover that had him dry-heaving in the airplane lavatory most of the way home, the material witness handcuffed to the arm of his seat.

Martines frowned more deeply.

"Young to be retired."

Burton was pretty sure he knew how that had happened. When they talked last spring, he'd gotten the feeling she was associated with Frank Vinson a little more closely than anyone down there might have liked. If the New Orleans department had been suffering one of its chronic house cleanings, she might have been forcibly retired. He wasn't going to complicate Martines's life until he verified that, however.

"Film at eleven." Burton looked at Martines pointedly. "That's all I have at the moment. I need to make some calls. It's an hour earlier down there."

Martines twisted his mouth, as if he had something more to say.

"Sounds like it could be touchy. Keep me in the loop."

Burton knew he was worried about outside pressure. The murder of a cop, retired or not, would trigger a deeper level of scrutiny and a stronger push for a solution. Even if Antoinette had been, as he suspected, bent, they could expect a certain level of interest from her former colleagues, once the news drifted south.

"Will do." He pulled the desk phone toward him.

Martines hovered in the cubicle's entry.

"At least this will keep you out of MacDonald's hair, right? That other thing?"

'That other thing.' The murder of a woman he'd known and loved. He stilled his face.

"Sure thing, boss. I'm not going to bother him at all."

25

"I'm sorry, hon'. It's going to be at least a month. There's a huge grant application due and Patryc lost her only writer this week." She made a spitting noise. "Quit to be a technical writer at Intel."

I had no idea what those words meant, except that Susan was now not coming back to Boston until September.

"If that's what you need to do."

"Don't go all hangdog on me. The last time we talked, I wasn't even sure you wanted me to be there at all."

I thought about that. In the heat of those moments, she might have been right. But not now. I'd believed—still half-did—that she had cheated on me. What bothered me more than not being able to trust her had been the feeling I didn't know her as well as I thought, whether she was capable of something like that. Or not.

"Of course I wanted you to stay. I was a little surprised by what happened is all."

"Shit," she said. "You still don't believe me, do you?"

How could I answer a question like that, except with the truth?

"Susan. We're grown people, aren't we? Does it really make sense for us to be having this conversation?"

Her silence felt dangerous, as if we were poised over a crack in the earth.

"You mean, does it make any sense for us to try and resolve this over the phone?"

"I'm where I've always been," I said. "You're the one who keeps leaving."

"Elder. You know I have to do this. I never pretended otherwise."

"I just didn't think it was going to happen this way."

"Maybe we're not grown up enough to have this conversation over the phone."

"Funny." My face felt hot. "I hear that as you telling me I'm not grown up enough."

"If the shoe fits, my friend."

I took a breath and said what I'd felt coming since the start of the call.

"Maybe we need to table this until we can be face to face."

"The conversation? Or the relationship?" Her voice was dry ice, cold and burning.

"Your choice. I don't have the energy to hash this out from three thousand miles away."

"Good enough." She cut the call so quickly I held the phone to my ear for a good five seconds before I realized she was gone.

26

Burton thought Elder looked a lot more content behind the bar than he'd been in the past year. It didn't escape Burton that the place he himself felt most comfortable was the Esposito. He snorted at the idea.

Late afternoon was a good time to be in a bar, too, close enough to the end of the workday he could have a drink and not feel like he was cheating the city. He had few rules about how he did his job, which was why he was in trouble so often, but not drinking while he was working was a cardinal one.

And this wasn't officially work anyway, in the sense that he wasn't authorized to follow any lines of inquiry into Marina's death. He'd made all his requests for information, the other phone calls he could make to kick-start the Bordaine investigation, and now he could focus on the task he cared about.

He stepped off the bottom step into the bar, almost deserted in that odd blue hour between day-drinking and after-dinner drinking. He'd always been a fan of the jazz guitar, so hearing Joe Pass finger his way through a complicated passage on "Autumn Leaves" made him smile and think of better days. He tipped his head toward the speaker up in the corner.

"Man can play."

Closer up, Elder looked unhappy about something. Maybe he was having a hard time readjusting to the night shift schedule.

"Knew you were coming."

"Your new cook around?"

Elder glanced back through the doorway.

"Getting ready for the dinner hour. Assuming there is one tonight. Sit and have a drink. I could use some advice."

Oddly, a straight-ahead request from Elder. Something was pulling at him.

"Sure. I declare it cocktail hour. What have you got?"

Elder held up a footed glass. "Whiskey sour?"

"I'm going to need hard liquor to hear whatever it is? OK."

The music shifted to John Pizzarelli doing "How High the Moon" and he realized Elder had constructed an entire playlist of guitar music. He tasted the froth on top of the greenish drink and felt that sense of home again.

"So. What's the problem?"

"Isaac."

Burton tried not to frown, rubbed the back of his hand where it emerged from the cast. He'd never liked the kid, felt like he took advantage of Elder. He was too smart-mouthed, too sure of himself, with an edge of self-interest he didn't always bother to conceal.

"The night manager."

"Whatever. I'm still trying to balance the books, but it looks like he's been stealing from me."

Burton sighed. Probably because he spent most of his days rubbing shoulders with crooks and other lowlifes, stories like this never surprised him. He'd never run Isaac through any of the police databases, which he had done on Elder's behalf on other occasions, but maybe he should have checked the kid's record. Now it would be locking the proverbial barn door.

"You don't have to verify anything," Burton said. "I know how tight an eye you have to keep on your books. You trying to convince yourself it didn't happen?"

Elder looked at the scotch rack on the back bar, then nodded.

"He also seems to have disappeared. After getting the shit kicked out of him."

"I hope that's not a surprise. If he's been stealing from you, he'd have to know you were going to catch up to it."

Elder shook his head.

"Evvie—you remember Evangeline, right?"

Shit. Elder had had an eye out for that girl before she left for New Orleans. Another user. What was she after from Elder?

"Sure. Rainbow hair and metal hardware."

"Not so much now. The two of them have been together since she got back. She says he's gone missing, too. Left without a word."

"Wasn't he supposed to go to college? Stanford or somewhere? It's close to the start of school. That's probably what happened."

Elder shrugged. "No way to tell, I guess. I just don't believe he'd rip me off."

"No. There's never a good reason for that." Burton felt bad. Elder had trusted the kid, tried to help him out, maybe even acted as a father figure. He didn't know the family situation, but it wouldn't surprise him to learn Isaac had no father present in his life. "Maybe he needed money for books?"

Elder frowned, as if Burton might be joking.

"It was a lot more than that. Let me go see if Syndi's free."

*   *   *

For someone who didn't have anything to hide, Syndi seemed a little too nervous about talking to Burton. He conducted her over to a table against the far wall where Elder couldn't overhear. He'd get more honest answers out of her if the questions stayed between the two of them.

"It turns out you were friends with Marina? Antonelli?" He tried not to show his tension.

Her shoulders raised, she darted her eyes around the bar as if looking at him directly would give something away.

"I didn't know her last name. But we were, like, the only two grownups in the classes, most of the time."

"She have any problems with anyone in particular? Arguments? Unhappy words, even?"

Burton knew Marina's temper well. She wasn't the type to put up with anything silently.

Syndi picked at a brown spot on the back of her hand.

"Look," he said. "I know it was a macho atmosphere. Lot of big-mouth talk, wandering hands. I'm trying to find out if there was anything egregious."

She shook her head.

"Anything that would make someone angry enough to kill her."

Syndi's eyes got big, the blue as pale as a morning sky.

"She's dead? Someone killed her?"

He kicked himself for hitting her with that, not easing her into the conversation.

"Yes. I'm sorry to say."

"I don't know about her pissing off any of the other students," she said. "I know she didn't get along with that Edouard Batarrh, the pastry chef. They had more than one argument. I think there was something sketchy about that school anyway. They had some kind of scam going on."

27

I stood behind the bar watching them—I guessed Burton wasn't as worried about talking to Syndi as he'd made it sound. I was aware of the worry rising as I heard a few of the words he was saying: "cooking school," for example. Burton was talking to Syndi about something to do with Marina's case, not whatever murder he was officially assigned to.

My stomach was sour. Mickey wasn't the kind of guy who gave out a lot of warnings. If I failed to divert Burton, I could expect some blow-back eventually. Telling Mickey how hard it was to keep Burton from doing what he wanted wouldn't be a revelation to Mickey, but I doubted he would accept my excuse.

The playlist shifted to a slightly frantic version of Django Reinhardt playing "I Can't Give You Anything But Love" as Burton walked back to the bar, carrying his empty glass. Syndi scuttled into the kitchen, looking relieved to be out of his orbit.

"Get what you needed?" I took the empty and turned it upside down in the dishwasher rack, and found myself hoping he was getting ready to leave.

He hitched himself onto the stool, looking as if he might want another drink.

"I don't know. I have to say nothing I'm hearing seems to rise to the level of a motive to kill Marina."

I knew what he meant. I didn't think a heroin overdose was a very certain way to kill someone. And, I admit, I felt some relief. Maybe he would back away for a bit on his own. I knew he wouldn't give up entirely, but if Mickey came around to threaten me again, at least I could tell him that much.

"Syndi says she thinks something shady was going on out at the cooking school. Which dovetails with a feeling I had, talking to them."

"White-collar crime? Something darker?"

"White-ish. But scammers and con men, they're not likely to kill someone. Attracts too much attention. In my experience."

He sounded bitter, as if his experience wasn't doing him any good and he knew it.

"I know you're the expert here. But what if this really isn't what you think it is? What if her shooting up really was an experiment? An accident?"

I was never going to convince him of anything he didn't already believe, but if I could dent his certainty a little, maybe that would help. It was not that I was so afraid of Mickey, but I could see how the focus on Marina's death could grind Burton down. If that was what he intended, Mickey would probably do a better job avenging Marina's death than Burton.

He shook his head.

"Just because something doesn't make much sense doesn't mean it's wrong. I haven't figured out the story yet." His gaze locked on me. "You have some kind of stake in this being accidental? You seem to want me to get off the case."

I held up my hands.

"Hell, no. Just playing devil's advocate." His instincts were too sharp for me.

"Well, play it somewhere else. You don't know fuck all about how I do my job."

That hurt, though I didn't let him see it. We'd often tossed around his professional problems in the bar. He'd told me more than once that an uninformed perspective sometimes jarred something loose.

"Fair enough. Are you going to kick me in the nuts if I tell you I'm worried about you?"

Silence covered that like a thick curtain. It wasn't the kind of thing we said out loud to each other.

He inhaled, deeply.

"Have I been eighty-sixed here? Or am I allowed another drink?"

That gave us the time to let my comment stop reverberating. When I returned with another whiskey sour, he inspected it as if the color might be off.

"This is the work I do, Elder. You wouldn't tell a teacher to stop teaching. Or a brickie to stop building walls. Even if this weren't about Marina, I'd be in it."

I wondered what he'd say if I came clean—I owed him more loyalty than I did Mickey Barksdale. Mickey had convinced me he was going to handle the solution to Marina's murder himself, that Burton would hurt himself by firing off in all directions, but Burton seemed to be handling the pressure fine. The more I thought about it, I wondered if I'd been realistic about Mickey's motives. There had to be some benefit to him in keeping Burton away.

"OK. But let me tell you something else." He'd be pissed, but I needed to get this off my chest. "You need to know."

"Elder? Sorry to interrupt."

Syndi stood in the kitchen doorway with a sheaf of papers in her hand. I wondered how much she'd heard, whether I could trust her disavowal of a loyalty to Mickey. He could have placed her in the bar as a listening post, to track whether I was doing what he'd asked.

"I found something that might help Mr. Burton."

"Detective," he and I said simultaneously.

She wrinkled her forehead.

"What are these?" he said.

She spread the papers out on the bar, pointed to one with an aquamarine fingernail.

"Right there, you see? I paid for my tuition in advance. Right?"

Burton leafed through the contracts. Paper was not his forté. I turned them around and scanned the receipts.

"Then they paid it right back? It looks like more than you put in."

She smiled, not innocently. She'd known something was off.

"They told me it was like a scholarship. And the rest was for books and stuff."

Burton picked up the paper.

"So basically they lost money on your going there? They paid you to go to their cooking school?"

She ducked her head as if he'd yelled at her, pulled on the sleeve of her shirt.

"What was I supposed to do? Turn it down?"

I would have asked questions, but who looked a gift horse in the mouth?

"Interesting." Burton tapped his fingers on the papers. "I wonder if they gave Marina the same deal."

Syndi nodded.

"We talked about it, how weird it seemed."

"Thank you," he said. "This will help move things forward. I can hold onto them?"

"I need them back."

"I'll make copies." He turned to me. "We'll talk about Isaac another time, OK? I've got to get this moving."

And he headed for the exit. Would I get another chance to tell him about Mickey? Now that he was refocused, I could see how badly I'd failed at what Mickey wanted me to do.

28

It was as if thinking about Mickey the night before conjured him to life. It was late the next morning. I was feeling pretty good. I had a nice fresh cup of coffee and the sports page of the *Globe*. It would never live up to the days when Bob Ryan wrote the basketball beat. The music was low and unobtrusive, some of Brad Mehldau's trio work.

I watched Mickey strut down the stairs. If you didn't know who he was and you didn't know enough to be frightened of him, you would take him for an MBTA driver or a baggage handler out at Logan. I folded the newspaper and tucked it under the bar.

"Morning, Mickey."

His pale Hibernian face darkened. Either he didn't like me calling him that name any more or he was irritated about something I'd done. Or not done. This was always the challenge of dealing with bullies. They made a point of keeping you guessing, keeping you off balance.

He pointed to my coffee and twitched his neck, as if he had a crick he couldn't get rid of.

"Is that fresh? I could use a pick-me-up."

I thought about asking whether Dunkie's had eighty-sixed him, but cracking bad jokes when I was nervous was a habit I needed to break.

"Sure. Fixings?"

He looked at me strangely. His pale blue eyes were the exact shade of Syndi's. They did share a genetic branch.

"Black is fine," he said. "I have a bone to pick with you."

My mother used that expression all the time, but it didn't scare me the way it did coming out of Mickey. I shook out my wrist so my hands wouldn't tremble while I poured his coffee.

He grinned, aware of the effect he was having on me.

"So." He sipped and nodded appreciatively. "Sulawesi? Very nice."

The last thing I'd expected was that he was a coffee snob. That didn't civilize him any more. Blood rose into my face. I felt warm.

"Mickey." I was ready to apologize. I knew damn well what bone he'd come here to pick—all I could hope was that it wasn't going to be one of my arms or legs. He'd tasked me with diverting Burton and I hadn't done it, though the more I thought, the better I felt about the fact I hadn't. Burton and I had a strange and touchy friendship, but it was a friendship.

"Elder. You don't mind if I call you that?"

His voice was soft as flannel, a rod of steel underneath.

I shook my head.

Imagination is not your friend in situations like this. I didn't know if he might pull a knife or a gun, or go nuts and start breaking up the furniture. The only small idea that comforted me was that Burton said Mickey saw himself as management, not labor. If violence or heavy lifting was in the cards, he'd use his minions.

"Elder. I'd prefer you call me Michael, if you don't mind." He pointed a finger at me. "Not Mike, mind you. Or Mikey. Michael."

"Of course. Whatever you like." That was weird, but it couldn't be the only reason he'd come by.

Inside, though, I was rolling my eyes. One of the many things that annoyed Burton about Mickey—Michael—was that he was what the locals liked to call a professional Irishman, someone who always marched in the St. Patrick's Day parade in Southie, contributed cash overseas discreetly, and could muster a brogue or a passable rendition of "Danny Boy" whenever the occasion demanded. The persona was another way he obscured his motives and agenda.

"Mi… Michael. You are correct if you're here to say I haven't had much success with what you asked me to do."

Better to acknowledge what we both knew and for me to find out right away what he was going to do about it. Because he was certainly planning to do something about it.

He raised a hand, as if he were a priest and my confession was running too long.

"That's all been very clear to me. Honestly? I wasn't confident exactly how much success you were going to have."

Which stirred me to anger, though I was careful not to show it. Why bully me into something he didn't think I could do?

"You know, a man in my position doesn't have a lot of friends." He laughed shortly. "Can't afford them, can't trust them."

There was no reply I could make that wouldn't get me in trouble, not that I was sympathetic to his whine. I had the wild thought he was trying to create a rift between Burton and me, so he'd have a better chance of Burton being his friend. It sounded like middle school stuff, but it wasn't impossible for a man with such limited emotional range.

He looked hurt, as if I hadn't responded sensitively enough. I shrugged.

"Lonely at the top, I guess."

He laughed again, a harsh bark.

"I came by to tell you everything is fine now. I know who caused all this trouble and I'm taking care of it. I don't hold it against you that Burton's still on the case, because I know he's not going to catch up to me. I'm sure you did what you could, though that doesn't appear to be much."

Relief buckled my knees the tiniest bit. He saw it and smirked, an evil smile that made me want to break his teeth.

"That's mighty white of you, Michael. I appreciate your coming all the way down to the fancy part of town to tell me."

He nodded at my sarcasm, but recognized it as *ex post facto*, not any kind of real resistance: an impotent yawp.

At that moment, before I could jam my foot any deeper down my throat, Syndi appeared in the kitchen doorway, with nothing in her hands.

Mickey perked up.

147

"Hello, cuz," he said. "What are you doing here?"

Another lie from a congenital liar—did he expect me to believe he hadn't known she was working here?

29

The fraud squad, as the two-person department was colloquially known, always generated comments about pencil-necked geeks and computer nerds whenever the topic came up. A lot of cops treated them as not really cops, since most of their work got done inside, off the streets. But they were responsible for anything related to fraud—financial, artistic, business—that originated in the city. Burton didn't think about them one way or another, except as a public service, like the library, a place to go when he needed something that fell into their bailiwick, which was almost never.

Francesca Gatoberri was not a woman that anyone who met her would call a pencil-necked geek or a nerd. She was taller than Burton when she stood up behind her desk to shake his hand, with a cropped cap of chestnut hair, large lively brown eyes, and a sense of fashion he suspected was both high-class and expensive. Both of the fraud squad people tended to dress well, he knew, though it must have been to impress each other, since neither of them was out of the office much.

The office, too, was more polished than the homicide cubicles. It was bright, with high windows that looked out onto Tremont Street and the edge of the Common.

Francesca's partner, who was the size of one of the sulky drivers at Suffolk Downs, stood up when Burton rapped on the door frame.

"I'm going for coffee," he said. "Get anyone anything?"

Burton shook his head, feeling out of his element in the

cool sophisticated space, with prints of paintings even he could recognize on the pale gray walls.

"Daniel Burton." He offered her his hand.

She raised her right hand, missing a knuckle of the ring finger and most of the pinkie.

"Shaking irritates the nerves. Nothing personal."

He was aware of his own nerves. This kind of crime—hell, he wasn't even sure there was a crime here—was foreign to him. Despite his middle-class upbringing and his liberal arts education, he thought of himself as a blue-collar cop. The idea of crimes that didn't involve blood and violence didn't quite resonate. Greed drove plenty of the crimes he dealt with, but it didn't seem like such a terrible thing when no one got hurt. Physically.

"No worries." He glanced around at the pastel walls, the wooden furniture that looked newer and classier than the World War I vintage he was used to. He caught a sandalwood scent in the air, spied one of those aromatic oil dispensers, two crossed sticks in its mouth. "Nice office."

That made her frown, a deep dimple showing in her right cheek. OK. No small talk. Probably a woman who looked like she did got hit on a fair amount, especially in the cop world.

He laid a folder on her desk and took the visitor's chair. Except for the neutral beige color, it was exactly the model they had in Homicide: hard molded plastic, uncomfortable in the extreme.

He winced. She smiled.

"Yeah. We don't want our visitors hanging around any longer than you guys do. What's this?"

She flipped open the folder. The single-spaced typed sheet inside represented everything Burton had been able to find out about the Blue Sash, which wasn't much. All the usual searches and sources had petered out quickly, much more quickly than they should have if the cooking school was legitimate. At least he thought so.

"Something funky's going on at this cooking school." He sat back, crossed his legs, and felt the chair creak. "Money-wise, I mean."

He'd searched Marina's files and verified that she'd been offered the same generous deal Syndi had. She'd paid for her tuition up front—a loan against the money she had in the bank—and a month later, received a "scholarship" check in that amount plus twenty per cent.

Once he finished explaining it, Francesca lapsed into thought, staring at a small black-framed print of Seurat's *Sunday Afternoon on the Island of la Grande Jatte*, a painting he recognized by name. He found himself wondering whether she liked jazz music.

When she returned from her reverie, she nodded.

"First thing we do is see whether they're on the Education Department list."

She pulled a laptop across the desk and keyed in a few strokes.

"Yep. If you're not on the list, student scholarship money is taxable income. The school is there, but it only got on a year ago. Which does imply something shady. Paying your students to matriculate isn't much of a business model."

"So what kind of scam would we be talking about?"

"You might not think so, Dan, but we are pretty busy over here. I know everyone else thinks we're eating lunch with gallery owners and going to openings."

He smothered a wise-ass remark he'd been about to make about solving the Isabella Stuart Gardner theft.

"This is in connection with a homicide investigation." He didn't like to big-foot her, but murder always overrode a money crime in his mind.

"An investigation you're currently assigned to, I assume."

He showed surprise before he could control it. She'd known in advance he was coming, that this technically wasn't his case. Which meant only one thing.

"You've met an article by the name of Liam MacDonald, then?"

Her brown eyes glinted and the smile widened.

"Tall fellow? Thinks he's God's gift? Maybe a little handsy?"

He relaxed. She hadn't liked MacDonald any more than he did. He wondered if it would gain him points to tell her he'd sucker-punched the man.

"I don't know about that last. The rest sounds familiar."

Her eyes sparkled.

"I would never countenance violence on another human being," she said. "But some humans ain't human."

A John Prine fan, to boot. MacDonald would have had to explain the splint on his nose. He spread his hands out, beseeching.

"All this financial stuff is totally outside my area of expertise," he said.

She measured him with a sharp look.

"I'm sure your expertise is quite varied. And deep."

Fuck. Was she flirting with him?

"So you think you can do some digging?"

The smile disappeared.

"If I open a file, it goes into the system. Which I suspect you do not want?"

He nodded.

"It's not so much I'm worried about pissing off MacDonald," she said. "But my official plate runneth over."

"If that's easier for you, it's fine with me."

"Good." She tapped the file with a pearl-polished nail. "I'll get with you when I have something. Maybe over a cocktail or two."

She was flirting. The last thing he wanted was to shut her down, but he did worry a little about later on.

"Sure," he said. "Do you like jazz?"

30

One of the things I always loved about the bar business was the occasional surprise on the upside. Thursday nights were well known in the hospitality business as the deadest night of the week, too close to the weekend for people to want to come out. For no good reason, this night was as busy a night as I'd had since my first round of ownership.

People started crowding in around eight-thirty, and by eleven, all the stools at the bar were occupied, as were all the tables but one. I was moving as fast as I could, but I never felt like I was in the weeds, and I felt as positive about what I was doing since I'd come back from Vermont. Even the music felt dialed in just right, the energy and volume keeping the party going.

Syndi helped me out on the floor without being asked, distributing plates of food, something Marina had always resisted doing. She stopped briefly at the bar after delivering cheeseburgers to a quartet of teenagers who were too young to drink. I knew, because I'd checked.

"Is this a normal night?" she said.

Her face was pink with the heat of the kitchen and the running back and forth, her hair covered by a yellow bandana.

"If only," I said. "I could afford to retire."

More importantly to me, this kind of crowd meant the business would support live music again. I was mentally running through the promoters and musicians I still knew in the city, trying to think where to start. My thought process on that screeched to a halt when the street door opened and Isaac jogged down the stairs.

Business in a bar comes in swells like the ocean, waves of intense demand followed by moments of respite. As Isaac crossed the floor, it seemed as if everyone finished their drinks at once. People stacked two and three deep at the bar for refills, while eaters carried their dinner checks, with fistfuls of cash, to the end of the bar near the register. I'd stopped taking credit cards as an experiment, trying to rebuild my cash reserves, and nobody seemed to mind.

Isaac looked ready to work, a fresh starched white shirt, a red bow tie, dark vest, the sleeve garters he affected. He avoided my questioning look and stepped behind the bar, slipped an apron on over his head, and started to ring people up at the register.

I needed his help at the moment too much to kick him out, but the sight of him touching cash and joshing with customers as if he'd been here helping all along, as if he hadn't stolen from me, burned in my stomach.

Syndi came out of the kitchen with plates. When she saw Isaac, she set them on the pass-through for him to deliver.

My frustration swelled as the damn business stayed strong and steady right up through last call. I had a few words to say to the youngster. We'd been dancing around each other behind the bar, careful not to collide, and all the conversation we had time for was as much of a dance. "More lemons out back?" "Need beer for that cooler?"

I was exhausted by the time we cleared everyone out, and not entirely because of the pace. Frustration and anger made it hard to enjoy the feeling of the most successful night the Esposito had had in a year.

Isaac cleaned up the table and the bar top while I pointedly emptied the register and took the cash bag out back to lock in the safe. It had a new combination, which I hadn't written down. By the time I came back out front, he was sitting at the bar with an open bottle of beer, an act of ownership that pissed me off even more.

Syndi walked out with her bag slung over her shoulder. Most nights, she would sit with me and have a drink before heading out, so we could both wind down. Tonight, she sniffed the air and headed for the stairs.

"Night, Elder." She wiggled her fingers at me and clomped up the stairs.

"Night."

And there we were. The sound system had developed a tear or a wrinkle in one of the speakers that made the Duke's trumpet hiss. That minor imperfection was enough to trigger my rage.

"You have a colossal fucking nerve showing up here."

I thought about pouring my nightly shot of Macallan, but if I'd learned anything about my drinking, it was that taking one in the middle of an emotional situation only increased the chances I'd take more than one. I hadn't had a serious slip in so long, I felt confident, but it would be stupid to risk it for him.

"I know it doesn't do any good." His face shone with perspiration, though he'd been sitting still for a few minutes. He wiped his forehead with a paper napkin. "But I am sorry. It had to be that way."

I changed my mind, fished down the bottle of Macallan and a dusty Waterford crystal shot glass.

"Had to be," I said.

I tensed when he reached into a pocket of his vest, but he only pulled out a square envelope, slightly crumpled, and laid it on a dry part of the bar. Charlie Haden segued into a duet with Don Cherry called "Out of Focus." And my anger rose.

"What's this supposed to be? An IOU?"

I said fuck it to myself and poured a scotch, drank it off in two swallows. The heat of it, its beautiful eloquent song, the love—all of it bent my knees and nearly dropped me. I exhaled. Where else could I find this love?

I refilled the glass.

"I didn't know where else to turn." He didn't sound sad enough for me. "It's not like I could talk to my parents."

That, strangely, quashed some of my anger. I'd been treating him like a man, but in many ways, he was still a kid, with all the short-term focus and impulsivity you'd expect from someone whose brain wasn't fully developed. In another neighborhood, with other upbringing, he might have been stealing cars, mugging people, fighting with other young men to burn off all that youth and testosterone.

"Your parents? You were expecting they might bail you out of this? What if I brought in the police?" I sank half of the second shot. "You think I'm going to just let this slide?"

He eyed the glass in my hand. I think he knew my story and in that moment, I could have sworn he was more worried I was starting in on a drunk than whether I was going to have him prosecuted.

"I wouldn't expect you to." He drank from his bottle, pushed the envelope toward me with a fingernail.

"Maybe this will help straighten it out."

"What?"

"Open it. I'm paying you back."

The envelope was too flat to hold cash. I ripped open the flap and extracted a cashier's check. I'd have to trust him on the amount—I hadn't yet gone back to calculate my loss—but the number looked about right.

I folded it and stuck it in my chest pocket, wondering how he'd spent all that money in the first place, and what he might have done to find the cash to repay me.

"It's a start," I said. "Doesn't make up for what you did."

If he thought I would magically forgive him, that we could return to the easy give and take we'd had, he was mistaken. He couldn't repurchase my trust.

His eyes narrowed and he sniffed.

"Why wouldn't that even us up? Or do you just like staying pissed off at me?"

He made it sound as if he were the aggrieved party, retroactively deciding to value the relationship we'd had. More evidence of how immature he was. If he didn't get it, I wasn't going to explain. He'd probably think I was whining.

"Never mind." I poured the rest of my whiskey into the sink gutter, not without regret. "Tell me why you felt you had to steal from me."

He slid the beer bottle back and forth between his hands, watching it like it contained a secret.

"Evvie," he said. "I did it for Evvie."

I'd half-expected to hear she was involved, which only brought my dislike for her act roaring back. It was sad enough that she could pimp herself out to a gangster in exchange for career help, but to push Isaac into a position where he felt he had to steal for her? Inexcusable.

"What? Vinson didn't give her plane fare to get home? She didn't squeeze enough out of him to set herself up here?"

Isaac's face relaxed. At a minimum, he cared about her. Maybe he thought it was love. Either way, it was the same kind of poison, chasing a woman like her.

"Rehab, Elder. She needed to kick."

It reminded me of how she'd looked the last time I saw her: the twitching, the bad skin, the way the little extra flesh she carried seemed to be melting off. I'd put it down to the aftermath of being with Frank Vinson, freeing herself, then escaping. But she had been living and working in a town full of excess and temptation while trying to keep the gangster happy.

"Meth?"

"Oh, God no. Just heroin."

Just. Though I understood how things could be even worse. Fentanyl, for one, hurt you harder and faster.

I blew out a sigh, puffing my cheeks like Diz. If I understood why he'd done what he'd done, it didn't erase the hurt of being stolen from, lied to by someone I trusted.

"Where is she now?"

He named a rehabilitation facility in Jamaica Plain, a familiar name. I whistled. It was the local equivalent of a Hazelden.

"No wonder you needed the money."

He nodded toward my shirt pocket.

"So. We're good?"

His hopeful question abraded my irritation.

"I wouldn't say so. No. The books are balanced, sure."

How could I make him understand how it felt to have your trust betrayed?

"I'm disappointed, Isaac."

His eyes went stony.

"I'm not your son, Elder. Not your nephew, not your boy. We aren't even pals."

That sealed my anger, made me store it away. I was foolish to think I'd connected with him in any real way.

"Is this the race thing?" I tiptoed toward that, remembering how hot he'd been last week.

"Not really." He stood. "Look, I have to get going." A smile pulled at his mouth. "Got to get my shit packed for California."

At least he'd decided to go to school, probably the best decision he could make.

"You're not taking her with you?"

He beetled his brows, looking older.

"She wasn't ever coming out there with me," he said. "That was her pipe dream. Literally."

But the clipped way he said it told me the decision had cost him something.

"How is she getting along?"

"Making it. The program is residential, so she's in there for three months. After that? She's an addict. You know how that goes."

That felt like a personal jab.

"She's on her own? No family around here?"

"Only way she's going to make it."

"Look. Isaac."

"You don't have to pay me for tonight," he said. "Think of it as interest on the loan."

He picked up his empty, walked behind the bar, and slotted it into the cardboard case. Then he headed up the stairs without saying goodbye.

Five minutes of heavy thinking later, I shut off all the lights except the bar back and climbed the stairs myself, recognizing the hot knot under my breastbone for what it was: loss, a touch of fear for his path going forward.

The early morning air on Mercy Street was sultry and still. It made me think of California, of warm days and nights, of where a young man's life might go from here.

31

After leaving Francesca at the fraud squad offices, Burton felt like he'd set everything in motion he could, as far as Marina's case went. Sometimes you had to start the process and wait for results, though he knew patience was not his best trick. He wondered what, if anything, Liam MacDonald was coming up with. As far as he knew, MacDonald still hadn't been anywhere near the Blue Sash, which was where the answers were going to come from.

Back in the precinct on Friday morning, he turned his attention to Antoinette Bordaine, a murder that looked an awful lot like inter-gangster warfare to him. That kind of torture was designed to send a message as well as elicit information, and he had a couple paths he could follow. Most urgently, though, he wanted to know what she'd been doing at the Blue Sash.

When he talked to her last year, he'd gotten the sense from a warning she'd given him that she might have been on Frank Vinson's pad in New Orleans. The fact that she'd been 'retired' early supported that. Nothing overt had ever come back to Burton on that score, but he remembered not telling her everything he might say to a fellow cop he trusted.

His voicemail contained a message from someone claiming to be the Public Affairs Office of the New Orleans police department. The man spoke in a languid syrupy accent that Burton knew people in the North thought connoted stupidity or slowness. His few interactions with cops in the South perplexed him. They tended to be aggressively polite and over-pleasant to your face, while hiding the usual complement of human meanness and frailty. That contrast always made him mistrust the person he was talking to.

He pushed the redial number and listened to the telephone beep and boop to make the connection.

"D'Anton."

It took him a second to realize the person was identifying himself.

"Dan Burton here. Boston PD."

"Yassuh." D'Anton's voice seemed to sweeten, as if he might be putting on the accent, the way a farmer up in Maine might do, as a joke and as camouflage. "You called us about an officer of ours?"

"Detective Bordaine. Antoinette. I believe she was Burglary?"

"Well. First of all, Detective Burton, that would be ex-Detective Bordaine. The lady has not been a member of our proud and illustrious force for some months now."

Nothing there he found surprising. He made his tone collegial, confidential.

"She get herself kicked off, did she? Who'd she kill?"

From what he'd heard, it was a feat to get booted from the force in New Orleans. His enduring image from the night Antoinette had taken him out on the town was an enormous Black cop—pro linebacker size—sitting astride a huge motorcycle in the center of Canal Street where the trolleys ran, smoking a cigar the size of a Little League bat. In uniform. He'd dead-eyed the two of them crossing the street, only nodding when Antoinette pulled back the hem of her jacket to show him her badge.

"I heard you Northern boys do not believe in foreplay. Do you?"

Burton's bullshit meter pegged red. Someone was trying to divert his attention.

"You did get the part of my message that said she was the victim of a homicide up here?"

"Most unfortunate."

Even for a PR guy, whose job was lying and spinning, D'Anton seemed curiously unruffled by Burton's interest.

"I'm trying to work up some background on the victim." He

leaned on the last word, trying to manufacture a little urgency. "Any idea why she'd be up here in Boston?"

D'Anton made a *tsk*-ing sound, like an old maiden aunt.

"Officially, my friend, all I can tell you is that Antoinette Bordaine left the force in April of this year."

The fact that he had her date of separation at his fingertips meant Burton's call had gotten the man interested enough to look up her records.

"And unofficially?" Dealing with cops in other jurisdictions had taught him there was as likely to be competition as any sense of brotherhood over the thin blue line. It sounded as if Antoinette had not had friends in the department who would protect her. "Must have been some kind of stink."

He hated phone conversations, where he couldn't see the face of the person he was talking to, be able to judge reaction and emotion. He pushed down his rising frustration.

"I can tell you this much." D'Anton's manner was smooth as a frozen daiquiri. "Her separation from the force was prompted by a Federal action down here in the city. Not something her local brother and sister officers were concerned with."

D'Anton *tsk*'ed again, making Burton think the man was less concerned with Antoinette's crimes than the fact she'd gotten caught.

"Didn't she work for Frank Vinson?"

Silence at the other end said he'd surprised the public affairs officer.

"My, aren't you well-informed? I do believe there were allegations of some sort of connection there, something to do with providing information she should not have. Altering records, perhaps."

He said it so lightly, it sounded like that sort of thing happened all the time, in every police department. His insouciance stuck in Burton's craw. The entire force could not be corrupt, but the attitude of this cop said he wasn't too concerned about the appearance.

"So, you can confirm she had ties to Vinson?"

Burton needed a connection, something he could follow to give him a handle on Antoinette's death.

"I'm actually not the person you'd need to speak to about that," D'Anton said. "I'm just the public mouthpiece here. Everything I've said is all I can tell you. I can give you some names, if you like."

He doubted it would do him any good to talk to Antoinette's former colleagues. The honest ones wouldn't want to admit they'd known her and the bent ones would nod and smile and tell him exactly nothing.

"Sure. But tell me this. Assuming you can, of course."

His sarcasm thickened the air.

"Are there major movements going on among your gangster populations? Fights over territory? Power plays of any kind?"

D'Anton emitted a tight polite laugh.

"You're a police detective, Mr. Burton. And no doubt a very good one. You know as well as I do, there's almost always something going on with the unwashed. These people thrive on chaos."

"That's not really an answer." Being polite wasn't getting him anywhere.

D'Anton sighed.

"There might have been a few extra *contretemps* this summer. I wouldn't guess whether it was the heat and the time of year, or whether something major was brewing. There has been a modicum of unrest, however, especially at the higher levels. Games of power, you know."

"Involving Vinson?"

"Well. Mr. Frank is the center pole of the big tent of gangsters in this circus, Detective. I'd be astonished if he wasn't in the middle of it somehow."

"That's pretty vague." Burton vented more of his frustration.

Even if Antoinette had been corrupt, he would have expected the fact that a cop had been murdered—OK, an ex-cop—would have inspired her former colleagues to help him out. Either D'Anton really knew nothing or, more likely, he wanted to keep the NOPD's dirty laundry in the city.

"You can't give me any more than that?"

D'Anton's voice chilled. He was done.

"Well," he said. "I'm mortally certain y'all have that Google up there. Don't you?"

* * *

He walked away from the phone call feeling he knew less about Antoinette Bordaine than when he'd started. The most obvious reason for her to die was if Frank Vinson was worried about her implicating him. He hadn't thought to ask D'Anton if that Federal "action" might have rolled Bordaine up as an informant. It was a method the Feds loved, putting the pressure on minor participants as a way to get to targets higher up the food chain. But even if that had been the case, why would Vinson want to kill her in Boston?

In fact, the only connection between Frank Vinson and Boston was through the two young women he'd lured to New Orleans with promises of stardom. One of them, Lily something or other, had come home and killed herself. And then there was Evvie, the woman Elder once had an eye on. He wondered if she'd ever met up with Antoinette.

Elder would know where to find her.

He checked himself out of the office on the white board outside Martines's office, empty already at four-thirty, and headed downstairs to the street door. Halfway down, he met MacDonald coming up. When he saw Burton, he squeezed over to the right and looked down at his shoes as they passed. That made Burton feel ashamed.

The Esposito was pleasantly cool, coming in from the street, and he wondered idly what Elder's air-conditioning bill must be like. While this hadn't been the hottest August on record, it was certainly one of the steamiest. The little window unit he had in his apartment could not keep up with the humidity, and he hadn't been sleeping well.

The sound system was pumping out some of that old-school jazz Elder was so stuck on, but low, in the background. Burton couldn't identify the names of the musicians off the top of his head, but he wished Elder would investigate some of the newer people, women in particular. Jazz was a shape-shifting genre, moving forward, sometimes back, and Elder's taste was stuck. Maybe he was just after familiar ground, given all the upheaval around the bar this past year.

Elder leaned against the back bar, staring into space. He didn't move when Burton climbed up on the stool and rapped his knuckles on the bar.

"You look like a seagull shit on your head," Burton said.

The only other customer this afternoon was the short squat guy who worked for one of the newspapers, an Esposito stool-sitter from the earliest days. Petey something or other?

Elder straightened up, refocused. His eyes were red and his thin hair messed up, as if he'd been running his hands through it.

"Everything all right, barkeep? How's Susan?"

He flinched as if Burton had touched an open sore.

"She's not here right now."

OK. Not going down that road, then.

"How about a beer?"

He fully intended to get a mild buzz on—sometimes it helped him think—but if he started pounding down whiskey sours, his night would be short and the thinking window narrow. And if he stayed half-sober, Elder would tell him what had soured his milk.

Elder banged the bottle down on a coaster.

"What? I don't rate a glass?"

He received a look of deep disgust, as well as a pint glass with the logo from a craft brewpub in Vermont. He poured and let the foam settle, looking for a neutral topic.

"Syndi working out OK?"

Burton could get what he wanted out of Elder—Evvie's whereabouts—easily enough, but he didn't want Elder to feel their ways had become transactional. His back and forth with Mickey had to be like that, tit for tat, but Elder was his friend.

"She's doing fine."

Elder drifted down the bar in response to Petey's raised hand, refilled his beer glass from the Rheingold tap, made change. The beer wasn't Rheingold, of course, the handle a vintage collectible.

"Better than fine, actually," he said when he came back. "She runs a very tight kitchen and the food's been better than average."

Burton felt a ping of irritation, as if Elder had made a backhanded complaint about the job Marina had done.

"So things are getting back to the old Esposito?"

"Getting there. Had a good crowd over the weekend. Maybe try out some live music in a couple of weeks."

"So why the horse face?"

Elder's shoulders stiffened. He crossed his arms. Burton was ready for him to dismiss the question, pretend nothing was wrong, but Elder took a deep breath.

"Isaac."

"Your kid bartender? What, he leave town on you?"

Wrong thing to say. Elder's face got red.

"Getting ready to, anyway."

That explained it. He'd watched Elder go all Dutch uncle on the kid, all the way back to last year, when Baron Loftus owned the bar, and Elder and Isaac were running those music popups. Elder had invested himself in the kid, helped him out, and Isaac had fucked him over.

"That was already baked in, wasn't it? That he might go off to school?"

"Not that he might go off to school with some of my money. I told you he stole from me, Burton."

Burton's natural cynicism about people in general and Isaac in the particular kept him unsurprised.

"I'm sorry. I know you liked him."

Elder looked surprised, as if he hadn't expected even that much sympathy. Which made Burton wonder what kind of friends he thought they were.

"He paid it back."

"You made it a loan?" He let his tone say what he thought of that, Elder forgiving the little shit, as if it were his fault Isaac had stolen.

"He took it to pay for someone's rehab."

Shit all over again. Isaac only cared about one person enough to steal for her.

165

"Evangeline."

Elder nodded. Burton read his conflict: the insult of the theft against the righteous use of the money. It was going to be harder for Burton to talk to Evvie than he'd thought.

"She's over in Jamaica Plain." Elder named the facility.

Burton swigged some beer.

"My question would have to be how he got the money to pay you back. I hope you didn't take a check."

32

I felt strange getting confessional with Burton. He would have had a different reason to come in than to hear my tale of woe. He had been looking for Evvie, though he knew now he'd have a hard time getting to her. Those rehab places like to isolate their patients while they work their healing. Or so I understood.

"Did she ever talk to you about her time with Frank Vinson?" he said. "What he was like? How he acted? She ever mention an Antoinette Bordaine?"

At one point last year, Isaac and I believed Evvie was being held against her will in New Orleans. Before we could mount any kind of rescue operation, she'd reappeared in Boston, shaken but not terribly harmed. Or so I'd thought at the time. She'd been quiet about the experience, but seemed physically OK, which said nothing for my powers of observation. She'd been harboring a habit.

"Never talked about it around me. I don't know if she got into more detail with Isaac. They were closer."

A touch of longing hit me, remembering the one night I had with her, what I'd thought might be a spark. It hadn't stayed lit.

Burton nodded. If he'd come in to drink, he was going about it very deliberately. He'd barely touched his beer.

"I just picked up a new case. You remember last winter? I told you I had a contact on the force in New Orleans?"

I nodded warily. Burton rarely brought up details of his work life.

"She turned up dead."

"Whoa. And you think she had something to do with Vinson, that whole thing?"

"I'm sure of it. But it happened here, Elder. She was tortured, shot in the chest, and left in an abandoned house in Hyde Park."

"Wait. A New Orleans cop killed here? That makes no sense."

"Ex-cop. But yeah." He nodded. "You see why I want to talk to Evvie."

My mind twisted with the possibilities.

"You don't think she…"

"How long has she been in rehab?"

I counted backward to when Isaac had stolen the money.

"Couple weeks? Ten days?"

Burton shook his head.

"Not likely it was her, then. And I don't know what Evvie would want to torture someone for."

We thought about that for a second.

"But the cop—what's her name?"

"Bordaine. Antoinette Bordaine."

"If she was working for Vinson, Evvie could have known her somehow. Maybe the cop was part of how Vinson kept people in line."

"What I was thinking," Burton said.

"What about Isaac? Trying to protect Evvie?"

Burton shook his head.

"That kind of stuff isn't as easy as it looks on television. He's a kid."

That wasn't the brightest thing I'd ever heard him say. Child soldiers, younger than Evvie and Isaac, killed people in conflict zones all over the world.

"Yeah. I can see him having the idea. But not being able to carry it through."

"It might explain why he took off so suddenly."

I shook my head.

"Why would he have waited all this time? And how would he have gotten this Antoinette to Boston? She'd have no reason to pay attention to him. Evangeline was a smaller part of Frank Vinson's world than he was in hers."

Burton nodded again.

"Got to run the idea down, though. She didn't come to Boston because she liked the chowder."

I couldn't wrap my head around the possibility Evvie or Isaac had killed this ex-cop. I wrote out Isaac's address on the back of a blank dinner check.

"This is where he's been living. He told me he was packing up for California, but that was only yesterday. He's probably still there."

Burton shoved the paper into a side pocket.

"If you decide to go see Evvie…" I said.

He raised an eyebrow. I knew what he was thinking.

"No, nothing like that. Just tell her she has people she can count on. After Isaac's gone."

"She's what, twenty years younger than you?"

"It's not that. You know Susan and I are together now. I don't want Evvie to come out of rehab feeling like she's on her own."

"Make me a whiskey sour. Maybe it will help me wash down this bullshit."

I was glad to step away from the disbelief, from my own anger. Until I'd opened my mouth, it hadn't occurred to me to feel responsibility toward Evangeline. It had nothing to do with affection, our momentary collision. I was remembering Lily Miller, the young woman who'd preceded Evvie in Frank Vinson's affections. And her suicide.

"The woman's a talented musician, a singer, Burton. The world doesn't own so much of that we can waste it."

Burton looked alarmed, as if I'd dropped too much philosophy into the conversation.

"I'm going to go over there," he said. "I have to. Her rehab's important, but so's my murder."

I nodded, unsurprised. He'd do what he had to do. But especially in the early stages, she would be focused, minute to minute, on withstanding the urge. She wouldn't have enough capacity for much more than that.

"Take it easy on her. She's bound to be brittle."

Burton set his jaw. I wasn't supposed to tell him how to do his job.

"If I can even talk to her. I won't go in unless her doctors say I can, all right? I assume they have doctors in this place. But I'm sure as shit going to try. Murder, Elder."

A couple of women in their mid-thirties opened the bar door and started down the stairs. Both of them wore business clothes, a bit of a rarity now that most white-collar employees worked from home. One was a creamy-skinned redhead with long messy hair piled up on her head, the other an olive-complected brunette. Both of them were a step above merely good-looking.

"As long as you're here," I said. "Talk to Syndi."

Burton was eying his untouched drink as if something was wrong with it.

"What the hell for now?"

"I think she knows more about the cooking school than she was saying. Something beyond the money scam."

His mind was still back on Evvie and what had happened to his ex-cop acquaintance. He sipped, then pointed with his chin down the bar.

"As long as I'm here. Why don't you take care of those two lovely ladies while I finish my drink. And maybe something a little less oldie-moldie on the tunes?"

He spoke loudly enough that the redhead turned a fierce green-eyed look on him. It wasn't like him to be rude that way. I hustled down the bar before they got irritated enough to leave.

"Evening. Can I serve you something?"

"Who's your dinosaur friend?"

It was their first time in the place—I would have noticed them before—and this was exactly the demographic I wanted to see more of, local folks to replace the dubious collection of one-timers and tourists Baron Loftus had left me with. I liked customers who were youngish, urban, reasonably well-heeled. I leaned in so Burton wouldn't hear me.

"Liquor inspector. You know how city employees can be."

The brunette nodded, only half-convinced. She had lovely hazel eyes.

"Makes for a less than welcoming atmosphere."

"Not much I can do about him. But since you're both new to the establishment—would it be too forward of me to offer you something on the house?"

The redhead was a bourbon drinker and the brunette ordered Dubonnet and soda, a mixture that tasted so much like medicine I believed people who drank it wanted pain with their pleasure. It was a very Puritan tipple.

I left them mollified, chatting, and walked back to Burton.

"Made some new friends?" he said. "That's certainly a better class of customer than you've been getting."

Still irked about something, he pushed the empty glass forward. I ignored it.

"Syndi. You want to talk to her or not? You are still working, I take it?"

A tide of flush rose up through his neck. His knuckles whitened.

"I am."

The brunette looked our way again, hearing his tone.

"Come on in the back, then. I don't think she's too busy right now."

It felt like he was about to explode. I didn't know why, but I didn't want it to happen out in the bar.

"Am I allowed another drink if I'm really, really good?"

I rolled my eyes.

"I'll bring it to you. Use my office."

He slid off the stool, mumbling, and headed for the end of the bar, passing the two women on his way to the kitchen. He tipped an imaginary hat as he walked by.

"Ladies."

Both of them stared at his back as he disappeared into the kitchen.

33

Burton ran the faces of the two women at the bar through his mental database. Something about them tickled his antennae. They gave off an aura of off-duty hooker, not that it was so easy to tell these days, with the way the internet kept the details of your hookups private, not to mention the occasional housewife looking to spice up her suburban life.

Elder's cook was wearing white earbuds and chopping onions, her hands and the knife a blur over the butcher block counter. He waited until she stopped, not wanting to startle a woman with a knife in her hands.

She plucked a tissue from the box on the window sill and dabbed at her eyes, took out one of the buds, and looked a question at him. He wondered if her skittish nature was native or a result of his being there, projecting his essential cop-ness. She seemed to be up on her toes and ready to run.

"What?" she said.

"Elder said the two of you were talking about the cooking school. Did you remember something else? Something about Marina?"

And if she had, why in hell hadn't she talked to him?

Her shoulders went rigid. She set the cleaver down and backed away from the bench.

"I don't know anything about that," she said.

Some days he felt as if whatever interview skills he had were eroding. He wasn't as patient as he used to be, when he could manage an informal conversation like this, even with someone as meek and skittish as Syndi, ease his way to what he wanted to know, then ease himself out again without anyone getting upset.

He leaned on the counter.

"Syndi. You're not in any trouble here, OK? The scam they were pulling, whatever it had to do with the 'scholarships'? It's probably legal, if not completely kosher. But you do not have any liability there."

Which reminded him of Francesca. He wondered if the fraud squad had found anything he could use.

"So tell me what you and Elder were talking about."

She crumpled the tissue and threw it in the trash bin.

"Marina talked about you a lot. Her cop ex-boyfriend. In a nice way."

That took him like a dart to the chest, that she'd embraced him when he wasn't there and pushed him away when he was.

"What else did you talk about?"

"She was poking around the school, I think. She never said what it was, but I think she wanted to bring something to you. Maybe evidence?"

"Of the scam?" The fact that she might have been playing amateur detective depressed him. Civilians got themselves in trouble that way.

Syndi shook her head. Burton marveled at her paleness, how bloodless she looked.

"It wasn't the money thing. It was something else."

"Then what?"

She tensed up again.

"You know she wasn't the first student at that school who died. There were at least two others."

* * *

He no longer had the urge to drink tonight, even in a minor way. Syndi had dropped that bit of information a little too casually, and nothing else. He couldn't shake the sense that her agenda was more complicated than he knew. But if it would lead to Marina's killer, he'd follow the faintest trail.

He walked out of the kitchen, past the two maybe-hookers. Elder looked up and said something to him, but Burton was chewing so hard on the idea that the cooking school might have some relation to Marina's murder that he was up the stairs and out the door before he realized it. And before he realized he'd left his change on the bar.

He snorted. Elder would happily drop that in the tip jar.

He was halfway to where he'd left his Jeep when his phone buzzed with a text message.

"Haymarket 9 p.m. Information for you."

He didn't need to see the elaborate graphic signature, an M twined with roses, to recognize Mickey as the sender. The fact Mickey had spelled out the word 'Information' reminded him of their quality time in the fourth grade in the clutches of that gray-haired grammarian, Mrs. Ward.

He considered the perils of going to Mickey for help again. He thought about the gangster the way he imagined a suburban homeowner thought of his plumber—not always present, but handy in a pinch. Mickey was someone Burton only needed occasionally, but when he did need him, he really needed him. Did he need Mickey right now?

Mickey also didn't play around, so if he had something for Burton, it was relevant. But to which of his cases?

He continued on to the Jeep and drove across the city to his apartment building. He and Mickey never discussed it, but Burton doubted his old classmate would be surprised if he recorded their conversation. A couple close calls in the last year had made Burton cautious and he'd bought some miniaturized gear he used to protect himself.

The street outside his apartment building was deserted, well after dark now. Most of the families remaining in the neighborhood had no kids, which was one reason he liked it. And the heat had abated so people could sit inside without melting. Not too many air conditioners on this street.

The door to his apartment was ajar about six inches. He unholstered his weapon and stepped left, so his back was against the hallway wall. Then he reached around with his free hand and shoved the door inward as hard as he could. It banged against the inside hall and he winced. Another divot in the drywall to fix.

"Boston Police. Show yourself."

He didn't yell, not wanting to frighten the neighbors.

No sound came from within. He was about to step inside, thinking whoever had broken in—some misinformed punk who didn't know whose apartment this was or that he owned little of value—was gone, when a cigarette lighter clicked, then someone exhaled. Smoke drifted out toward the hallway and tickled his nose.

Coupled with the text message, it was no coincidence.

"Mickey Barksdale. Open a fucking window, will you?"

Mickey's low laugh—the pleasure of putting one over on him—turned into a cough.

"As soon as you put your little gun away. Come on in, why don't you?"

Burton frowned, looked up, and saw the bright eye of a tiny camera clamped to the door above his head. That was why the door hadn't closed, and how Mickey knew he was armed.

Mickey stepped into the doorway, a filterless cigarette stuck between his fingers, reached up, and plucked down what looked like a tiny plastic insect.

"Pretty neat, huh?" He flicked his ashes onto the hall carpet and stowed the camera in his pocket.

"Little high-tech for a high school dropout from Charlestown, isn't it?"

"Gotta move with the times, Daniel. You know that. Come on in."

This was brash for Mickey, breaking into his apartment. Their unspoken understanding was that any connection between them, any conversation, was purely professional and needed to stay discreet. Mickey sometimes gave him information that helped, but he never suggested a *quid pro quo* or pushed into Burton's personal life. This was a violation of their rules.

They walked inside, Burton shutting the door but not locking it. He turned on a floor lamp to brighten the dimness and opened a window on the street side.

"You're going to smoke, do it over here, will you? My cleaning lady hates the smell."

Mickey looked around the room, ran the butt under the faucet in the kitchen, and tossed it in the waste basket.

"Sorry, Daniel. Sometimes I can't withstand the urge to wind you up."

"Wind me up? We're in a British farce now?"

Mickey, having eschewed his senior year of high school and ignored the benefits of post-secondary education in favor of advancing his career, was very sensitive about his vocabulary. Unless Burton wanted them to spar all night, he needed to ease off the smart-ass and let Mickey talk.

"I thought we were going to meet up later," he said. "And I'm sorry for the crack—it wasn't relevant. I know you wouldn't have come in here if it wasn't important. So what is it?"

Mickey seemed mollified, though with him that was a fragile state.

"Before we go down to Haymarket, where I'm going to show you something you'll like, we need to have a wee chat."

He paused. Burton nodded, trying for patience. About the only benefit Mickey took from these conversations was the chance to tell his story, draw it out enough to make it clear Burton would never have found the information without him. It was useless to press, because he reacted so unpredictably. You'd think you understood him, then he'd pull some wildly unexpected trick and blow all your assumptions out of the water.

"Mickey, I'm tired." He saw the thug start to flare. "Don't get me wrong. I'm grateful. I just really need to get some rest."

Mickey set his jaw.

"You telling me you're too tired to hear who killed your girlfriend?"

Burton felt himself heat up. How was it Mickey thought he could do a better job finding Marina's killer than he could? His secondary reaction was curiosity. Mickey did have sources and went to places in his daily rounds that Burton had no access to.

He forced himself to unbend.

"I could make some coffee."

Mickey's shoulders dropped from up around his ears.

"Too late in the day for me. It'll keep me up all night. But go ahead."

Always taking the other side of the argument. Burton shook his head, sat down in the armchair across from the couch, spread his palms.

"Come on, Mick. Give."

"Antoinette Bordaine."

That was the last name he'd expected out of Mickey's mouth.

"I assume you know the name?"

Burton tried to connect the dots, how Mickey would have run into her, and what that had to do with Marina. He nodded.

"Cop from New Orleans. Met her a couple years ago on a trip down there."

Shit—had Mickey killed her? That would murder whatever fragile relationship he'd had with the man. He couldn't let anything like that slide.

"You have some way I could contact her?" Mickey was ultra-casual about the ask, which emphasized it.

Burton's immediate thought, that Mickey might have killed her, sluiced away under hope. If he was looking for Bordaine, he probably hadn't killed her. Which didn't mean he didn't want to. Or maybe he was trying to establish an alibi for it ahead of time. Mickey was capable of any number of head games.

"You try the police station down there?"

Mickey twitched, as if Burton had said something stupid.

"She's not a cop any more," Mickey said. "But you probably knew that, am I right?"

Mickey's stubby fingers rose toward the cigarettes in the pocket of his short-sleeved shirt. Burton measured Mickey's interest by the fact he didn't whip out the smokes and light up again. He was doing his best not to irritate Burton, which meant he wanted something.

"I did know that. The gossip was that she walked over to your side of the street. Down in New Orleans, of course."

"Fuck!" Mickey slapped his thigh. "I knew she was up here for something like that."

"Like what? What's your interest?" Bordaine had been teaching at the Blue Sash. Was Mickey connecting that to Marina's death somehow?

Mickey leaned forward on the sagging sofa, hands on his knees. He looked worried, an emotion Burton was not used to seeing and one he doubted any of Mickey's worker bees had seen, either. Burton felt oddly favored, as if they were friends.

Mickey started to speak, then clamped his mouth shut.

"What?"

"Nothing. That was the thing I needed to know." His worried face was taken over by a smirk that made Burton want to slap him. "I knew it was going to be helpful some day, having you as a pal."

Burton's gut flipped.

"Not your pal, Mickey. Don't make that mistake."

He knew he walked a dangerous line with Mickey, taking his help, but he didn't ever want the man to think they were friends.

"Hold on. What does any of this have to do with Marina?"

Mickey looked sympathetic, which unsettled Burton. Any show of his humanity would only complicate things—it was easier if the bad guys stayed bad guys.

"I hope I told you how sorry I was about that. Because I was. I am. A decent part of your life gets ripped away. You must be pissed."

This was weird, Mickey trying to console him.

"Pissed might be the weakest way to say how I feel. She will have her day." He bore his gaze onto Mickey. "Regardless of who might be involved."

"Whoa, brother. I'm trying to help you out here, believe it or not. I will tell you this much. I've gone up and down my business ladders, talked to everyone who works for me. No one I'm associated with had anything to do with it." His voice got ragged. "I really shook the trees."

"Well, I thank you for that, though I'm sure you didn't do it only as a favor to me. But again. Where's the connection? What is it that makes you so convinced it wasn't an accidental overdose?"

Mickey gave him a you-stupid-fuck look. Burton should have known his reach went all through the city.

"It's a hypothesis. You know what one of those is, right?"

With the return of Mickey's sarcasm, they were back on familiar ground. He didn't enjoy the idea Mickey might have been feeling sorry for him. Or patronizing him.

"Mick."

"Sorry." Not sorry. "The only reason I can think of for an ex-cop, especially one who might be mobbed up, to be running around Boston and talking to my people, is that she represents an advance guard. Someone trying to horn in. You know I don't do any dope. Buy, sell, distribute. I won't touch it."

"Gold star for you. You think someone's trying to come in and take that business up?"

"Exactly. Which is why I need to find this woman and see what her story is."

This was a very elaborate setup, if Mickey had killed her and knew she was dead.

"So where does Marina come in?"

Mickey looked uncomfortable, as if his contribution to the conversation wasn't going to match what Burton had given him.

"Her name came up in passing. Out of Bordaine's mouth. Something to do with the cooking school. That's all I know."

Burton felt a slight shock, that the two murders might be related.

"I'd like to talk to this Bordaine." He wasn't going to tell Mickey she was dead, see where things led.

Mickey nodded. "You and me both."

"When she does show up, Mickey, she better be healthy. I'd hate to have to pay you the wrong kind of attention."

Mickey had few tells, but Burton believed he was telling the truth.

Mickey shrugged.

"I love the consideration. I try and do you some good and what do I get in return but threats?"

34

The only way I can explain what happened is that I must have thought I'd lost Susan once and for all. I hadn't heard from her in several days and the last time we talked, the air was fraught with kiss-off and goodbye. I figured it was my fault, that I was such an inconstant man and so easily disconnected.

The two ladies at the bar acted conscious of me. I caught more than one long look in my direction, and even when I wasn't seeing that, I felt the sense of awareness you get when someone is paying you attention or talking about you. So I wasn't all that surprised when the brunette stood up, leaned over, and pecked the redhead on the cheek.

"Big day in court tomorrow," she said, loudly enough for me to hear. "Can't stay out late like I used to."

I smirked to myself, wondering whether I would take the bait. Apparently they'd made whatever negotiations they needed to make over who got what. Something like this only happened to me once or twice a year, but it was clear enough what was going on. It was always flattering, occasionally comical, and normally I could disengage myself without offending anyone or getting in too deep. Tonight felt different.

I poured a shot from the one bottle of Pappy 23 I kept under the bar, for the guy who worked in the financial district and was willing to pay the $35 a shot price when he came in.

"If you're a bourbon drinker." I pushed the glass across the bar with my fingertips. "You really need to try this. I'm Elder, by the way."

The redhead gave me the one eyebrow cock. I nodded.

"I don't believe I can afford to develop any more bad habits," she said with a smile showing perfect white teeth.

I read her concern. Any single woman in a bar would be leery of a man she didn't know offering her a free drink.

I brought the bottle over, poured a second shot, then drank the first one myself. She seemed less than impressed, though she did pick up the glass.

On the other hand, I was dumbstruck with the beauty of what I'd just poured down my throat, the smooth brown-sugar jolt of the bourbon running through me like hot sap through tree limbs. I wanted to wiggle and dance, a reaction so unlike the dour way I felt when I drank scotch that I wondered how I'd been missing this joy all my life.

She hesitated.

"I have been pouring drinks for you all night," I said. Meaning if I'd had nefarious intentions, I'd already had a chance to exercise them.

She tipped her head to one side, acknowledging the logic. Her ginger hair had streaks of a darker red blended in, the artistry of an expensive hairdresser. Her dark green suit was tailored and the smile lines at the corner of her eyes set her age in the early thirties, old enough to know what she was doing.

She picked up the glass with the blood-red pinkie nail extended, a parody of high-class tea-drinking, and sipped. Her green eyes, too much a match for the color of her suit to be anything but contacts, widened in surprise.

"Now you've done it," she said. "Ruined me for the cheap stuff."

I smiled. The bourbon made me feel playful, not a reaction I was used to. "It's what I do."

She pushed the glass with her original drink off to one side.

"All done with that rotgut, then."

I nodded at the glass of Pappy.

"Mixer? Ice?"

She mocked me with a grin.

"Not with the nectar." She extended her hand over the bar. "Lucinda."

I moved down the bar to serve a couple other customers, watching her out of the corner of my eye. She sipped the bourbon thoughtfully, the way whiskey like that ought to be respected. I appreciated her appreciation. The question of how far I was willing to take this entered my mind.

The place cleared out slowly. I anchored her to her stool with the offer of another shot and promised myself one more, after the bar was empty and my cleanup was done. When Syndi came out of the kitchen to leave, carrying a light windbreaker, she stopped short at the sight of someone still sitting at the bar.

A look passed between them—recognition?—but I was busy counting out the register and didn't give it my full attention. Then Syndi was up the stairs and out.

I flipped the playlist to a string of Miles Davis ballads and while the piano intro to "Stella by Starlight" slipped out into the darkened bar, I took up a spot on the other side of the bar from Lucinda. She nodded once, which I took to mean we were agreed.

"Thanks for the recommendation." She tapped the shot glass with a dagger fingernail.

I sipped my second shot of Pappy and thought about those nails raking my back. Where had this sudden surge of desire come from? I was too old for one night pickups, instant lust. Or so I'd told myself.

"I have a place on Commonwealth Ave. A chair that's a little more comfortable than a bar stool."

"Is the music just as good? Because I adore Miles Davis."

I tossed back the bourbon, its seductive warmth spreading all the way out to the ends of my fingers.

"Better," I said.

She tipped her head toward the bourbon bottle, which I'd left handy on the back bar.

"Maybe we could carry your friend along for company?"

At that point, I was enough of an ass to bring the three hundred dollar bottle along, though if we drank much more of it, we might as well be gulping Old Crow.

"Sure. You need the ladies' before we go?"

She shook her head, meeting my look.
"I'm just fine right now, thank you."

* * *

The streetlight over the one empty parking space in front of my
building was burned out. As I parked, I wondered how Lucinda
had gotten to the Esposito in the first place and whether she would
expect me to take her home afterwards.

We walked up the granite stairs. She leaned into me, carrying
the bottle of bourbon by the neck. I'd finally fixed the latch on the
street door after years of Mrs. Rinaldi leaving it open and the new
lock resisted the key for a bit.

She hesitated in the open doorway, as if having second thoughts.
I'd already discarded my own uncertainties. Once I decided to do
something, I didn't generally reconsider. Not always the smartest
stance, but at least I was consistent.

"Pretty nice address," she said. "You own the whole building?"

The question seemed a little off, but I let it go. Buying the place
was one of the few financially intelligent things I'd managed before
the drinking really took me over.

"Coming in?"

If she wasn't, now was the time to say it. I wasn't trying to hide
her presence from anyone—neither of the other apartments was
occupied right now—but I didn't want her to feel forced.

She stepped inside, up onto the bottom step, and turned to
put her hands on my shoulders. Her face level with mine was an
invitation and I accepted it.

Her perfume swirled in my head. Her lips were soft, but cool.

She turned and started up the stairs. Her skirt was some kind of
miracle linen, thin and unwrinkled, so I could appreciate the sway
of her hips. At the top of the stairs, she stepped aside to let me
reach the lock with my keys.

"I don't know when the right time is to say this." Her voice was
quiet. "But Olivia said I should be sure to ask you for my fee ahead
of time. Would you like to do that now?"

"Olivia?"

Was she saying what I thought she was? That this was not a mutual seduction but a transaction?

She dropped a tiny pout at my obtuseness.

"The woman who brought me into the bar? I'm interning with her."

"Interning." All I could manage at the moment was to repeat her words. Mostly, I wanted to guffaw at my own idiocy, the stupidity of mistaking an apprentice—intern?—hooker for a pickup.

Her expression rippled. Suddenly, she looked bovine to me.

"I hope you didn't think I was the sort of woman who let men pick her up in bars."

That was so convoluted I didn't even try to parse it. I was still helplessly amazed by my own stupidity.

"Well, Lucinda. I'm afraid…"

The sound of the lock on my apartment door clicking open sent a shower of ice down my back. I clenched my keys. Lucinda looked at the opening door, her eyes wide.

"Elder?" Susan threw the door open. "What the hell is going on out here?"

And in less than an instant, Lucinda had turned and started clattering down the stairs, clutching the bottle of Pappy, her only fee.

35

Burton met Francesca Gatoberri the second time for brunch at Legal Sea Foods in the Prudential Tower. Since it was the last couple weeks of summer, tourists abounded, and Francesca told him she needed the camouflage of the crowd. She was working on a situation with a City Councilor who had an overblown sense of the tribute her new political position entitled her to. The subject lived in the Back Bay and Francesca had interviews to conduct in the neighborhood later. She didn't want the woman to notice her.

Which Burton thought would be difficult, given how striking-looking Francesca was. Intelligently, she'd gone in the opposite direction from trying to downplay her looks. She wore a wide-brimmed lavender straw hat, enormous round Iris Apfel sunglasses, and a yellow linen jumpsuit with short pants that emphasized her long tanned legs. No one was going to be looking at her face.

Burton himself was a little distracted by her beauty. More than one male walking across the restaurant developed a hitch in his step when he saw her.

"That school is running a long ton of cash through its books." She speared a raw oyster dressed with a dab of mignonette. "Way, way more than it's taking in. And way more than they're paying out in the scholarship scam. Which only went to two students, by the way."

Marina and Syndi. That was curious.

She tapped the tiny fork against the oyster plate, making it chime.

"You listening to me, Burton?"

Flustered, he crumbled some more oyster crackers into his clam chowder.

"Of course." To be honest, he only wanted to ask her how her love life was.

"It's a little too obvious to be really smart," she said.

"They're not trying to get caught."

She shrugged.

"Every one of these assholes thinks he invented the scam he's running. But most of them are older than the history of hookers."

He sipped some water. The chowder was still too hot to eat.

"A money laundry? How the hell do you pick a cooking school to do something like that?"

She ate another oyster. He watched her throat work as she swallowed. She frowned at him, then started to tick off possibilities on the long fingernails matching the color of her hat.

"There's linens. Produce and meat. Alcohol. Cutlery and dishes. Most of them can be cash transactions. And you know who those businesses are usually connected to."

"The mob."

Was the Blue Sash Mickey's, then? And had the man been trying to gaslight him? Fake that he knew nothing about what was going on about the school or Antoinette Bordaine teaching there?

"You think this could be our fair city's resident chief gangster?" he asked.

He wasn't sure he wanted the answer he already suspected, but he needed it to move forward. If Marina had stumbled into a scheme of Mickey's and threatened to bring it to Burton, the man had a fine motive for killing her. Though the presence of heroin didn't fit.

Francesca shook her head.

"Maybe. But you said he doesn't touch the drug trade with his pudgy little hands, right?"

"Drugs involved, too?"

"Those other two deaths you found? One was an overdose, one happened in a fight over a deal. Both of them were students at the school. Like your victim."

186

So, possible, but unlikely it was Mickey. But who'd have the balls to go up against him in his own town?

"New kids on the block?"

"Possibly." She picked up her cocktail fork again. "That's all I have for you right now, Dan. Eat your chowder. Enjoy your lunch."

*　*　*

She'd given him too much to think about to go off and do what he normally did with a Sunday afternoon, grab the Sunday *Globe* and a six-pack, put a ball game on the tube and unwind. He did not believe Mickey had suddenly decided to take up the drug trade after being so adamantly opposed to it for so long, but Mickey was nothing if not nimble. Maybe the pressure of keeping his organization going in the twenty-first century had forced him in that direction. The idea of the cooking school as a money laundry, on the other hand, was exactly the kind of scam Burton would expect from him. One of the axioms of high-level crime was that you had to have a way to clean up the cash.

So he agreed with Francesca's estimation, up to a point. The Blue Sash was a money laundry, and probably Mickey's. But the deaths associated with heroin dealing implied that heroin was also flowing through the enterprise somehow. The question was whether Mickey knew or approved of that. Was that why Antoinette was working at the school? Was she the vanguard for Frank Vinson muscling his way into Boston?

He wasn't going to be able to relax. He might as well go to work. Early afternoon on a summer Sunday, the precinct would be deserted, anyone who wasn't off the clock was out in the field trying to catch and interview the witnesses they hadn't gotten to during the week.

So he was more than a little surprised to see the back of Liam MacDonald in the break room, fussing with the recalcitrant coffee maker. Burton scuffed his feet on the carpet as he walked in, not wanting to startle him.

Which didn't help much. MacDonald turned, the glass carafe in his hand, and looked alarmed when he saw Burton. He set the vessel back gently on the hot plate, picked up his full mug, and started for the door.

He paused in the doorway. Burton prepared himself to duck, if MacDonald threw something. MacDonald shook his head and continued out into the bullpen.

Burton looked at the sludge in the pot and decided against coffee. He walked out, directly to MacDonald's cube. The man wouldn't look up from his laptop.

"Fuck off, Burton. I've got nothing to say to you."

Burton leaned into the opening and the fabric-covered cubicle shifted. If he didn't heal this up somehow, maybe somewhere down the line a murder didn't get solved. And regardless of how he felt about MacDonald, that was unacceptable.

"You know this thing they have on Twitter? AITA?"

MacDonald stared at him, as if it were beyond his ken that Burton even knew what Twitter was. Though politics had made them all experts in it recently.

"Reddit, actually. Am I the Asshole? Sure. What about it?"

"I was the asshole," Burton said. "I had no right to tee off on you the way I did. I apologize."

He chuckled to himself at MacDonald's reaction—he tensed up like a dog expecting a beating, his eyes pinched with suspicion. He wasn't going to last long in this city without a tougher skin.

"So what?"

And he wasn't ever going to be hard enough to pull that look off. His fingertips drifted to the fading bruise around his left eye, the scab on his cheekbone.

Burton shrugged.

"OK. So nothing. There it is."

He wasn't going to grovel. An apology had two sides, and he'd been clear and unequivocal, not one of those sorry-if-I-offended-you jobs. He couldn't force MacDonald to accept it.

He walked back over to his side of the bullpen. It was the right thing, but he couldn't get too self-righteous about it. Losing his temper was a fuck-up, but like all his fuck-ups, he was prepared to live with the consequences.

The quiet in the precinct made him restless. He had no more strings to pull, no calls he could make on a Sunday afternoon that would move him forward. He tried to write down everything he knew about the two cases, looking for commonalities, but it was so skimpy he tossed the pen down and stared at the acoustic tiles in the ceiling. His brain didn't operate in that logical a fashion.

He paddled around in his own impotent thoughts for a while, until a shadow darkened the opening of his cubicle. He looked up to see MacDonald staring at him, coffee cup in hand, and wondered if he'd have to duck a dousing or let MacDonald hit him once to even the score.

MacDonald took a long deep breath, down to his toes. Burton braced himself.

MacDonald stepped inside the cube, set his mug down on Burton's desk, and sat down in the visitor's chair, crossing his long legs and arranging the crease of his khakis over his knee.

"Burton. The name Frankie Vinson mean anything to you?"

36

"Nothing," I said to Susan. The trailing scent of Lucinda's perfume hung in the hallway as a telltale. "Nothing's going on."

She cocked her head and stared into my face from her bantam height. She appeared calm, but an artery jumped in her throat, suggesting some effort to control herself.

"Didn't look like nothing."

I desperately clutched at a story that might be believable.

"Prospective tenant. She works nights."

"Please." Her voice caught. I felt like an asshole. "You really thought I wasn't coming back?"

"Mrs. Rinaldi's place."

No lie I could sustain would salvage this. I spread my hands, stepped inside, and shut the apartment door. Her red roller suitcase stood on end in the living room, handle extended. Coming? Or going? A glass of white wine sat on the table next to a bottle I'd never bought, half-empty.

She brushed at angry tears.

"You really believe I slept with someone else out there?" she said. "You trust me that little?"

She stomped across the floor and sat in my leather recliner, folding her small bare feet underneath.

"So that makes what was happening out in the hall what? Revenge?"

I shook my head, embarrassed. If I could ever tell her, she'd find it hilarious I'd been duped by an apprentice hooker, but that wasn't a story for tonight. Maybe ever.

"I don't know."

"Ah. The old I-lost-my-head argument. It doesn't look like you got too far. This time. Intent is everything."

I walked to the cupboard over the sink for the Macallan bottle. She jumped up and blocked my way, smelled my breath, and nodded.

"Not tonight, bucko. You've already been into it."

My temper flared, but she was right. More whiskey wouldn't help a thing.

"Are you back for good, then? You're staying?"

She eyed me.

"That depends on you, Elder Darrow. That's what we're going to find out, I guess."

"I don't know if I can handle a relationship talk at this hour."

I followed her out of the kitchen, not relaxed enough to sit down. I stood by the bay window, looking down into a deserted Commonwealth Avenue. The air conditioning was drying my throat. I could feel the tickle in my nose.

"Could you ever?"

I didn't know where to go with all this, where she wanted to take it. No question I was in the wrong, that what I'd been about to do—at least until I found out I was supposed to pay for it—was a betrayal of her. Of us. But what about her contribution to the chaos? The chronic running away to the West Coast, her inability to wind up her business out there?

I had no answers. All I knew was that the frustration had erected a wall inside me, with my anger and impotence pulsing behind it like a slow building tide. I didn't want to be here with her when it broke down.

"I'm going for a walk." I started for the door.

"Elder. I'll still be here when you come back." Her voice was sad with hurt and the knowledge of how I always ran from unpleasantness. "It's three a.m. I know the city's safer than it used to be, but it isn't that safe."

She wasn't so worried about that, I knew, as the fact I was

fleeing the problem, hoping it would resolve without me. And I feared my own temper—I couldn't discuss anything sensibly when I was this angry.

What was the big deal anyway? We weren't married. We had no legal entanglements to worry about. Why were we trying so hard to salvage something neither of us seemed ready to commit to?

"I've lived here my whole life. I guess I know how to take care of myself."

She sighed loudly. I knew why. The conversation had leaped the bounds of what was important to something entirely tangential. She lifted a hand and flapped the back of it at me, dismissing the words, dismissing the whole relationship, for all I knew. At the moment, I could not care.

My vision clouded and I knew I had to leave before I threw something or broke something or shouted at the top of my lungs.

"Don't wait up." I banged my way out through the apartment door.

Stumbling down the stairs, I smelled the faint taint of Lucinda's rich perfume still hovering in the air. I shook my head at my own stupidity and tried not to let the thought enter that the bourbon had made me do it. All the alcohol did to me was release the parts of my character I usually kept under wraps. My self, my weaknesses, my fear that I didn't deserve someone like Susan, maybe? That was what made me do it, nothing as simple as bourbon.

I'd just stepped down onto the bottom step outside when a dark bulk rushed at me from the shadows of the stoop next door. I didn't even get my hands up before a hot line bloomed along the left side of my rib cage. I twisted away from it and as I fell, thought it would surely piss me off that Susan had been right, that I could get mugged literally on my own door step.

The granite step slammed into my chest and drove out the air. I grunted and tried to roll, but only managed to smack my skull against the stair too, and before the unyielding stone slammed me into blackness, Susan was above me, shrieking like a banshee.

"Get off of him! Get off!"

I came around to the sounds of Burton and Susan arguing.

"What the hell are you two into now?" she said.

I smelled rubbing alcohol, disinfectant, the rubbery scent of bandages. My head cleared slowly. It felt the size of a summer watermelon and twice as thick. I was lying on the couch in my apartment with no memory of how I'd gotten there. The faintest movement of my back threatened to send my legs into rigid cramps and I wondered vaguely if I'd injured my spine, bruised something important with that impact against the stone.

Eyes closed, I tried to remember what had happened, but the immediacy of the pain drove everything else out.

"You didn't tell me he was still drinking," Susan said. "I thought we agreed you would do that much, at least."

"This didn't have anything to do with his drinking. He didn't fall down on his pocket knife."

While I absorbed the knowledge that the two of them had been talking about me behind my back, the mention of knives reignited the line of heat along my ribs. I groaned.

"Elder," Susan said.

The end of the couch dipped as she squeezed in next to my feet.

"Don't try and sit up yet. We need to make sure those butterfly bandages are going to hold."

I looked across the living room at Burton, sitting in my recliner with a bottle of beer in his hand. He must have brought it with him.

"You want the doc or someone?" he said. "EMTs?"

I didn't want to shake my head.

"No. I got stabbed?"

"More cut, really. Very shallow. Who all did you piss off tonight?"

I saw the knowing look and remembered the reaction he'd had to Lucinda and Olivia in the bar. Maybe the two of them had been running a weird variation on the badger game? Or Lucinda had been pissed off enough about how our evening had ended that she hung around in case she had a chance to take it out on me? None of that made sense, and it wouldn't be intelligent to broach the possibilities in front of Susan.

"No one I'm aware of."

Susan was throwing me knife-sharp looks, no doubt thinking what I wasn't saying.

"Then none of this means anything to you?"

Burton showed me a photo on his phone. It looked like the door of the Esposito, graffitied with bright yellow paint, the word 'Killer' in stylized round letters with red drips of paint from the bottom of each.

If I was concussed by the blow to my head, all this did was compound things. I shook my head, gingerly.

"This had to have happened tonight. It wasn't there when I closed up."

37

Elder brought Burton up to date about the two hookers while Susan was in the bathroom.

"I had a feeling," Burton said. "I would have warned you, but I wouldn't have guessed you were in the market for those kind of services."

Elder glanced at the closed bathroom door as if Susan might hear them through it. It was an old building. He didn't have to worry.

"Yeah, well. Me either." Elder was blushing, but Burton couldn't bring himself to joke about it while his friend was down. "But I would think it was pretty unlikely this was Lucinda."

He hovered his hand over the exposed slice in his pale rib meat, held together with the ghostly white fasteners. The blood had crusted into a thin black line.

"You're sure?"

The way he described it, Lucinda wasn't an experienced hooker. That didn't mean she wasn't strange or violent.

"So I'll ask you again? You aggravate anyone other than me recently? Eighty-six someone from the bar?"

Elder shook his head stubbornly. Burton got the sense he was holding something back.

"What?"

"I know I said Isaac was angry with me. Mostly because I didn't forgive him on the spot. But this isn't like him."

He wished he could convince Elder how often people acted in complete contradiction to their normal patterns, most often when someone they cared about was threatened. Isaac might have been worried that Elder was going to report the theft. That would have shot down the kid's Stanford career before he ever got there.

"I'd agree," he said. "A white-bread kid like that, he doesn't go around stabbing people to get what he wants. He'd have his daddy sue you."

Susan returned from the bathroom, her face red, as if she'd been rubbing it with a towel.

"Burton," she said. "I think you better go and let this boy get some sleep. Did you two decide whether to take this to the real authorities?"

Ouch. Susan was pissed at him again. Despite her sketchy history before she met Elder, she was the law-abiding type, a believer in process and procedure and appropriate legal responses. He was a cop, mostly bound by all that, though he stretched it occasionally. But Elder? Not so much.

He'd always been the type to do things himself, from fixing the dishwasher in the bar to throwing out drunks. He liked to pick up problems in his own two hands and deal with them as best he could. Handing something over to an outside authority would feel like failure to him.

Elder ignored her jab.

"The graffiti on the door must have something to do with this." He shifted up into a sitting position and winced as Susan helped him into a Black Watch flannel shirt.

"Who's this killer?" Burton said.

"You looked pretty deeply into Syndi's background?"

Susan looked confused. Elder had a lot of explaining to do.

Burton climbed out of the chair and set the empty beer bottle on the table, paced the living room. Susan glared at him. It was a matter of minutes before she got angry enough to throw him out.

"I didn't. Except for the basics. She did go into the convent as a novitiate. She also did flunk out, then stay and cook for them for a while. And the habit."

"Well, I haven't killed anyone lately." Elder's joke wasn't funny. "And I can't think of anyone else it might mean."

Burton picked up the empty and tucked it in the bag with the rest of his beer.

"It's not too late to initiate an official response to this." He said it to mollify Susan. He knew what Elder would say.

Elder pulled himself to his feet using the arm of the sofa. Susan stayed close, as if she'd be able to hold him up if he fell. Burton felt a pang of loss for Marina that made his chest hurt.

"No. I'm fine."

"Get some rest, then. I'll come by tomorrow and we'll talk some more." Burton turned to Susan. "Glad you were here. This could have been much worse."

She ducked her head and he smiled to himself. Another person who couldn't take a compliment.

"Thank you for coming, Burton." She sounded as formal as a hostess.

He hitched the bag of beer up under his arm and left, waiting in the hallway until he heard the locks click shut.

The Jeep was parked three cars north of Elder's stoop. Burton left the beer on his hood, then returned to the scene of the stabbing.

Blood had dried black on the granite step where Elder had hit his head. He was lucky it had been a glancing blow or he would have had worse than a mild concussion. He said the assailant had come at him from his right. The knife had tagged Elder's left side. Probably a right-hander.

The space between the buildings' staircases did not catch light from either fixture, the one on Elder's building or the one next door. A perfect pool of shadow formed between for someone to hide in.

He flashed his penlight around in the trash between the stairs, caught a glint of broken glass, then a longer thinner reflection. Slipping a plastic bag over his hand, he bent and picked up a folding knife, blade out and stained. The words etched on the steel were 'Opinel Savoie France.' A wood-handled picnic knife.

He nodded. It didn't make complete sense yet, but it did give him a reason to go back to the cooking school.

197

38

By Monday, I'd had enough rest and recuperation. Susan's solicitude was starting to annoy me, which meant I was feeling better. Both of us tiptoed around the conversation we'd started to have before I was attacked.

I called Syndi early and told her not to come in until the dinner hour, giving me a little extra time by myself. I was surprised, after a three-hour nap on the couch, not to feel worse. My headache was gone, I was stiff in places I normally didn't feel, and the wound along my side pulled when I twisted my torso, but the butterfly stitches held. As I looked at myself in the mirror after a long hot shower, even the bruises didn't look so fearsome. I gave myself a sardonic salute in the mirror.

"You are not going to work," Susan said when I came out in my usual black pants and a fresh cotton shirt, brushing my hair back.

I felt adequate to the day, if not on top of it.

"Who else is going to do it? I can't afford to take time off."

"I could fill in for you."

The offer was so tentative I knew she didn't want to.

"Thanks. But I'd just have to explain how I do everything. Easier to do it myself."

She frowned, as if I wasn't appreciating her enough.

"And. I'm not trying to avoid what we were talking about. I know we have to continue the conversation we started. Just not today. OK?"

Her mouth opened—I was sure she wanted to argue—but she surprised me.

"All right. But soon, yes?"

The table was laid out with a bowl of scrambled eggs, English muffins, butter and marmalade. I beelined for the coffee pot.

"At least let me drive you in."

I needed to be by myself for a bit, to think about what had happened. And the few times I'd ridden in a car she was driving had shaved years off my life.

"I think I can manage the power steering. But thanks."

She smirked. She'd been setting me up and I warmed to the feeling maybe we were back on the same side. We could work through the rest of it.

* * *

I turned down the alley entrance alongside the Esposito building and parked the Volvo by the loading dock so I wouldn't have to walk down the front stairs inside. Then I remembered the graffiti Burton had shown me last night and figured I better walk around front and see how bad it looked. Assuming the vandals hadn't used some kind of unerasable paint, I'd call a cleaning company to remove it.

My walk hitched, a little out of rhythm as the stitches pulled at my side. When I rounded the corner, hand on the brick wall for support, I saw someone crouched in front of the bar's door, scrubbing away.

"Isaac?"

I walked up, surprised to see him, but gratified. I doubted he would have come to clean it up if he felt guilty about doing it. But could he be the killer the graffiti meant? I didn't see how.

He straightened up, a spray bottle in one hand and a clutch of bar towels in the other. I smelled bleach. He'd gotten most of the garish color off, but you could still see the ghostly outlines of the letters, bulbous and fat like a midnight artist's tag. Isaac wouldn't look at me directly.

"You don't have to do that." I needed to step lightly. I had no idea why he'd come back, but I wasn't in any shape, mentally or physically, to argue with him any more.

He eyed the cleanup work skeptically, squirted more cleaner on the shadowy outlines.

"Some kind of industrial paint. You must have pissed someone off pretty good?"

Same question Burton had asked.

"If I knew who, we'd both know." I saw no guilt or guile in his expression. "I'll assume you're not cleaning up a mess you made yourself."

A flash of irritation stiffened him, quickly squelched. The door to the bar was open. Like the business genius I was, I'd forgotten he still had a set of keys.

"No." He wadded the towels together and pulled the door open with his other hand. "I might have come by to apologize."

Then he stepped in front of me and started down the stairs.

He threw the dirty towels on the laundry bin and stowed the bottle of cleaner before I made it halfway down the stairs, wincing all the way. I might have been too optimistic about the way my body felt. The pulling of the bandages set me itching along the incision and my low back felt as if it had been pounded with a meat mallet.

"You OK?" Isaac looked concerned as he met me at the bottom of the stairs. His arms hung like he didn't know what to do with them, like he might have to catch me.

I paused at the bottom, one hand on the railing.

"I'm fine," I said. "I appreciate the cleanup work. You didn't have to do that."

He ducked his chin.

"I was acting like an asshole. You were always decent to me. I had no right to…"

I held up my hand, feeling steadier now that I was on flat ground.

"No need. What we needed to say, we said. You did the right thing, even if you went about it the wrong way."

"She's doing good," he said.

"That's excellent." And I meant it. I tended to forget that I had more money than ninety five percent of the population, and that it did no good locked up in a bank somewhere. "But she's in for a long program, right?"

"Another eight weeks, minimum. I'll be gone to California by the time she gets out."

He sounded guilty. I inferred he was asking for something.

"Someone will keep an eye on her," I said. "If she's up for it. Maybe even if she isn't."

He nodded. He hadn't wanted to ask outright, but that was part of why he'd come back to talk to me.

"I still owe you something. You look a little rocky. You catch the flu or something?"

"Or something."

"Let me set the place up for you, then." He grinned an irrepressible grin. "Might be the last time I get to screw up your system."

39

Burton thought long and hard about how he wanted to tackle the Blue Sash the second time around. He had questions about Antoinette Bordaine working there, among other things, and decided a quick look early Monday morning wouldn't hurt. He went by around six, since the brochures about the school made a point of how it tried to mimic the hours of the restaurants and other establishments the students might end up working in.

He had no more facts than he'd had the last time, except for Antoinette's presence there, only suppositions and inferences from the research Francesca had done. The best he could hope for was to rattle some cages, but there was no law against lying to the people he wanted to talk to.

He was surprised to find Pierre Macaron, the chief administrator, in conference with a lawyer, as well as a man who looked like cheap muscle dressed in chef's whites, a short guy with dyed black hair and shoulders like a bull. Nobody, fortunately, was wearing a toque, which would have crowded the room.

"Arvette," he said pleasantly.

He knew Arvette Coleman by reputation, though it was the first time he'd met her in her not-inconsiderable flesh. She was of counsel to Brown and Sarton, one of the old-line law firms downtown, with offices in the Pru. She was their criminal troubleshooter, the renegade attorney every firm kept around for dealing with the inevitable client problem that couldn't be handled by lawsuit, contract, or some other form of paper-shuffling.

She was a dumpy Black woman, lightly freckled, with curly hair kept semi-natural. She looked dismissable, but her courtroom reputation was such that rookie ADAs rolled their cases over and settled when they heard her name.

"Not really getting your presence here this morning," she said in a high fluty voice.

"As I explained to Macaroon here the other day…" He nodded toward Pierre.

"Chef Macaron, please." Coleman waved Pierre silent.

She sat very straight in her chair, exuding that fake outrage lawyers did so well. Something felt off. She must have known pulling an attitude would make him more curious, wonder why she was here so early on a Monday morning.

"One of the cooking school's students was murdered." He held off connecting up Antoinette's death for now. "I wouldn't think there'd be any question you'd want this cleared up."

"And I would think that working a case to which you haven't been officially assigned might cause your superiors to ask some pointed questions."

He nodded, unfazed. The threat didn't bother him as much as knowing someone in the department was talking to her. MacDonald?

"I don't usually take investigating advice from a defense attorney."

She raised a stubby forefinger. "I completely understand your interest, Detective. If my fiancée died under circumstances that were less than clear, I would be involved as well."

She'd done her homework, and needed to prove it. He'd expected no less when he walked in and heard her name. But how had she known he was coming in this morning?

"Now that we have all the, uh, wagging out of the way?" he said. "Can we get to business?"

Her eyes tightened. Useful to know she didn't like being challenged.

"Out of respect for law enforcement," she said stiffly, "and for your personal interest, we are willing to submit to questions. I'm only here to protect the interests of the school."

Whose ownership was buried under shell corporations and

layers of obfuscation Francesca was still sifting through. His money was still on Mickey.

He took a croissant off the platter and tore off a piece. As he put it in his mouth, he nodded at the other man sitting in the corner. He looked every bit the movie thug: swarthy, mustached, thick muscles clenched against all potential threats.

"I've met Chef Pierre," Burton said to her. "And you come with a reputation."

She smiled insincerely.

"But who is this gentleman?"

The man started to speak. Coleman cut him off with a brusque gesture.

"Chef Edouard is the Blue Sash's pastry instructor. He made the croissant you're eating."

He put the pastry down.

"And he's here because?"

"We were actually having a meeting before you appeared. Chef Edouard was also one of Ms. Antonelli's instructors. I thought he might be able to provide you some context."

Edouard grinned, his teeth dark here and there.

"She was quite good with the sucrée pastry. The sweet." He leered.

Burton frowned at Coleman. It was gratuitous for one of the school's instructors to try and provoke him.

"Excellent. I'm actually interested in the school's scholarship program. It seems counterintuitive that you would essentially pay a student to matriculate here."

Coleman relaxed. She was prepared for this question.

"I'm sure you're not aware of the full details of the program. But I'm happy to explain."

She raised her eyebrows, waiting for him to ask. He nodded. It wasn't the first time he'd had to drag information out of a lawyer.

"If you would." He popped the tail of the croissant into his mouth and looked at Batarrh. "I've had flakier, by the way."

Edouard scowled.

"The Blue Sash was founded by an anonymous benefactor in the food service industry." She recited as if from a marketing brochure. "This person understands too well how precarious employment in the industry is for everyone—the cooks, waitstaff, kitchen help, and so on. In addition to providing state of the art culinary instruction and business training, the principal behind the Blue Sash likes to provide adult students of promise with cash grants to allow them to work a little less and study a little more. Simple as that."

"Two adult students." Syndi and Marina were it, as far as he knew. And he doubted it had been that simple until he started questioning it.

"The number of recipients, of course, varies with the composition of the student body." Coleman had all the answers. But the explanation sounded contrived, an exoskeleton of logic cobbled together over the real reasons.

"It's been suggested," he said. "That the payments, and the school itself, are a little less altruistic than that. That the Blue Sash is functioning as a money laundry."

Pierre's hand flew to the blue checked scarf around his neck.

"Never! That is absolutely not true!"

Burton found it interesting that Macaron didn't have to stop and think what a money laundry was.

Coleman side-eyed the pastry chef, who stood and spoke a few words into Macaron's ear. Pierre rose from his chair, stared hate at Burton, and let Chef Edouard guide him out of the conference room. Interesting dynamic.

Burton didn't protest. With only him and Coleman in the room, the conversation might get real.

She waited a few seconds after the door closed before turning her full attention on Burton. Her dark brown eyes looked amused.

"Your phone," she said.

"Excuse me?"

"Your telephone. Give it to me, please."

He pulled it from its inside pocket, pressed the power button to turn it off, and showed her. He noticed she didn't offer to turn her own phone off. No matter. He always watched what he said around lawyers.

"It's probably better for the both of us if there isn't any record of what I'm going to tell you."

"You are going to tell me I'm right," he said. "And also that the fact the school is laundering money has nothing to do with Marina's death. Or the death of the other two students."

She raised her eyebrows. She hadn't known he knew about the other two.

"There is nothing in the operations or the finances of this cooking school that would not stand up to the light of day. I am an officer of the court, and while I know you don't necessarily believe it, I take that seriously."

Still, she looked like she were judging how straightforward she could be, which also meant how much she could lie.

"And by 'you,' you mean the cops? Or me personally?"

"I don't know you well enough to judge, Detective. Let's say that, as an entity, the Boston Police have shown a preponderance of contempt for the work I do."

Burton decided he liked the woman. She took no shit, but she seemed like he could work with her.

"So you'll have to wait and see."

"Whether I can trust you? Most definitely. Just as I will have to convince you of my own probity."

"The easiest way to convince me this all is innocent…" He picked at the flakes of the croissant. "Give me the name of this so-called benefactor. The man with so much money he can afford to give it away."

She was shaking her head before he was halfway through the sentence.

"You know I can't do that."

"It would be a very short and simple conversation. To verify the story you're asking me to believe."

She pouted.

"So you don't trust me."

"Trust but verify," he said.

"I didn't think there were any Ronald Reagan fans left in the world."

"You could help me eliminate a whole line of investigation."

It would be provisional, but an easing there would help her with her client. She seemed to consider it, but she was too much of a lawyer to accept his first offer.

A lock of her hair had escaped one of the barrettes, springing out into space. She shook her head again.

"We both know you can't make me that kind of promise." She stood and picked up her phone. "Give me a minute, will you?"

She stepped out into the hall, a veteran move. If she'd asked him to step out, she wouldn't know whether he was wandering the halls, talking to people she didn't want him talking to. He had the sense he might have pushed a button that would release some information, though he had no idea what it would be.

Her voice rose and fell on the other side of the hollow-core door, though he couldn't distinguish words. When she returned, thumbing her phone off, she was laughing, which softened her face, made her more likeable.

"Well." She reseated herself at the table. "That's always a chuckle."

He was impatient.

"Are you going to tell me his name? Or hers?"

She shook her head, the stray curl bouncing like a spring.

"You do not want me to say his name out loud, I'm certain. Or so he said. Leave you some plausible deniability."

"Which I need because…?"

"This is someone you have a relationship with." She smiled at his confusion. "Someone with a philanthropic bent you haven't known about before."

Elder? Burton could see him doing something like this anonymously, helping out Marina. Hiring Syndi. But he'd have no reason for Burton not to know. And the financials went against Elder's grain—he wouldn't run a business at a deficit to give away money. Nor would he need the shell corporations and layers of secrecy.

He shook his head. Fuck. He knew. But he wanted confirmation.

"We can sit here all day and let me guess. Just say the name."

She was enjoying this too much for his taste. He guessed he was getting paid back for all the times a cop had jerked her around. She finally dropped the bomb he was expecting.

"Your childhood pal?" She nodded. "There you go."

Son of a bitch. Mickey Barksdale owned the Blue Sash? It made sense. He'd spent considerable time and effort in the last few years trying to legitimize his gangster businesses. Apparently he hadn't been able to resist using a legitimate business for some shady cover.

"That's not a name I'd use for a childhood pal," she said. Her smile widened.

"Sorry. Did I say that out loud? We were never pals. And are not now."

Coleman dipped her head to one side.

"What our mutual acquaintance did say was that Ms. Antonelli's death has nothing to do with the operation of the school. What he has said to me, candidly, is that you know he would not want you to have to come after him." She eyed Burton with a little more respect than she'd shown. "It sounds like the two of you have a rather fraught relationship."

"No relationship at all." He stood up. "But thanks for the information. I'll be sure to tell Mickey how helpful you were."

Saying Mickey's name out loud made it less likely she could use this conversation against him, if she did happen to be recording it.

She tucked the errant coil of hair back and re-snapped the barrette.

"I trust this will help you move forward," she said. "And eliminate the Blue Sash from your concern."

"Nah," he said. "I'll probably be by again."

Burton's reward was the slightest hitch in her smooth composure. Good enough for him.

40

I hadn't expected Isaac to stick around and work, but he must have seen I was feeling rocky, and jumped right in. A trio of tourists from somewhere Nordic, all bright white teeth, blonde hair, and rolling consonants, were the first people through the door for dinner. Syndi had overcome whatever was bothering her about Isaac; they worked together and handled the moderate dinner rush without snarling at each other.

I wasn't out of commission altogether, but the knifing and the lack of sleep had doubled up on me. If it got busy, I could pitch in, but for now I was content to sit on a stool and watch, husband what energy I had.

In a lull around seven, Isaac stepped down the bar to where I sat.

"You don't look that perky, Mr. D. You want to take off?" He nodded at the kitchen. "We can handle this all right."

Someday I'd have to ask why they'd been so hostile with each other.

"I'm fine. A little washed-out feeling. It's going to be busy later."

His smile faded. He was remembering I still didn't trust him.

"Anything new on Evangeline?" I said. "Rehab's going all right?"

The rest of his good humor evaporated. That woman would be a tender topic with him for a very long time.

"You didn't tell anyone where she was? What's she's been going through?"

"Only Burton."

He frowned some more. He'd never trusted Burton, but I was starting to understand it wasn't personal.

"You trust him not to say anything?"

"He wouldn't have any reason to. You know he's not one of her fans. The subject came up, he'd probably avoid it."

Isaac nodded, walking away to smile at a single woman who'd come in and sat at the bar. She made me think of my ridiculous evening with Lucinda and whether I was going to be able to paper that over with Susan.

When he returned, I realized what was bothering him.

"Someone went by to see her there?" I said.

"Their security is very good.'"

That alarmed me.

"Keeping her in? Or other people out?"

"Both. Someone came to the place asking about her. They wouldn't confirm she was there."

"Not me. Not Burton."

The music switched over to what I thought of as drinking jazz, soft brushes on a snare drum, muted trumpets. His face worked with worry.

"She must have family. Friends? Maybe one of them heard about it and wanted to visit?"

He twisted the water out of a bar towel over the sink.

"No sibs. Her dad left when she was two. And her mom died last year."

"New Orleans?"

"That's what worries me. She was telling us all a different story when she came back than what I saw when I went down there."

I stood up and walked behind the bar so we could talk more quietly. My torso was stiffening and if I didn't move, my joints were going to lock right up.

"You think it was Vinson?"

I'd made some assumptions about the devil's bargain Evvie had made with the New Orleans gangster, but I hadn't rechecked them when she returned. None of my business, except that Isaac was worried now, and that felt like it should be my business. Maybe the break with Frank hadn't been as clean and voluntary as she'd told everyone.

"The man fell hard for her," Isaac said. "The way I heard it."

"Frank Vinson fell in love with Evangeline?"

He touched his bow tie, as if the idea choked him.

"That's what she said. And I did see a little bit of it. He got obsessed, had people watching her all the time. Controlling where she went and who she saw. And it was starting to cause him business problems."

"Lucky she got out when she did, then. Was that when she started doing dope?"

"She didn't escape, Elder. They sent her home. Some of Frank's minions. His business was suffering. He wasn't taking care of things."

"She told you all this? She wasn't high when she did?"

I understood addicts well enough to take their stories with a handful of salt. The engine of addiction ran on all kinds of negative energy, including lies and paranoia.

"She was not."

Pain roughened his voice. No matter what he thought, Isaac was going to have a tough time leaving her for California.

"You think Vinson's here looking for her?"

"Or some of his people. The ones loyal to him. Maybe they want to make sure she isn't tempting him any more."

He air-quoted the word 'tempting.'

"Kill her? That would be insane." The logic was there, but it was too difficult for me to believe. "You need to tell Burton."

Isaac shook his head.

"I can't, man. I promised her I'd keep it quiet."

"Not intelligent, Isaac. We're not talking about a pinky-swear here. She could be in real danger."

"Burton's not going to want to get involved unless someone dies."

If he believed that, he didn't know Burton.

"You don't want to wait for that to happen, do you?"

He was struggling with it, his loyalty commendable but dangerous.

"Let me tell him," I said. "You may not trust him, but I do. He'll do the right thing. Maybe he can order up some protection."

The woman at the bar raised her empty glass at Isaac. He nodded. The music slipped once, as if the wireless had hiccoughed.

"Just the bones of it?" he said. "It doesn't have to be a huge deal."

41

Burton felt his anger simmering, hot as the afternoon, as he parked the Jeep down near Haymarket. The farmer's market was winding down for the day, but he didn't bother looking for Mickey among the stalls and vendors. Making change and bagging carrots wasn't Mickey's idea of a good time.

He'd never been naïve enough to think Mickey looked out for anyone but Mickey, but Mickey had also never outright lied to him, especially about something Burton could corroborate. But here he was, playing the dunce about the Blue Sash when Burton asked about it. Which called into question other things Mickey had said to him lately. About looking for Antoinette Bordaine, for example.

Burton slipped in through the warehouse door into the sanctum Mickey maintained as one of his legitimate endeavors. The crates of fruit, summer-ripe and jeweled and plumped up, glistened under the periodic spray from the plastic tubing that hissed above the displays. The concrete floor was wet and slippery. He wondered if Mickey also supplied all the produce for the cooking school, a believable double-dipping.

He stepped past the aisles, through the hanging plastic strips at the back, thinking that on such a hot day, Mickey might be hiding behind the insulated door to his office. He opened the door.

The inner room was set up like a downtown barrister's office with heavy dark furniture, glass-fronted bookcases, a large Oriental rug in shades of blue and cream. The air was dry enough to keep the moisture out front from affecting the books on the shelves.

He leaned over to look at titles and grinned to himself. Readers' Digest Condensed. If that didn't define Mickey's self-image, nothing did.

The rancid smell of an Italian stogie slipped in. A faint outline of light showed in the back wall and Burton pressed on the panel. A catch released and a rough doorway appeared, letting in bright sunlight and the heavy stink of the cigar.

"Close the door, for fuck's sake," Mickey said. "You have any idea what air conditioning costs me?"

He sat on an upturned plastic five-gallon bucket, bright orange with the black logo of a home improvement supply company. He took a last puff and ground the butt out on the asphalt at his feet. The lingering smoke smell battled with the scent of rotten fruit.

"Took you long enough to catch up to me."

He smirked, took out a bottle of hand sanitizer, and rubbed some on his palms. He offered it to Burton, who shook his head.

Now that he was here, Burton reined in his temper. He'd never gotten anything useful out of Mickey by going head-on. And he had to believe allowing Arvette Coleman to reveal who funded the Blue Sash was a decision that benefited Mickey somehow. The ground out here in the alley was slipperier than inside with the wet.

"It's always a bad idea to lie to the police, Mick. As I've mentioned before. And it's a worse idea to lie to me." He felt a churn in his chest. "You wanted me here to tell me you killed her? Or had her killed?"

Mickey straightened up fast on the stool and looked insulted.

"You think I killed your girlfriend? Absolutely not. I would never."

"And I'm supposed to just believe you."

Mickey crossed his legs and rested his folded hands on his knees, as easy a pose as if he were sitting in an armchair sipping sherry.

"You are not a stupid man, Burton. Though I have to say, you sometimes act like one. I wouldn't be friends with a stupid man."

"Mickey. We are not friends. Maybe in the third grade? But not now. Don't make that mistake."

He looked hurt, which made Burton wonder if the gangster was getting soft. Why would he care, all of a sudden, what Burton thought of him?

"Something you don't realize, my friend." He leaned on the word, sending Burton a message. "What you would call my business? I have certain boundaries. Guard rails, you could call them. I drive inside of them. It's good business and it keeps me out of trouble. Mostly."

"You're saying you didn't kill Marina because it wasn't in your business interest?"

"Sounds harsh, I know. But basically correct. That kind of sloppiness only causes trouble."

Burton believed him, but not because Mickey wouldn't kill someone who got in his way. If he'd killed Marina, Burton would come after him with everything he had, and that would disrupt all of Mickey's businesses, legitimate and not.

"Not one of your clowns or clones? Some asshole trying to grab favor with you? Or make you look bad?"

Mickey considered that, as if he hadn't thought of it himself. His manner iced.

"I would never allow the discipline to slack that way."

"OK. So. The cooking school. What's the story with that?"

He lifted his shoulders.

"A try at something new. Vertical integration. My cousin put me onto it."

"The cook at Darrow's place? Sydney?"

"Syndi. No. She's not involved."

He was adamant about that in a way that interested Burton.

"I had a pressing short-term problem," Mickey said. "A good deal of cash and no way to get it into a bank."

Legally. Without tax trouble.

"The scholarship thing was a little convoluted."

"That was for Syndi. And Marina. A little extra help."

Burton read what Mickey wanted. Giving Marina extra money was supposed to help Burton think better of him.

"You know someone's been selling dope over there?"

He didn't look surprised.

"I heard that. I'm looking into it. I'm getting out from under the school even as we speak. Could have been some of the students."

Mickey had tells when he lied and Burton recognized this one, the pull at his lower lip.

"Marina was killed by an overdose of heroin."

"You think I don't know that?" Mickey stood up, so close Burton smelled the stale tobacco. "You think I would allow something like that to happen? I hate drugs."

Burton didn't know why, but he did know Mickey refused to traffic in them.

"Besides. Antoinette Bordaine." Mickey said, his face twitching. Not a tell.

"What? You knew she was dead when I talked to you, didn't you?"

"I think she was the one who killed your girl."

"The girl has a name, Mickey. Marina. Antonelli."

"Marina." Mickey bobbed his head.

"You think Antoinette had something to do with that?"

"I knew she was working at the cooking school."

"You told me you didn't know who she was."

"I didn't remember her name, the first time you said it. I knew she was from New Orleans, teaching that Cajun cooking."

"You kill her, Mickey?"

Mickey fumbled out the little cardboard box of cigars, printed in the colors of the Italian flag.

"That sounded like a horrible thing. I don't torture people."

But he knew she'd been tortured before dying.

"You think Frank Vinson sent her up here? To horn in on your world?"

Mickey flicked the head of the wooden match with a thumbnail, lit up.

"You know I won't sell drugs here in the city."

'My city,' Burton heard, and bristled. His city, too.

"There are drugs being sold here, though."

Mickey nodded.

"And I know who's peddling them. I have a certain amount of influence over how big the business gets, what happens in that market segment."

That was a thin line to draw, between not selling the dope and controlling the market, though it apparently made Mickey feel better. Burton had heard rumors about Mickey helping out people in the old neighborhood who'd gotten sucked into drugs, proving once again how complicated people could be.

"You're a prince, Mickey. The school."

Mickey stared into the ancient brickwork of the warehouse across the alley. In anyone else, Burton would have guessed the expression as regret, but Mickey was an actor.

"I only invested in the school for the, uh, cash situation. A month ago, I started hearing rumors. Right around the time the Bordaine woman came on. About students selling horse."

Burton smiled to himself at the old-school name for the drug.

"At first, I thought amateurs, you know? At the retail level like that, they either get taken off the board or incorporated into whatever organization is selling the shit."

Whatever. If Mickey didn't know who that was, Burton would eat one of his cigars.

"Who is it, Mickey?"

Mickey waved him off with the hand that held his smoke.

"One of the Cambodians. Not a serious player. But it wasn't him."

And not someone Mickey would allow to become a serious player.

"So. Bordaine?"

"I heard she was trying to organize the half-dozen or so peewee dealers there. Probably on behalf of her boss."

"The cooking school's pretty small potatoes."

Mickey doubted Burton with a look.

"Nose under the tent, my friend. You establish yourself in one place, then you expand."

"So, she was working for Vinson, but she didn't know you were involved with the school? That's pretty shitty intelligence."

"Yeah, well. I'm not sure the guy I've got running the place is all that sharp. Though he does look legit. Or it might have been a big fuck-you. To me."

"So you took her off the board."

The hard question pulled at his certainty that he understood Mickey. The man enforced his own discipline with the local troops. But if he'd killed Antoinette, any fragile détente between him and Burton had just crashed to the ground. Third-grade classmates or not, Burton would bring him in.

Not surprisingly, Mickey shook his head. Convincingly. And Burton wanted to believe the man would stop short of a torture-murder.

"Swear to God, Daniel. I never touched her. Even though I'm ninety-nine per cent sure she hot-shotted your… Marina. I would have done it for you, you know."

Burton let that pass.

"Why would Bordaine kill an innocent, Mickey? Why take the risk?"

"No idea. Maybe Marina found out about the dope ring? And threatened to tell you?"

Burton had to separate what he believed from what he wanted to believe, and he couldn't do it standing here talking to Mickey. The sun had moved off, leaving the alley in shadow, but the air was stiller, more stifling.

"Then who did Antoinette?"

"I'm working on that." Mickey's face closed down. "I don't know yet, but I'm going to find out."

Bad for business, other people killing people in Mickey's sphere of influence.

"I don't want to find you in my way, Mickey."

Mickey tightened up. He didn't love being told what to do any more than Burton did.

"Seriously."

Mickey thought their relationship protected him. But they'd never tested the boundaries. Burton let him believe, for now.

"It's my problem," he said. "I would think you'd want revenge. For Marina."

Burton shook his head. His initial rage over her murder was banked. He'd seen too many cases blown up, too much justice deferred, because someone let emotion run an investigation. He could keep the personal at bay.

"I want justice, Mickey. However that's possible. People don't kill people here and get away with it."

Mickey stared at Burton. "Bullshit. You want revenge even more than I do. You just can't make yourself say it out loud."

Burton shook his head. "Enough with the psychobabble, OK? I'm serious. If I find out you killed Antoinette Bordaine, or anyone else, you know I'm going straight down your throat."

Mickey grinned, as if the challenge amused him.

"And you know I don't choke. Grab a bag of plums on your way out, pal. On me. They're choice right now."

42

I'd been too optimistic about how I'd felt. The slice along my ribs only throbbed a little, but I was as physically tired as if I'd run a marathon, all my body's energy directed toward healing, I suppose. My reserves were flat and I appreciated that Isaac had come back to tend bar for the night while I sat on my ass.

Syndi exited the kitchen around ten, a canvas bag over her shoulder.

"I tried to tell you before, but you were busy." She glanced at Isaac, chatting over the bar with a middle-aged couple. "I have to take off early."

I wasn't so turned in on myself that I couldn't see the strain on her face. She'd been doing a good job and I hadn't been paying her much attention.

"Everything OK?"

She smiled, a bit weary.

"Yeah. A couple of things I have to handle."

At ten o'clock at night?

"OK. Look, you are doing a terrific job back there, you know? People always say how much they enjoy the food."

I always felt clumsy handing out praise, but she must have needed this, or something like it. Tears rose in her eyes.

"Thanks, Elder. I like it here. See you tomorrow."

I watched her walk up the stairs and wondered what was pulling on her coattails.

And I thought again about who might have wanted to stab me. The question stymied me. The aborted interlude with Lucinda was the only out-of-the-ordinary occurrence recently, and I couldn't imagine someone who wanted to be a hooker reacting like that. The attack had felt clinical in a way, the violence emotionless.

Isaac floated back down the bar. We were down to a half-dozen hardcore drinkers, late-nighters who were probably postponing the trip home. Once the Esposito started hosting music again, we'd have a much different crowd.

"Forgot how much I liked this part." He looked pleased. "Yapping with the peeps."

"You are a gifted schmoozer."

"You want to take off and go home," he said. "I can close up."

"That's fine. I'll stay around."

It came out quickly enough that he knew why I'd said no. It deflated him, but he nodded.

He untied the apron and pulled it over his head.

"Best be going, then. Early day tomorrow."

"Heading out to San Francisco."

He didn't recognize the lyric.

"Palo Alto, actually."

I stood and gave him a one-armed hug.

"Thanks," he said. "Not going all boy-band on you, but you helped me out."

"Someone, one of us, will check in on Evvie."

"I'd appreciate that. And she will, too. Eventually."

"Write if you get work."

He gave me that confused look again and loped off up the stairs, out of the Esposito, and presumably out of my life.

* * *

Susan showed up about half an hour before closing. Everything was put away, the counters wiped down, the kitchen clean. I was down to a Jeff Bridges wannabe in a Hawaiian shirt drinking White Russians, who looked up when she came hopping down the stairs and shook his head as if he might be hallucinating.

He vacillated between ordering another drink and leaving. I was relieved when he scooped his change off the bar and pocketed it. He gave Susan a wide berth as he headed up the stairs.

She gave me a tight smile.

"Still knocking them dead, aren't I?"

"Surprised to see you. I'd have been home in another hour."

"I thought it would be easier to talk here."

That sounded ominous.

"Get you something?"

"Not if it means you have one, too."

I held up my hands like she'd pointed a gun at me.

"Let's talk, then."

She seemed to lose whatever momentum had carried her here. I'd known we were going to have to have the relationship talk, but I'd been hoping it would be a full daylight conversation, both of us awake and rested. Right now, I was so sore and distracted I could barely stand up.

"The big question," she said, "is whether this friendship can be saved."

"Friendship."

The decision that word implied was obvious.

"We still have that, right?" she said. "The connection, the history. A certain care about what happens to each other?"

"I'd have said it was a little more than that."

"I'm a pretty simple woman, Elder."

I suppressed a snort.

"Not the way you mean. My life: I want my work, my friends, a little pleasure now and then. Love would be nice."

"And we didn't manage that for you?"

"All of that and more," she said. "It's the more that's the problem."

I shook my head. "Not getting it."

"The crime-fighting stuff," she said. "I don't know how it happens, but there always seems to be violence around you."

"It's not like I go looking for it."

She shook her head.

"It is you. I don't think I really understood it until tonight. You were ready to sleep with a stranger because you were looking for a charge. You and Burton, strategizing over who had enough of a grievance to want to stab you. You weren't afraid, which would be the usual reaction. You were excited. You liked it."

She was correct that, in the past few years, circumstances had pulled me into some odd situations, some violent, some merely out of the regimen of my daily life. It never occurred to me I might be inviting them.

"You can't run away from everything," I said. "I have to take care of myself."

"But how is it you keep getting into situations where you have to do that? If you're not inviting it, somehow."

I had no good answer. What she saw as something I was seeking out seemed more like the random motion of the universe, molecules of weirdness and violence that occasionally pinged off of me.

"So that's a good reason to break this off?"

"I'm afraid, Elder. I'm afraid of what happens to you if we stay together. And to me. What gives you juice only scares the crap out of me."

It wasn't worth arguing. It never was when, as now, her mind was set.

"I'm going back to Oregon this week. For good. Go ahead and advertise the apartment for the first of September. There's no reason for me to hold onto it."

A lassitude washed through me. I leaned on the bar.

"If that's what it is, then that's what it is." I could process all of this later. Right now, I had to close up my establishment.

43

Martines looked about as comfortable as a long-tailed cat in a room full of rocking chairs, with both Burton and MacDonald in his office at the same time. No matter how much the younger detective had been sucking up to Martines, he had not warned the lieutenant he and Burton had agreed to work together and Burton approved. He always approved keeping your business to yourself. If Martines wondered why they were suddenly acting like partners, he kept it to himself.

"So. Bring me up to date."

Martines was in a no-smoking phase, though twice now, Burton had seen his hand flutter up to his shirt pocket, that smoker's unconscious gesture of comfort.

"MacDonald. Start. Where are you on Ms. Martinelli's case?"

"Antonelli," MacDonald corrected before Burton could snap. "I'm following up on something at the cooking school where she studied."

Burton focused his attention. What had MacDonald found out there?

"Details." Martines flicked his fingers impatiently. He really hadn't gotten any better at managing the squad. He still preferred to sit in his office all day and have the information come to him. Burton wondered when he'd finally get promoted and they'd be rid of him.

"There seems to be a gangster element involved in the school." He glanced at Burton. "Not sure what it is, completely. Rumor is that some part of the staff there might be involved in selling heroin. I've got a call in to Narcotics, see what they know."

Burton relaxed a fraction. MacDonald hadn't uncovered Mickey's ownership or the fact that Burton's victim, Antoinette Bordaine, had been teaching there. He still had a chance to solve Marina's murder first, which was the whole point of making nice with MacDonald.

Talking to Mickey had recharged his rage. The gangster's take on what had happened, that Frank Vinson had sent Antoinette to muscle into Boston and Marina had been collateral damage, felt right to him.

"Who's this Edouard Batarrh character?" Martines held up a flimsy paper. "And what's the request?"

"Interpol," MacDonald said. "Pastry chef hired on about six or seven months ago. From Marseille. The one in France," he added when Martines looked blank.

"Why?"

Burton chafed. He preferred it when Martines didn't pretend to get down in the weeds with his detectives. You had to explain everything to him, and it slowed them down.

"Marseille, Loo." He saw the chance to look like he was supporting MacDonald without giving away too much. "One of the oldest criminal cities in Europe. The French Connection?"

MacDonald frowned at Burton's sudden helpfulness.

"Right. More rumors that someone was trying to push into Boston. New York has gotten very tight." He stared at Burton. "Dope is the one kind of crime that never really flourishes here. Like there's a vacuum. Maybe someone's trying to fill it."

Was MacDonald hinting to Martines about Mickey's connection to Burton?

"It's believable," Burton said. "That's about the only thing Barksdale's outfit doesn't dabble in. Even if he lets it go on."

"So." Martines rubbed his hands together. "Progress on that front, then. Keep me in the loop on this Interpol thing. Maybe it's as simple as that, a new group of thugs trying to push out the old ones and Ms. Antonelli got in the way."

There were logic holes in that you could drive a taxi through, but Burton wasn't going to educate his boss.

"Burton, Antoinette Bordaine. Where we at?"

Burton was careful about what he was going to give up. MacDonald didn't know this yet, but Burton knew that once he pinned down Antoinette's killer, he'd know who killed Marina. He didn't want MacDonald to have everything he had and get there first.

"Not too much to report. She was a cop, and it looks like she got thrown off the force for something, maybe bribes, maybe consorting with gangsters." That sounded vague enough.

MacDonald raised an eyebrow. Martines shook his head.

"That's it? That's all you have? Where was she a cop?"

"New Orleans." He doubted Martines would remember any of the confusion last winter, the killings and their connection to the Crescent City. "Recently separated. Maybe six months ago."

"I don't care about her marital status. What was she doing here?"

Burton wasn't ready to give up the fact she was working at the cooking school, if MacDonald didn't already know that. Or that she'd been organizing the low-level heroin dealing.

"Not sure yet, Loo. I'm still checking to see if she had family locally. Or friends. Or whether she was working." He threw that in to cover himself, in case MacDonald did find out she'd been teaching at the Blue Sash.

"You know, when you keep calling me Loo, it feels like you're trying to put something over on me."

That was the smartest thing Martines had said to him in a year. He reminded himself not to take the man for granted.

"Sorry, Lieutenant. All I'm interested in is what we all want, building the case."

Though that wasn't all he was interested in, once he got his hands on who'd killed Marina.

"OK. Out of here and back to work, the two of you." Martines touched his shirt pocket again. "MacDonald? Good work. Looks like you're on a good track. Burton: Are you dogging this somehow? Get off your ass."

He shrugged that off, more of Martines's half-assed management technique, as if they were a football team and just needed to get downfield and hit someone.

A dozen feet outside of Martines's office, out of the lieutenant's hearing, MacDonald braced Burton.

"You're telling me you didn't know your vic was teaching at the cooking school?"

Shit. Maybe MacDonald was smarter than he looked. Burton arranged his face in surprise.

"No shit? No. I did not know that."

MacDonald's eyes crimped at the corners.

"Nothing you want to share, Burton? Like maybe you're thinking the two cases are connected?"

He pretended to consider that, shook his head.

"I don't know anything more than you do, Liam. Maybe less."

"Why do I think when you call me Liam that you're trying to put something over on me?"

"Don't know. I'm sure we'll get this resolved."

He hadn't intended it as a challenge, but MacDonald flushed.

"One of us will, Dan. And that's for shit sure."

44

Susan and I spent early Tuesday morning in a numb, if companionable, silence. Both of us were ignoring the fact she'd decided to leave me. She inspected the butterfly bandages along my rib cage and pronounced me a disgustingly quick healer. It was hard not to hear a subtext in that comment, and her solicitousness was no doubt calculated to remind me what I'd be missing.

We ate bagels from Finagle a Bagel with lox and cream cheese and after that, she went downstairs to the apartment on the second floor to pack what she needed to take with her, clean out the refrigerator, and perform the other tasks she had to finish to turn the place over. The fact that I was dulled to any sense of regret convinced me we were doing the right thing. I'd suspected I was too far immured in my adult habits and prejudices to make much of a domestic partner anyway.

Still and all, I was not in a peak mood when I showed up at the Esposito around ten-thirty and found Burton leaning on the brick wall with two coffees and a bag from Dunkin' in a cardboard tray. The ghostly outlines of the letters on the door were more obvious in the sunlight.

"You could change the name of the place," he said as I unlocked the door.

"'Does it go in the ear like honey? Or does it go in the ear like broken glass?'"

Burton frowned. "Too early for philosophy."

"Eddie Condon," I said. "You want to drink in a bar named Killer? It's not a euphonious name."

He followed me down the stairs.

"Instead of one named after a hockey player from the ancient past? Not too much difference there, I'd say."

He settled himself at the bar. I walked into the kitchen and turned on the grill and the fryer. He was prying the plastic cover off one of the coffees when I came back out.

He looked tired and angry, as if he hadn't rested much since the last time I saw him. The tired I understood—he never looked completely rested.

I opened the bag and peered inside, extracted a Boston Kreme doughnut.

"You look pretty ticked off about something. They forget the sugar?"

I pointed at his coffee. He nodded, biting off the end of a plain cruller.

"Pissed at myself. I haven't been taking this seriously enough."

"Marina?" I thought he was, if anything, taking it too seriously.

"I'm working with people who are paying more and better attention than I've been able to. Fact is, I've been doing a shitty job. Emotionally involved."

Which was, I gathered, why Mickey had wanted me to try and discourage Burton. I was relieved to have that off my shoulders.

I had no idea who he was talking about, but I'd heard him talk more than once about the sagging middle of a case, the point in an investigation where he'd put in all the background work, assembled his facts, developed a theory, then had to slog through a long period of routine and heavy thinking to shove the whole mess forward. He'd described it as a place where you could paddle your feet a hundred miles an hour and feel like you were going nowhere.

"I'm not privy to the facts," I said. "But I'm pretty sure you've been doing everything you can."

That was about as close as I could get to blowing sunshine up his ass and not having him dismiss me. He didn't react, which told me what he'd said wasn't the usual bitching.

Halfway down his coffee, he spoke again. The cruller was crumbs.

"I should be angrier," he said. "It's like this has become just another case to me."

"You always say you try and treat each one the same."

"Feels like it should be different. When it's someone you know." He looked at me, then went on.

"It makes me feel like she and I weren't that close. Like the whole relationship with her was a mistake."

I bit into the doughnut, but it tasted dull. Neither of us normally ventured into emotional conversation, and I wasn't sure what he wanted from me. If anything. I had my own emotional baggage this week, with Susan leaving. Thinking about it all made my head hurt.

"Can't stop time. Can't go back." My coffee was cold and bitter. I poured it out into the sink. "People change. Things."

Burton shook his shoulders like a dog coming in out of the rain.

"Thank you, Dr. Phil." He straightened up, finished his coffee. "I actually came here to do a little work."

"Here. The Esposito?"

"Where's your cook?"

I looked at the clock over the kitchen doorway.

"Due in half an hour."

He balled up the bag and the waxed paper and shot them like a basketball at the open trash can.

"Your kitchen skills up to making me a fried egg sandwich?"

"If you tell me what you want with her."

"You're not screwing her, too, I trust?"

"Too? Who? What are you talking about?"

"Susan called me."

"Of course she did." I stepped back from the bar. "Her decision, Burton. Not what I wanted."

I did wonder if she shared her reasoning with him, that the two of us hanging around together was too dangerous for her to feel safe.

"You should not let that woman go," he said.

This was deep water for us.

"I'm not sure I'm going to take relationship advice from you." I meant it as a joke, but I saw it sting.

"Fine. No reason we shouldn't both be miserable, then."

The street door creaked open at just the right time, before I said anything else that might strain the friendship. The buddy-buddy emotion confused me.

"Over easy?" I grabbed an apron off the hook.

Syndi hesitated halfway down the stairs, as if she sensed she might be walking in on something. Burton looked at me, his light blue eyes sad.

"Sounds good." He tipped his head toward Syndi. "You can sit in on the conversation, if you want."

45

Burton confronted Syndi before she got to the bar. He had a theory Mickey had placed her here, part of pushing for a stronger connection between the two of them, Mickey trying to make Burton believe they were friends. Her sudden appearance, just when Elder needed a cook, was too well-timed to be a coincidence.

"Hang up your coat. We need to talk."

She tried to look surprised, but she was no actress. The result was a teeth-baring grimace that made it look as if she was in physical pain. She looked at Elder, who was carrying out a plate with a fried egg sandwich but he shrugged. She slipped past him into the kitchen to hang up her bag.

Burton nodded thanks and sent Elder back to the kitchen. He'd get a straighter set of answers if he spoke to Syndi alone.

When she returned, she was carrying a cup of coffee, which she set on the bar between them. She pulled the apron on over her head and tied the strings, calmer now.

He started her off with an easy question.

"I don't suppose you know who stabbed your boss?"

"What? No!" She picked the mug up, slopping coffee on the bar. "I don't know anything about that. When did that happen?"

He measured her reaction: believable, maybe.

"I thought you showing up here was a little pat," he said. "Right at the moment Elder needed a cook. Why don't you tell me what's really going on?"

She relaxed, wiped up the spilled coffee with a bar rag. It happened sometimes, when people got caught—the relief let them

232

accept whatever fate was due. They could give in to the inevitability. Still, she tried.

"I don't have any idea what you're talking about, Detective. What do you want me to say?"

"Why is Mickey trying so hard to be my pal?"

Her thin shoulders slumped.

"I told him this was a stupid idea. You hardly ever come in the bar anyway."

Though he was happy to have the confirmation, he didn't look forward to telling Elder. Another woman who'd fucked him over. Still, her admission she'd been Mickey's clown in this circus meant he was getting somewhere.

"You weren't actually going to school at the Blue Sash."

She folded her hands in front of her as if she were back in parochial school.

"You already knew how to cook at that level. I talked to the nuns."

"Lot of fun, aren't they?"

"You can make me drag it out of you. Or tell me the whole story."

She sighed, touching the mug.

"You already know Mickey's my uncle."

He knew better, actually.

"Yes. Come on."

"Well, shit. Between you and Mr. Darrow, I can't always remember who I told what."

He could have reminded her the truth was easier to remember than lies, but that wouldn't have helped.

"Uncle Mickey asked me to do him a favor. Not a lot of people he trusts for that." She preened a little, which made Burton sad.

"And what favor was that?"

"He told me he owned part of the school. He thought someone might be ripping him off."

"Ripping him off how?"

"He wasn't sure. That's why he put me on the inside."

She was full of pride, which made him wonder how smart

she really was. The nun he'd spoken to remembered her as "a flighty thing." In criminal families, loyalty often outweighed the importance of smarts.

"So you went undercover."

She smiled.

"Look. Mr. Burton. I liked Marina. A lot. She was the only other person there who wasn't running around with their head up their ass. Like some half-shit cooking school was going to turn them into Ina Garten or Bobby Flay."

He had no idea who she was talking about.

"What happened?"

"I never saw anything out of the ordinary." She sounded disappointed. "A couple of the chefs were real assholes. This one woman from New Orleans, talked through her nose? She liked to pinch people. And the pastry chef was slimy, like he was always thinking about getting you into a closet."

"Heroin?"

"Rumors, but nothing I could take to Uncle Mickey. You know he's death on drugs."

Which made Burton wonder again if he'd been death on Antoinette Bordaine. He didn't really have another suspect.

"That was when he pulled me out," she said. "After the first OD."

"Huh. Why's that?"

She reached into the pocket of the light pants she wore under the apron, showed him a pink enameled medallion.

"You know what one of these is?"

He didn't need to read the tiny print.

"Recovery coin."

"I'm one year clean last week." She took a ragged breath. "He was worried I might relapse."

"So he pointed you here instead. To spy?"

She shook her head, as if a little truth now entitled her to lie.

"Syndi."

"He knew I was looking for work after the nuns kicked me to the curb. And he knew I liked to cook."

"I could tell Elder all this, let him decide to fire you or not. If you don't quit screwing around, I'll do that." And he might do it anyway.

"OK, OK. Mickey knew Mr. Darrow was looking for a cook, after he took the bar back over."

"And what were you supposed to do?"

Her good sense warred with her loyalty to Mickey. She did seem to feel bad about fooling Elder.

"Nothing heavy. Really. Keep an eye out."

"What does that even mean?"

"He wanted me to watch out for you. He knew your girlfriend getting killed was going to make you crazy. He was worried about you."

Probably more worried Burton might do something to threaten his business.

"I was supposed to pay attention, listen, tell him what you were doing."

Burton doubted Mickey's motives. But he hadn't been in the Esposito that much since Marina was killed.

"That's it? Truly?"

She dipped her chin. The intimidated look, which he suspected now, was back in place.

"Who stabbed Darrow, then?"

"Shit. I don't know, I said. That's too bad. I liked him."

"Past tense?"

"Well, you're going to tell him about all this, right? Fuck me over with this job?"

"You tell him. He's a big boy—he can decide. Tell him the whole story, though."

She huffed, but she knew he'd do it if she didn't.

"Don't take this out on Uncle Mickey. He was worried about you, really. He doesn't have a lot of friends, you know."

Which was about as much of the absurd as he was going to swallow today, Mickey wanting to be his pal. He levered himself up from the bar stool.

"You tell Elder. All of it. Or I will. Understood?"

She nodded.

He took a bite of the egg sandwich, but it was cold and rubbery. She headed back into the kitchen. He headed for the stairs, wondering what he could do with this new random knowledge. It didn't seem to add up to a whole lot.

46

I was going to have to open up the bar in half an hour, but what Syndi was saying threw me. I should have known something major was up when Burton stomped out without saying goodbye. He was a moody man, but rarely impolite.

"You only came to work here because your uncle asked you to?"

She ducked her head as if I were throwing things. In the last week, it felt like she'd come out of her shell. I'd hoped she was getting comfortable with the idea of being a permanent part of the Esposito.

"That's only how it started." Her voice grated, whiny. It mocked what I'd thought was her fragility. "I like it here. I like cooking. And I'm good at it."

"But what would Mickey want with me? Or the bar?"

I was still trying to figure out why he'd asked me to discourage Burton. Maybe he wanted to turn the Esposito into a money laundry too, the way Burton told me he'd gotten involved in the Blue Sash.

She fidgeted, pulling at the strings of her apron.

"I don't know, exactly. But it wasn't you he was interested in."

"Who, Burton?"

"My uncle is a strange man." I let her take me off on the tangent—maybe it would lead somewhere sensible. "He has a lot of power. And a lot of people want things from him."

Poor Mickey.

"Uneasy lies the head that wears the crown?"

She stared like I'd lapsed into a foreign language.

"Whatever. I think he was trying to do something nice for Mr. Burton. Show him they were friends."

I shook my head.

"Burton is the most ethical cop I know. He couldn't be friends with a gangster."

She looked at me as if I'd missed the message.

"They meet all the time," she said. "They talk."

Burton never said anything to me about that. But why would he? He didn't ask for advice about how to do his job and I didn't offer it.

"I listened in on them. Uncle Mickey's told him things that helped him solve some of his cases."

I wondered if Burton knew she knew. Or even if Mickey did. Could he be recording the conversations, for pressure on Burton? That still didn't explain why he'd planted her in my bar.

"You're saying he sent you here to look out for Burton."

Mickey was the one to call me in Vermont and say he was worried about Burton. Maybe this wasn't so far-fetched.

She looked exasperated, as if I were missing a point she'd already made.

"He wants to be friends with Burton."

The idea was so preposterous I laughed.

"I think the words Mickey's looking for are 'fat chance.'"

"I kind of knew that. I think he was trying to cut you out, too. You and Burton are already friends."

Ah. Now the request to discourage Burton made weird sense. If Mickey could drive a wedge between us, he thought he had a better chance for them to be pals. Still…

"I'm not buying this. Burton has a very stiff neck. And he doesn't spend anywhere near the amount of time in the bar he used to."

"I told Uncle Mickey it didn't make sense." She retied her apron. "He doesn't listen all that well. But that's the whole story. And Mr. Burton knows it, too. There's nothing nefarious about it."

Unless you considered the chief gangster in Boston wanting to be your friend, whether you wanted to be or not. A memory flashed through me.

"Isaac knew, didn't he? That's why you and he didn't get along."

"He saw me talking to Uncle Mickey one day. He knew who he was." She set her mouth. "But I saw him buying heroin, too. Isaac."

I frowned. For Evvie?

She put her fists on her hips.

"So, am I out of a job?"

"I don't know, Syndi."

I hated being played. And I hated not being able to trust people, especially ones who worked for me.

"You're sure he's not trying to squeeze anything out of me? Use the bar for something criminal?"

Tears came up, almost believably. She didn't like that word.

"No, Mr. D. Everyone knows everything now. I'm not trying to hide. And I really need this job."

I would have liked to consult Burton. But for now, it made sense to keep her where we could see her. Maybe Burton would use her as a conduit back to Mickey, for false information or real. I didn't try to hide my irritation with her.

"I don't know. You came to work here under false pretenses."

She sagged.

"You need me today, though."

On a folding chalkboard outside, I'd been advertising a cheap lunch special, trying to raise some extra business on the slow early days of the week. I nodded.

"Today? Fine. After that? Let me think about it."

She brightened, as if I'd commuted her execution.

"Go to work," I said. "I'll put the board outside."

Of course, the lunch was as busy a daytime rush as we'd had since I bought the bar back. It didn't help me decide whether to keep her, though I decided not to ask Burton what he thought. Whatever passed between him and Mickey was their business, and I wanted no part of it. Mickey had gotten me to try and manipulate Burton, which I no longer believed was for Burton's benefit. Mickey had called me back from Vermont for his own reasons, not to help Burton out.

I wondered if I could believe Syndi's interpretation, that Mickey

239

just wanted to be friends with Burton. That notion tangled up the motives, but Burton could see the razor blade in that apple. I regretted agreeing to anything Mickey had asked me to do.

The afternoon slowed into the rush's aftermath, clearing the tables and washing the dishes. It let me lay off of the heavy thinking for a while, the kind where the decisions aren't obvious.

47

Burton didn't know whether to be pissed off at Mickey or grateful, or both. He could always rely on the fact the man's motives were multiple. Even if he had placed Syndi in the Esposito to look out for him, that wouldn't have been the only reason. What he liked less was Mickey's assumption that Burton wouldn't have been rational about doing his job in Marina's case. At first, of course, all he'd wanted to do was rip the killer's heart out with his bare hands. But he was a pro at this. Letting his emotions rule hadn't ever gotten him a successful result.

He stepped out of the stairwell onto Mercy Street, and stopped. Speak of the devil and he did appear.

Mickey was parked in a loading zone next to the mouth of the alley that led to the back of the bar. The white ragtop on the dark purple 442 was down, the finish sparkling in the late afternoon sun as if chips of mica were embedded in the paint.

Mickey raised a hand.

"Come for a ride with me."

Not a question. Burton hesitated. Usually when they met, it was more discreet than this.

He glanced up at the sign on the lamp post.

"What? You going to write me a ticket?"

He could say no, but Mickey always found a way to get what he wanted. He wouldn't put it past him to show up at the precinct, claim Burton as his friend, and take him out to lunch. And worse, Burton had always been a slave to his curiosity.

"Hold on."

241

He pulled out his phone, took a picture of the license plate, and texted it to Elder with a message: "Mickey B."

He opened the passenger's door, the hinges smooth and quiet. Mickey's restorations were meticulous. The white leather sighed as Burton settled in.

"Just had a nice talk with your niece."

Mickey squealed the tires away from the curb.

"Jesus. You have to do that?"

"Riding with a cop doesn't buy me any leeway?"

"Not this cop."

"She's a nice kid. She likes cooking. I hope you didn't screw that up for her." As if he already knew what Burton and Syndi had been talking about.

"Not sure what your point is."

"Helping her find a job, you mean?"

They crossed Stuart Street and headed up the back side of the Public Gardens, the air rushing over the car making it difficult to hear. Mickey ran up the windows.

"I was just doing her a solid, Burton. And Elder, too. Didn't he need a cook?"

"I'm not your friend, Mickey. You're a source. A confidential informant. Unofficial."

If the reminder bothered Mickey, he didn't show it.

They looped through Charlestown and over the Tobin, though Burton didn't know anyone who didn't call it the Mystic River Bridge. They drove out on Route 1 north, passing the lot where Frank Giuffrida's Steak House used to stand, with the plastic cows and the cactus. When they hit 95, Mickey dropped his foot and let the engine roar, the Oldsmobile headed for New Hampshire.

"I do have to work tomorrow," Burton said.

Mickey grinned.

"All love and respect to you, Daniel, I didn't pick you up for an overnight."

They rolled in silence for half an hour or so, Mickey slipped the car through the slower-moving vehicles, a cabdriver's rhythm.

He took the first exit at Portsmouth Circle, the US 1 bypass, and drove through a mostly residential area until they came to a small commercial strip on a curve: a half dozen shops on either side of the street, a noodle bar, butcher, a housewares and tchotchkes shop.

Burton recognized the back entrance to the shipyard as they passed through town, Mickey still driving too fast.

"Kittery Point? Nice neighborhood."

"Maine's actually a little more independent-minded than New Hampshire," Mickey said. "Despite the Live Free or Die bullshit."

He pulled into a dirt driveway a couple hundred yards beyond town, next to a well-kept bungalow with dark green siding and yellow trim. A yellow bug light burned in the front porch fixture and two fan-backed rattan chairs cast shadows. Someone sat in the farthest one, his cigarette red in the near dark. The nearest street lamp to the house was out. Burton put his hand on his belt, near his weapon.

Mickey closed the car door with a click. Burton followed him up the flagstone path, seeing Mickey's gait roll, as if his hips hurt. None of them was young any more.

"Everything jake?" Mickey said quietly.

The red coal bobbed up and down.

"You can take off."

Burton didn't see another car—maybe the watcher was local. But what was he watching? Or guarding?

Mickey climbed to the porch and sat in one of the chairs.

"Sit down, Daniel. Before we go inside, I want to tell you a little story."

Burton was starting to get irked with the byplay. But curiosity had carried him this far, and he was certain Mickey hadn't brought him all the way to Maine to do him harm, if only because he wouldn't have to.

"Feels a little secret squirrel, Mick. Even for you. But sure."

"Sit." Mickey's tone hardened. "I don't have all night for this."

Burton felt the rattan creak under his butt, the scoop in the seat a comfortable cradle. His nerves ratcheted up.

"What is this?"

"I've known you a long time, Daniel. And better than you think.

Boy from the old neighborhood makes good?" He chuckled. "Or at least makes a clean break."

Burton hated talk like that. He never used his background as an excuse, or a brag.

But the best thing to do in this circumstance was let Mickey run his mouth, do whatever they'd come up here to do, and go home. Why they were in Maine for this talk was the only mystery.

"When Marina was killed, I had the feeling it would fuck you up. OK? So I called your pal."

"You called Elder?" The effrontery amazed him. "You think you have those kind of rights in my life?"

Mickey patted at the air, trying to calm him down.

"Was I wrong?"

He thought about the first day, his immediate reaction to her death, and tipped his head in agreement.

"Still. You had no right."

"We should always appreciate what our friends do for us, Daniel."

Burton nodded, wondering if Mickey was why Elder had been trying to get him not to work Marina's case.

"What is it we're doing here, Mick?"

"I was as angry as you were, believe it or not. Maybe for different reasons. But when an innocent girl gets caught up in something like that..."

"Woman, Mick. She was a woman."

He shifted in the noisy chair, uncomfortable with Mickey's solicitude.

"I need to know how serious you are about avenging Marina."

"What is it you're not telling me?"

"I know that Antoinette woman was dead when you asked about her. I had to find out that part myself." His tone was aggrieved, as if Burton owed him something. "And that she was part of the heroin business at the school."

"So there was heroin at the school? Did you kill her?"

"I did not. But I don't know how to convince you of that. Especially since I have something inside to show you."

He stood up and cracked his back.

"Fucking bones. Cannot road-trip the way I used to."

"Can we quit fucking around and get this done?" Burton's anger flared. "Whatever it is?"

Mickey opened the heavy front door to the bungalow.

"Leave us go, MacDuff."

Trust Mickey to mangle the quote.

The floor layout inside was standard, reminding him of those Sears Roebuck kit houses popular in the thirties and forties. You sent away to the catalog and Sears delivered the components of the house of your dreams.

The two front rooms off the central hallway were square, the one to the left set up as a living room, with old slumped couches and stuffed chairs, a big screen TV. Video game controllers sat on a short-legged coffee table. Obviously a hangout for Mickey's guys, though Burton saw no empty beer bottles or fast-food wrappers. Or dust, even.

The den, back and to the right, contained an ergonomic chair in black wire and metal, pushed up to a glass-topped table, with a cable to connect a laptop to the large display, laid across the top. No pictures on the wall, nothing to personalize the space. He supposed this was another refuge for Mickey, far enough from Boston no one would know about it.

He heard a sound out ahead of them, a whimper like a sick dog. He followed Mickey toward the kitchen, the only room where the lights were on.

Lights so bright, in fact, he had to blink several times as they stepped into the kitchen. It wasn't only the lights but the scene before him that stung his eyes.

A blue plastic tarp was spread out on the floor and taped down around the perimeter with silver duct tape. More or less in the center of the tarp sat a solid-looking dining room chair. The man sitting in it had his right arm secured with more of the silver tape to the arm of the chair, though the fingers were free. A pair of Vise-Grips lay on the floor where someone had tossed them, rusty brown at the jaws. Scattered bits of bloody flesh and fingernail sparkled at the bound man's feet. The ends of three fingers were raw-red and oozing.

Burton's stomach lurched. He'd always assumed Mickey wouldn't put him in situations like this, where Mickey had done something so egregiously criminal that Burton would have to act. Mickey had shattered a norm. But why?

"Jesus, Mick."

Mickey held up his hands.

"I know you won't believe me, but we found him this way. You don't think I would do something like this, do you?" He sounded disappointed.

Burton's mouth puckered dry.

"You need to untie him right now, get this man some medical help." He pulled out his phone—no bars.

"Not yet, Burton. I want to know how pissed off you really are about Marina. Because this is the man who killed your girl."

Stunned, Burton took his first close look at the man bound to the chair. He was smallish, maybe five-six, a hundred and fifty, some of those pounds the belly pushing out against a once-pristine white shirt. His head drooped, chin on chest, so Burton could see the thinning black hair plastered across his skull, still in order after everything he'd been through.

Feeling Burton's scrutiny, he raised his head. Whoever worked him over hadn't touched his face.

"I did kill her." A faint lisp lingered in his words. "As you say."

Mickey backhanded him casually across the face.

"You killed nobody. You paid someone else to do it. You'd be the kind of boss who doesn't get his hands dirty."

Meaning Mickey was somehow superior? The man nodded.

"Of course, of course. I paid Antoinette to kill her. As you say. She was threatening my business."

Burton stared at Mickey, disgusted.

"This is Frank Vinson."

Mickey smirked.

"The original. Not too impressive, is he? Once he discovered what happens when you come into my city." He twisted Vinson's ear. "Come after the king, you better not miss."

Mickey was in a quoting mood.

"He did it, Burton. You heard him confess. He sent that Antoinette broad up here to set up his supply chain. Using my school. Your Marina walked into some things she shouldn't have."

Burton's rage rose. Mickey's story made a rough sort of sense, but where was the evidence? Frank Vinson, with someone pulling out his fingernails, would have copped to the Gardner heist. But as the American military had learned not long ago, torture didn't always get you accurate intelligence.

"Now what, Mickey?"

He was appalled by what Mickey had done and it bothered him he was showing him all this, making him an accessory. Mickey must have killed Antoinette, given the similarity in style here. What did that mean for what he wanted Burton to do?

Mickey reached under his Hawaiian shirt and pulled out a flat black automatic. Burton hadn't even noticed he was armed, though he should have assumed.

"Now we stop this thing in its tracks. And you get your revenge for Marina."

He shoved the mouth of the pistol against Vinson's forehead, denting the flesh. Vinson whimpered, the same sound Burton had heard from the front hall. Then Mickey swapped ends on the gun and offered it to Burton.

"Unless you'd care to have the pleasure yourself?"

48

I didn't recognize the man walking down the stairs, other than to note he didn't look like he was entering the bar with a drink in mind. He was tall and very thin, making me think of a praying mantis. I tensed as he walked directly to where I stood by the cash register.

Back in the bad old days, I kept a Little League bat under the bar, but I was glad it wasn't there to tempt me now. His face looked like he wanted to fight: someone, something, anything.

"You're Darrow?"

"Elder Darrow. What can I do for you?"

He brushed aside the pleasantries with the back of his hand.

"Where's Burton? I know he hangs here."

Even in the more civilized years of the Esposito, I never gave up the whereabouts of a patron. Wives could call looking for husbands, secretaries looking for bosses, I wouldn't give them up. I thought of it as a breach of the bartender's code.

"I know at least three people by that name. Did you have a particular one in mind?"

He squinted and put his hands flat on the bar, as if he were thinking of coming over. I slid my phone out on the shelf below the bar and tapped in a 9 and a 1.

"You do not want to fuck with me." His fists clenched at his sides.

"Which begs the question." I stuck my hand out. "As I said. I'm Elder Darrow, owner and operator. To whom am I talking?"

He did not take my hand or respond to the calmer tone, but pulled out a small leather case. He flapped his credentials at me in the quick negligent way I'd seen Burton do, as if someone might try and grab them.

"Liam MacDonald. I work with Burton. Daniel Burton, to be precise."

"Funny. I've never heard him mention you."

MacDonald flushed, as if his blood pressure had soared.

"I don't believe that's here or there."

At least he'd moderated his voice. My three solitary end-of-the-night drinkers went back to their deep thoughts. I had told MacDonald, in so many words, that I did know Burton.

"I need to speak with him. Urgently."

MacDonald was not easy to read, but he did not come across as someone who'd be on Burton's side. And hadn't Burton told me his boss assigned someone else to investigate Marina's murder? I shook my head.

"Saw him a little earlier." I gave him that much. "And he left."

"Drunk?"

"Absolutely not." I would have said that if Burton had walked out of here on his knees. MacDonald had the air of a cop who'd be happy to cause me trouble for overserving a customer.

I saw him will himself to relax. He put his hands in his pockets and took a breath. I read the next stage in his strategy.

"I suppose you'd like a drink?"

"I'm a scotch man." He scanned the bottles along the back bar. "Is that the Macallan 18 I see? Wouldn't have expected that here."

Was he making a point about the Esposito? Either way, he wasn't making a pal out of me. For all I knew, he'd researched my own taste in tipple.

I took the bottle down, dusted it, and poured him a standard shot, not a tenth of an ounce over, set a small glass of water on the side. Keith Jarrett was playing "Jasmine" and I felt a momentary grief that his stroke meant he'd likely never play in public again.

"That's twenty-seven dollars."

MacDonald held the glass under his nose, inhaling it like a lover's perfume.

"Lovely business." He looked at me. "Pretty steep price, however."

"Police rate."

I crossed my arms and stared until he reached for his wallet. The two twenties he offered me were crisp and new.

He went back to sipping the whiskey. It was an experience I could have described in more detail than anyone was interested in: the cool crisp bite on the front of the tongue, the burnt sugar, the heat down the back of the throat and into the body. Liquid well-being. He eyed me.

"If we've turned the temperature down?" Now he extended his hand. "My name is Liam MacDonald and I do work with Burton. And I do need to speak with him urgently. We're working on a case together."

"Marina Antonelli."

His eyebrow twitched.

"You knew Ms. Antonelli?"

He couldn't have done much research or talked to Burton much if he didn't know that. Which probably meant Burton wasn't cooperating with him.

"She was my night cook here. For several years."

Irritation, likely at Burton, brought his color back up. He segued into interrogation mode.

"Any signs of drug addiction when she worked for you?"

The question made me angry on her behalf.

"No. And it seems as if someone should have been asking questions like this a couple weeks ago."

MacDonald picked up his shot glass. His red face had returned and it wasn't the booze.

"Which would have happened, if someone had mentioned the connection."

He was definitely pissed at Burton, who must have been holding back information because he wanted to solve the case himself. I felt a bit of sympathy for MacDonald. Wouldn't two people on the case give a quicker result than one? Especially if one of them wasn't fueled by guilt and old love?

"Burton is not an easy guy to work with, or so I've heard."

"No shit. So do you know where he is or not?"

"Really. No."

He slipped the rest of the whiskey down his throat so fast he couldn't have tasted it, grabbed his change off the bar.

"Tell him to get in touch, when you see him. I have some information he wants to hear. Needs to hear."

And he was up the stairs and out of the bar before I realized the cheap bastard hadn't tipped me.

49

Burton stepped outside into the driveway, wondering if his phone would work any better. He told Mickey he wanted to think about his offer for a minute, but he needed the time to figure out whether to call local law enforcement or the Maine State Police, neither of which he had any contacts in.

As he stood there, a crack sounded inside the house, the sound of a big tree branch breaking, but muffled. He stiffened.

Mickey appeared on the porch, unscrewing something from the end of his pistol and Burton felt himself fall into despair. That had been Mickey executing the competition and taking a great leap across any boundary Burton had tried to maintain with him.

Mickey didn't hurry, but he moved with purpose, taking the flat holster off the back of his belt and storing the gun and holster in a steel toolbox in the 442's trunk.

He climbed into the front seat and turned on the engine, Burton still standing outside the car.

"I don't mind giving you a ride back," Mickey said. "But we probably don't want to stand around here all night."

Burton roiled. Assuming Mickey had just executed Vinson, what was he supposed to do? Ride in the passenger's seat back to Boston with a killer, a killer who could incriminate Burton with the fact of his presence? He had been fooling himself about who'd managed whom all this time, believing Mickey's protests that he was mainly a businessman. He'd been acting as if he could rub against the man without getting dirty himself.

Mickey revved the motor.

"Let's go."

"I'm driving," Burton said.

Mickey's piggy little eyes grew. He shook his head.

"It's not what you think, Daniel. I didn't shoot the fucker, though I have the perfect right. I scared him. Someone will come by in the morning and let him loose, put him on a plane back to the Big Easy."

"I'm driving," Burton said.

Mickey looked nervous, which thrilled Burton. A siren doo-wopped down in the business district, which seemed to convince Mickey. It was unlikely the police were responding here already.

"Fine." Mickey slid out the driver's seat and held the door open for Burton like a valet. "But let's get our asses out of here. It's getting late."

Burton slid onto the white leather, stepped on the clutch pedal, and dropped the Hurst shifter into reverse. As Mickey walked around toward the front of the car, Burton popped the clutch, reversed hard and fast out into the street, dropped the transmission into first, and screeched off down the pavement in the direction of the highway. His last glimpse of Mickey, open-mouthed in the rearview, made him want to smile.

He understood he'd escaped an attempt by Mickey to own him, and he wondered what had changed to make Mickey so desperate. The man was badly mistaken if he thought he could suborn Burton that way.

Before he made it to the highway, he stopped at a phone kiosk on Route 1A, maybe the last public phone in the Northeast, called the Kittery police, and reported gunshots at the address Mickey had taken them to. If Frank Vinson were dead in the house, the locals would probably have to call in the State Police anyway. They would be able to tie things back to Boston eventually, and if they didn't, Burton could help out, discreetly. He couldn't let on that he'd been there.

He hung up the phone and hustled back to the car, turned around so he could head back to Portsmouth Circle and pick up the highway south. It was full night now and when he hit 95, he hammered the gas pedal and flew the muscle car down the dark straight road like he was piloting a jet. The tires skimmed on a layer of air.

He was all done with Mickey now—should have been sooner, he realized. He'd been dancing along a very thin tightrope.

When he looked down and saw he was running over a hundred, he backed off, letting the car fall back until it was running along with the traffic. It would be a whole lot easier if no sign of his presence in Maine tonight ever appeared. A ticket, even one he slipped by waving his badge, would be dangerous.

He thought about leaving Mickey's car with the keys in it in a dark industrial area near Mattapan Square, where it would be stripped or stolen within hours.

Instead, he parked it in front of the Bunker Hill Market in Charlestown, put up the top, and tucked the keys up under the visor. No one in this part of town would not know whose vehicle it was, and Burton didn't want to trivialize the rift Mickey had just ripped between them. Trashing the car might make Mickey think Burton was just irked—he needed to understand that he had blown up whatever understanding they'd ever had between them.

He climbed into a cab at the taxi stand, knowing the driver probably knew Mickey, even if he didn't work for him.

"You look familiar," the cabbie said. "You live around here?"

Burton gave him the address of his apartment building and sat back to think.

Frank Vinson trying to come into Boston was a sign of something Burton had been thinking about for a while. Local control of criminal activities was weakening in a lot of cities. Like the global economy, crime had become less about neighborhoods and allegiances and more about the opportunities everywhere, regardless of geography. Easy travel, the internet, and law enforcement focus on the political all supported that. The realization may have threatened Mickey, made him understand his days as the ruler of a small discrete kingdom might be numbered. All the borders were porous now.

It was a short ride. Burton only had a twenty.

"Sorry. Don't carry change." The driver mumbled and took off when Burton hit the sidewalk. Maybe Burton hadn't looked that familiar.

He climbed the stairs to his apartment. Mickey had a great deal invested in Frank Vinson as the source of his troubles. Especially if Mickey had, as Burton believed after tonight's show, killed Antoinette Bordaine.

He wasn't buying Vinson as Marina's murderer. Taped up and tortured, he would have said anything to stop the pain. Mickey had been working a little too hard to sell that version of what happened. But did that mean Mickey had killed Marina?

He locked the apartment door behind him, uncapped a beer from the refrigerator. He didn't want to believe it, but why else would Mickey be trying so hard to sell Vinson as the killer?

It was too late to talk to Elder tonight. Tomorrow, maybe. He swallowed some beer. He was starting to feel like he was too close to the forest to see any trees.

50

I locked the street door and finished up the rest of my chores, cleaning off and wiping down the tables, restocking the supplies behind the bar, running one last load of glasses through the dishwasher, when I realized I wasn't hearing anything from the kitchen.

Mildly irked—if she was finished, why wasn't Syndi out here helping me?—I stepped back into the kitchen to find it deserted. The counters and cutting boards were clean, all the other surfaces shining, and the appliances were turned off, including the little radio she'd brought in to listen to seventies' rock.

"Syndi?"

A whiff of cigarette smoke made me sniff. She must be outside the back door, grabbing a smoke while I was cleaning up. Time to exercise a little managerial muscle.

I stalked down the corridor toward the fire door, which was propped open with a brick. I pushed at it, but something on the other side was blocking it. I had to shove hard to make enough room that I could slip out between the steel door and the jamb.

The yellow bulb in the cage above the door only lit a small circle of the alley, but it was enough to see Syndi's body, slumped on her side where the door had pushed her over. Her eyes were wide open but not seeing and she was very still. Her lips were a grayish blue.

My heart thundered. I pressed my fingers into the side of her neck, which was very hot, and saw a dot of blood inside her right elbow. Her pulse was fast and irregular.

I ran back inside. I used to keep a serious first aid kit, back when the Esposito was a rougher place, a box with more than bandages and iodine.

I fumbled it off the high shelf in my office and pulled out what looked like an Epi-pen, the needle you carried if you were allergic to bee stings. It was so old, I didn't know if it would still work, but it was all I had. EMTs would never get here in time.

I ran back down the hall, stripping off the outer wrapping and twisting off the protective cap. Back in the alley, I knelt and jabbed the naloxone needle down into the outside of her thigh, pressed the plunger. And waited, my heart skittering in my chest and my head light, as if there wasn't enough oxygen in the air. Burton had told me about her addiction, that she'd been sober a year. What had caused her to slip?

The naloxone, if it worked, was supposed to bring someone back from an overdose fast, but I hadn't known how fast. Less than a minute and a half later, Syndi's eyes opened, blinked a coupled of times as if the lids were sticky.

"Syndi."

"What."

A whoosh of air left me as I realized she would live. I picked up what looked like a vape pen cartridge and smelled it—sweet.

She pushed herself into a sitting position against the bricks, leaned to the right, and vomited into the alley, the spasms making her cry out, as if her stomach muscles hurt.

I stood up now, allowing my anger and sadness to push out the fear. I thought I knew something about addiction, but this was much worse, much deeper.

I extended a hand and helped her to her feet. She was still groggy, in the aftermath, but I was surprised all over again by how quickly she'd come back. I didn't understand the pressure against doctors and EMTs having naloxone available, unless it was some Puritan punitive reasoning.

She wobbled, put her hand on the wall, pasted on a sickly smile. "I guess I owe you that one. That was as close as I ever came."

My empathy yielded to anger. This was the kind of crap I'd

spent years working out of the Esposito. Addicts shooting up in the alley had never been part of the business plan.

"What happened?" I said. "Something must have triggered this."

A sad and haunted look passed over her face. She nodded, and her voice was small and helpless.

"I know you're not going to believe this."

"Burton said you were doing so well."

I brought her inside and pulled the fire door closed, followed her to the door of the washroom. She wet a handful of paper towels and cleaned her face, swished water in her mouth and spit it out.

When she turned back, she was pale as paper, a blue vein showing high on her temple.

"I didn't shoot myself up."

I shook my head. Here was the one similarity between our addictions—denial. It was common as air.

"Syndi. Come on."

"No. I went out back to grab a smoke. Then I was going to come in and help you close up. Someone sprayed something up my nose and I went out, in like two seconds. The rest? I don't remember a thing."

It was a pretty elaborate story to use to relieve herself of responsibility. If she'd been attending NA meetings, she knew that kind of thinking wouldn't help her stay clean.

"Look." She held out her wrists.

The blood had dried inside her elbow, but a ring of bruising was coming up on the pale skin around her wrists. As if someone had grabbed that arm.

"Why would someone want to do that to you?" I said.

The aftereffects of the drug and the antidote shuddered her thin body.

"I don't know. But it was really fucking cruel."

I didn't know whether to believe her, though I was leaning in that direction. Burton's bullshit detector was better than mine.

"I'm calling my friend Dan. He needs to hear your story."

"The cop. All right." She shrugged, resigned to my not believing her. "But here."

She reached into her pants pocket and pressed something into my palm.

"Take this. I can't have it any more."

I looked at the cold metal coin in my hand, a pink sobriety marker. And then I started to believe her.

51

Burton arrived at the Esposito just after the EMTs and parked behind their truck, which was too wide for the alley alongside the building. He ducked to his right as the two medics wheeled a gurney down the bumpy surface. Syndi's pale white face, eyes closed, showed above the blanket. He continued down the alley until he rounded the corner.

Elder sat on an upturned plastic bucket, staring into the night. Medical debris, a single purple nitrile glove, the wrappings from a naloxone syringe, were scattered on the ground.

"She live?" Burton said.

Elder nodded.

"I thought she was coming out of it. I gave her the jab and she was up on her feet and talking. She went out again as the EMTs got here. It was easier to get her out the back door."

He lifted his chin. Burton felt sympathy for him. It was another try on Elder's part to give a break to someone who needed it, then have the effort tossed back in his face. First that Isaac kid, now Syndi.

"Why don't we go inside?" he said. "She's in as good a set of hands as she's going to be."

Dull-eyed, Elder stood and picked up the bucket. He nudged the brick out of the door and pulled the door closed once they were inside.

"Tell me." Burton followed him up the hall into the bar.

Elder flicked on a couple lights and took up his usual place behind the bar.

"Drink?"

Burton took a stool, thinking Elder could use something to do with his hands.

"Sure."

He was feeling the exhaustion of everything he'd done tonight, the drive to Maine and back, the adrenaline dump of dealing with Mickey and his Frank Vinson fantasy, the lateness of the hours. He wasn't sure why Elder had called him, other than to complain about Syndi screwing him over.

"You can't be too surprised," he said, as Elder set a foaming rocks glass in front of him. He would have preferred a beer at this time of night, but he picked it up anyway. "Once a junkie…"

Elder was more distraught than he ought to be. Burton waited for him to spit out what was bothering him.

"She says someone else injected her."

"With heroin?" He snorted. "No surprise there. Junkies aren't known for owning up to their shit."

Elder nodded, pulled down a bottle from the premium shelf, poured himself a hefty measure in a tumbler. Was that bourbon? That was new.

"I believe her."

"And how did this mythical someone accomplish this feat? While she was working in your kitchen?"

He hated to see her buffalo Elder. The simplest story—a junkie had relapsed—was almost always the correct one.

"She went out into the alley for a smoke. She thinks someone knocked her out somehow. Some kind of spray, not a punch. Then shot her up."

Burton pulled out his phone.

"Easy enough for them to check. I'll have the docs do a tox screen for anything besides heroin."

But he was doing it for Elder more than because he believed Syndi.

Elder knocked back half of his drink. Burton hoped that didn't mean he was heading off on a toot. It had been more than a year since his last lapse. He didn't think the one-drink-a-night regimen included an eight-ounce glass. And what was the deal with bourbon, for a guy who'd always been a scotch drinker? But he kept his mouth shut. He wouldn't have tolerated Elder commenting on his drinking habits. None of his business.

"And I also remembered something you told me about Marina. How you knew she hadn't injected herself."

"Because I knew she wouldn't do that."

"Beyond that. The awkwardness. How she would have had to inject the dope with her off hand."

"So?"

"Syndi's right-handed." Elder looked into the darkness, validating his memory. "The needle stick was inside her right elbow."

Burton felt a tiny thrill.

"Any bruises?"

"Around the wrist. Like someone grabbed her."

"But she survived." Burton's job was to find the weaknesses in a theory.

"Pure luck. That I had naloxone."

It was believable, just. The similarities to Marina's death were enough. But why would someone want to kill the cook in a neighborhood bar? Who also happened to be related to Boston's chief gangster?

He sipped his drink, hoping it would help him think.

"Nothing happened in the bar recently? You didn't tick anyone off with your bar-side manner?"

Elder shook his head.

"It has to have something to do with her uncle, right? Nothing else odd has happened."

Burton had come to the same conclusion sooner, though he knew things Elder didn't: Frank Vinson's attempt to get into the drug trade in Boston, Mickey's torturing the man up in Maine, maybe killing him.

"Almost certainly."

Their contemplation of what to do next was interrupted by a pounding on the street door. Someone out on Mercy Street yelled.

"Closed!" Elder shouted back. "Idiots."

The pounding and shouting continued. Burton jogged up the stairs, opened the door a couple inches, and yelled himself.

"Hey! What do you want?"

"Burton? Is that you? Where is she?" Mickey pushed his way inside. "I swear to God, I'm going to kill somebody."

52

Mickey shoved past Burton and careened down the stairs so fast I was afraid he'd trip and fall and split his head open. What kind of trouble would I be in then, the owner of the bar where Mickey Barksdale suffered a concussion?

Since Burton was there, I didn't start to worry until Mickey came around the bar and stepped right up into my face. I grabbed my whiskey glass, feeling as if I were facing off a rabid giant bat with a fly swatter. His breath was horrid, as if he'd been chewing garlic cloves marinated in nicotine. I put a hand up and he grabbed my wrist and started to twist. I wound up with the heavy tumbler, ready to plant it in his teeth.

"Michael!"

Burton's voice boomed. He banged his closed fist on the bar. I was shocked and relieved to see the pistol in his other hand. I set the glass down on the bar very carefully and shook my arm free.

"Mr. Darrow is not the source of your problem."

I'd never known the details of their relationship, but had the distinct feeling it had changed radically, and recently. Mickey was compliant, almost meek.

"Sorry," he said, shocking me further. An apology from Mickey Barksdale?

He walked back outside the bar and slumped on a stool. I tried to catch hold of my galloping heart rate, my lightheadedness.

Burton put his gun away and raised his eyebrows. I nodded. I'd be fine.

"Let me buy you all a drink," Mickey said.

After his display of ire, I wasn't going to remind him legal drinking hours were over.

"What'll it be?"

His face crinkled, as if I'd asked a hard question. He looked like he wanted to cry, or explode again.

"Gin and ginger ale." He turned to Burton. "She's all right?"

Burton sipped his drink, placid. I mixed Mickey's concoction and served it to him without making a face at the combination. I thought about turning on some music and decided it didn't matter.

Burton pointed at me.

"You owe Mr. Darrow an apology. Your daughter would have died in that alley if he hadn't responded so quickly."

And happened to have naloxone handy.

Mickey looked suitably chastised. The dynamic between him and Burton made me curious.

"Wait. His daughter?"

Burton nodded. Mickey took a long suck of his drink through the straw.

"Not from your marriage, though," Burton said. "I have that right?"

Mickey Barksdale, a married man? Wait. Of course he was. In his world, a forty-something bachelor would be suspect.

Mickey's face twisted, either from worry about Syndi or pain at the intimate knowledge Burton had. And that I had now, too. He nodded.

"Neither one of you has a kid, am I right?" He didn't wait for a reply. "You have no idea how hard it is, especially when they fuck up in ways you can't control."

"Heroin," Burton said. "She's the reason you never wanted that kind of trade?"

Mickey stared into the mirror behind the bar.

"Partly. And partly because, well, you know, I've been trying to straighten out the businesses a little. Make myself less vulnerable."

Burton had told me this, that Mickey longed to be at least semi-legitimate.

Mickey slurped some more of his drink, slumped like a teenager at a Brigham's soda fountain. A dangerous teenager. His face hardened when he spoke to Burton.

"You should have killed him, you know."

A bar of ice replaced my backbone. Burton shook his head, but he knew what Mickey was talking about.

"I don't deal with things that way. You ought to know that by now."

"Twenty-odd years I've been dealing with her shit." Mickey focused on me. "I owe you one. She was alive when she left here?"

I nodded, not trusting the thickness in my throat not to squeak my words. Out of nowhere, I heard what Susan had accused me of, that I liked brushing up against criminal doings. Wrong. The ice had spread into my gut. I was only upright because I was leaning on the bar, and I could think of a thousand places I'd rather be.

"She was alive, Mickey. She told me someone else did it to her. Held her down and shot her up."

Anger rose into his face like a tide. He gripped his glass and faced Burton.

"Like I said. If you'd taken care of Vinson…"

Now I was confused. Frank Vinson was involved in this?

Burton looked at Mickey, almost sympathetically.

"If I'd taken care of him, you would have owned me. Wasn't that the plan? And besides, I heard you shoot him yourself."

"I shot into the wall, to scare him, keep him there thinking until my guy cut him loose. I can deal with him without having to take him out. What I don't understand is how he got down here so fast."

"Mickey. You had the man taped to a chair. He didn't teleport himself down 95 to do this."

"I got here that fast, didn't I?" Mickey sucked on the straw and the ice cubes rattled. "Besides, he must have people here. All he had to do was make a call."

He was winding himself into a rage again.

"I am going to kill that fucker. I should have done it when I had the chance."

Burton nodded. He seemed relieved about something.

"And if you do? I'm going to come at you with everything I have."

This felt like more of the change I'd sensed, as if some boundary between them had hardened and left them unequivocally on opposite sides.

Mickey's silence was menacing. Then:

"You think that worries me?" He stood up. "Come after me whenever you like. Just don't miss. Right now, I'm going to see my daughter."

He started for the stairs at a quick walk. As the street door sighed shut behind him, I looked at Burton.

"You mind explaining all that to me? Because I definitely feel like I'm behind the eight ball."

53

Burton slept poorly, a combination of too much adrenaline burn from the trip to Maine with Mickey, then Elder calling him out. He couldn't do anything about Syndi, but he was glad he'd been there in the bar when Mickey came roaring in to accuse Elder. Mickey was a volatile son of a bitch at the best of times, and probably worse when his daughter was in jeopardy. And despite Mickey's certainty, Burton doubted Frank Vinson was a viable suspect for Marina's murder.

He was still foggy the next morning when he looked up from the mileage report he was filling out and saw Liam MacDonald and Francesca Gatoberri standing in the opening to his cubicle, both of them grinning like lottery winners. It was either his age or the day's deep fatigue, but he felt like he hadn't known that gleeful anticipation they were giving off in years.

"What?"

Francesca's smile got wider. He noticed how close she stood to MacDonald. One more reason to hate the guy.

"Throwing a party?"

MacDonald waved a folded paper.

"Just got the warrant to take apart the Blue Sash. Francesca finally connected up enough dots."

She looked irked, as if MacDonald was implying she hadn't worked fast enough.

"What do I care about money laundering and fraud?" Burton said.

Francesca looked disappointed. MacDonald shrugged and started to turn away.

"OK. Don't say I didn't try."

"Wait. If she's looking into fraud, why are you going along?"

MacDonald tapped his temple. "Got me a suspicion," he said. "That we might find some evidence of something other than financial scamming going on over there. You remember the two overdoses before Ms. Antonelli? On top of what happened last night?"

Burton was startled he would know about Syndi's overdose. MacDonald grinned some more.

"You think you're the only cop in Boston who works after hours? Syndi was connected to the school, too."

Francesca interrupted MacDonald's declamation.

"The warrant is for financial documents, computers, records. But who knows what might show up in them?"

The quirk in her smile, a warmth directed at him, told him she didn't want to deal with MacDonald by herself. Burton pushed himself up out of his chair.

"Let me get my gun," he said, nodding at her.

54

Later that morning, I unlocked the Esposito's door, still ghosted with the graffitied letters, and walked down the stairs. Mr. Giaccobi's coffee shop had been tagged the other night, and he thought he knew who the responsible punks were. He'd been in the neighborhood long enough that I could leave the solution to him.

The air inside was cool, but tasted stale. I didn't bother turning on the grill and the fryer. Syndi might be in the hospital for another day and it didn't make sense to bring in a temp until I knew when, or if, she was coming back. I laid her pink sobriety coin on the back bar where I could see it.

Assuming all this happened as she claimed, why? And why here? The heroin drew a connection back to the cooking school, but she hadn't been in any position to do damage to the Blue Sash or its reputation. And I doubted she had any idea who'd killed Marina or she would have told Burton.

I wondered if it could have been a veiled threat toward Mickey. I hadn't known she was his daughter, but that didn't mean it wasn't common knowledge among the local criminal class. It might be as simple as that, Frank Vinson or one of Mickey's competitors trying to send him a message.

I shook my head. Life around the Esposito had been interesting for long enough. Burton would eventually figure out who'd killed Marina and why, but I wasn't feeling the need for closure. Instead, I was totaling up my losses, including Susan. If I kept on involving myself in situations like this, I could lose even more.

My confrontation with the enraged Mickey last night had firmed up my sense I didn't belong near his world, or Burton's.

I started a fresh pot of coffee and opened the *Globe* on the bar top. The sports section was all the excitement I needed today.

55

"You guys understand we can't just go inside and start banging around looking for things, right? The warrant is very specific."

Francesca must have been reading his mood, his excitement at the prospect of finding some answers, not to mention the prospect of action after a couple weeks of fiddling around.

MacDonald felt it, too. He sat in the back seat of Burton's unmarked, his leg juddering as they drove to meet the officers Francesca had dispatched.

"Plain-view," MacDonald said, catching Burton's eye. "Who knows what we might see in plain sight?"

Burton nodded. Maybe he'd underestimated MacDonald's commitment to the job, though if Liam thought they were going to find out who'd killed Marina, he hadn't shared that yet.

"I'm serious, you guys. This could mean my job."

She was sitting in the passenger's seat, her window cracked at the top. Burton knew he wasn't supposed to think this way, but she smelled wonderful.

"Nobody wants this to turn into a shoot-em-up," he said.

Burton pulled in behind the marked BPD van and looked at MacDonald in the rearview mirror. MacDonald reached his hand to where his weapon rode.

* * *

"My lead," Francesca said on the sidewalk in front of the Blue Sash. "Seriously."

Both of the Homicide cops nodded. She walked off to organize the entry team.

"You want Pierre or Batarrh?" Burton asked.

He accepted that while he'd been following Mickey's lead and obsession with Frank Vinson, MacDonald had developed a much more likely theory, that Marina had uncovered some criminal scam at the school and was killed to prevent her from telling Burton. It remained to be seen whether Mickey knew anything, but the fact was they had no evidence, only supposition.

"Batarrh's more likely to be the one," MacDonald said. "His Interpol sheet came back with a hundred different varieties of nasty. Even for a city like Marseille, he was a tough. I'll take him, you take Pierre."

Burton wondered if MacDonald also thought Batarrh would be too much for Burton, if he put up resistance. MacDonald was younger and fitter, but more importantly, he'd earned the bust. Burton would have cherished an unguarded minute or two with Marina's killer, though.

"You wearing your vest?"

Liam grinned, a familiar gleam.

"Why, Daniel. Didn't know you cared."

"Go fuck yourself, then." Burton's righteous anger built, fueling his energy. "Shall we do this?"

Francesca rejoined them at the front door of the school, looked at them like she could read their tiny minds.

"Guys. Don't screw up my case. I need you to follow, for once. Not lead."

Burton followed MacDonald, Francesca, and the clutch of uniforms she'd brought to do any heavy lifting through the wide double doors, which were painted a bright cobalt blue.

Francesca led her posse to the reception desk, waving the search warrant in front of a woman in a teal chef's jacket behind the telephone console. MacDonald and Burton peeled off to the left down a long corridor that led to the administrative wing.

Through the open doors to the office suites, the floors were carpeted, the lighting soft, the art on the walls more sophisticated than pictures of vegetables. Handily, the office doors were tagged with plastic nameplates colored to look like brass. Or gold.

"Liam."

Burton pointed to the first door on the right.

"Your man. Let's get the two of them wrapped up before they destroy anything Francesca needs. Or jump out a window."

MacDonald drew his weapon and put his hand on the knob. Burton regretted one more time that he couldn't make that particular arrest himself, but MacDonald had done the work.

Footsteps behind him said Francesca and her troops were catching up.

"Go."

"Burton!" she called.

He continued down the hall to Pierre Macaron's office. Pierre was too much of a wimp to be anything but Mickey's chief lieutenant in the money laundering, but if the front desk had had time to warn him, he was probably shredding papers as fast as he could.

Burton pulled his pistol and pushed the door open with his other hand. The office was as he remembered it, spacious, well-lit, CEO-quality furniture. The laptop connected to a huge separate display would have run thousands of dollars.

The office was empty. Burton cleared the space under the solid-front desk, the coat closet, the en suite bathroom with shower and a bidet. Apparently, Pierre did think of himself as a Frenchman.

Francesca crowded into the doorway as Burton looked more closely at the carpeting in the floor of the coat closet. Whitish powder was ground into the fiber and indentations showed where the feet of two heavy suitcases or duffels had sat.

"He isn't here." Disappointment weighed his words down. "And it looks like he might have been the source of the dope."

Francesca looked relieved, as if she'd been expecting him to do something rash if he laid hands on Pierre.

"The file cabinets first," she instructed the two beefy cops with her. "Then the computer. If it's password-protected, don't fuck with it. That's what we have Tech Services for."

Another uniform, a forty-ish sergeant who looked as if he couldn't pick up a box of cotton balls without straining himself, ignored her and walked to the computer. Knocking his leg against the desk more or less inadvertently, he saw the screen illuminate, then frowned.

"The fuck does this have to do with anything?"

Before Francesca could tear the cop a new one for disobeying her, Burton stepped over to the desk. A set of Google directions and a map displayed on the screen, the destination an address Burton was very familiar with, on Mercy Street in the South End.

"Shit." He holstered his weapon and started for the door. "You've got this, right?"

"Always did, Burton." She sounded irked.

He felt she was relieved to see him go. As he stepped out into the corridor and started for the exits, a shot exploded behind Edouard Batarrh's office door. He hesitated, then kept going. MacDonald could take care of himself, and if not, there were plenty of other cops around to help.

He bolted past the curious faces mobbed in the foyer and jumped into the unmarked sedan. The tires left a film of rubber on the street as he pulled away, headed for the Esposito.

56

I called over to Mass General, and after an inordinate amount of backing and forthing with one of the charge nurses, obtained the information that Syndi was resting without significant aftereffects, and would likely be released tomorrow. That relieved me. I'd done the right thing not to throw that old first-aid kit away, and I'd have to see if I could replenish the naloxone over the counter. I didn't intend to be around anyone's overdose again, but I was happy to be prepared.

I finished the paper and climbed the stairs to unlock the front door. The picture of Bobby Orr flying across the goal mouth in the old Garden was off-kilter a little and I straightened it as I went by.

My first customer of the day was, well, bland, as Caucasian as Velveeta, with watery blue eyes and a thick sweep of silver hair. He didn't look like the degenerate type of drinker who needs one to start the day, but I knew better than to assume.

I followed him down the stairs and took the last few chairs down off the table by the stage.

"Good morning," I said as I walked over toward the bar.

He'd stopped next to it, near the opening by the kitchen, his hands in the pockets of his linen jacket pulling the material out of shape. In the undimmed morning lights, the sweat glistened on his forehead.

"What can I get you?"

As I passed him to walk in behind the bar and serve him, I felt a hard pinprick in the meat of my shoulder. I grabbed onto the bar to catch myself, but my knees unlocked almost immediately and I was falling, face first onto the hard wooden duck boards. The last thing I remembered was Grant Green picking his way through the coda to Wes Montgomery's "Road Song."

57

For the first time in his life, Burton understood the expression "heart in the mouth." As he bucked the unmarked sedan through the sluggish midday traffic, his chest felt too small to contain him, his heart, and his worry. He sometimes forgot Elder was an amateur, despite his tendency to get involved. He had no business being threatened with death or injury solely because he knew a Boston police detective.

He double-parked next to a straight-body truck delivering tonic to the little convenience store up the block. The driver, pushing a two-wheeler stacked with cardboard cases up the sidewalk, started to complain.

"Police business," Burton yelled, and belted for the Esposito's open door.

He paused at the top of the stairs, preparing himself for whatever he was walking into. The lights were all the way up and behind the bar, in shadow, he saw the bulk of a body lying on the floor. He drew his weapon.

"Fuck."

Pistol leading, he started down the stairs, keeping his feet to the wall side where they made less noise. The sound system was playing some of that loopy, lazy jazz guitar Elder liked so much. Wes Montgomery, maybe. But was that voices he heard underneath the notes? Vocals?

He crossed the floor to the opening that led behind the bar and into the back of the house, and relaxed. The body lying on its stomach on the boards wore orange Crocs, which ruled out Elder.

The least formal footwear he'd ever seen his friend wear behind the stick was a pair of black athletic shoes.

The body showed no wounds or signs of blood. Burton prodded it with a toe in the rib cage, provoking a groan and a wet cough. The person's arms were caught underneath his body. Burton knelt and rolled him over.

Pierre Macaron's wrists were strapped together in front of him with thick clumsy wraps of duct tape. An egg with a tracery of blown capillaries protruded from his forehead. As he opened his eyes, Burton saw the left pupil blown so big it occupied most of the visible orb. Chef Macaron was the proud owner of a king-hell concussion.

"You are under arrest." Burton holstered his pistol, but left off the handcuffs for now.

Maybe he'd underestimated Elder, if he'd disabled the man and trussed him up like that. He'd been getting the feeling Elder was pulling away a little lately, unwilling to be involved in some of the things he'd been happy to do in the past.

He turned off the sound system and then he did hear the voices, which went silent as soon as the music did. He reacquired his weapon and stepped into the kitchen.

"Mr. Daniel Burton, ladies and gentlemen!" Mickey stepped out of the door to Elder's office down at the end of the hall, jazzed about something.

"What in the actual fuck are you doing here?" Burton said.

Mickey eyed the pistol, then spread his hands widely, as if Burton had just praised him. He was carrying a cosh looped around his wrist, the old-school leather-and-birdshot sap that used to be standard equipment for street cops. Burton nodded at it.

"Going headhunting?"

"In the nicest possible way. You just walked past my latest creation."

"You must have whacked him pretty hard."

Mickey's face darkened.

"Why don't you come inside here and catch up on the story before you start pissing down my leg?"

He stepped back into the office. Burton followed, his throat tightening at the thought of what he might see.

Elder sprawled in his office chair, feet raised on a red plastic milk crate from Hood's. His eyes were bloodshot and bleary and his shoulders slack, but he was alive. Burton felt a grand charge of gratitude. Then he saw the tan boxes on the desk, the wrappings, the discarded syringe.

"Jesus Christ."

Elder's smile was weak and weary.

"He wasn't helping much. Almost turned me into another kind of addict."

"Yeah. A dead one," Mickey said.

Mickey would never not claim credit for what he'd done, especially if it bought him favor from his third-grade classmate. But Burton had learned his lesson—Mickey had taken things too far this time for Burton to protect him.

"Somebody want to tell me what happened here? Without all the who-shot-John?"

Mickey looked at Elder. Elder nodded easily at him. Burton remembered how having your life saved could make a bond with someone, even someone as evil as Mickey. He remembered a time at the ballfield over by the Charlestown Navy Yard where Mickey had saved him once.

"You tell it," Elder said.

Mickey shook himself down, like a fat little bird settling his feathers.

"I went to the hospital to visit Syndi this morning."

"Mickey. I don't need the Old Testament version." He still didn't know why Pierre Macaron would have come after Elder.

Mickey glared. He would tell it his own way, or not at all.

"Look. Your pal here? Having that naxo stuff saved my daughter's life."

Elder smiled dreamily, limp and drained.

"Syndi had this idea, I should replace what he used on her. In case it ever happened again." He looked flustered. "Not for her. Just in general."

He addressed Elder directly.

"I know you think you made the place too fancy to worry about shit like that. But it's gotten fashionable again. You want to watch out."

"So this is a coincidence?" Burton said. "You just happened to walk in at the exact moment you could save Mr. Darrow's life."

Mickey looked irked again, as if Burton were accusing him.

"What's the matter? You should approve of the outcome."

A politician's answer, if there ever was one. Burton doubted he would get anything more honest. But there was the fact that Elder was alive to be grateful for. And he now had Marina's murderer in custody.

"Hey!" A flat, angry voice shouted from out front in the bar. "Someone going to move that fucking shit box? I got deliveries to make."

Mickey pointed the sap at Burton and chuckled.

"I don't know, pal," he called back. "Maybe you ought to call a cop."

58

By Sunday afternoon, I was still feeling the aftermath of the overdose and rescue, not the least of which was that tiny interval of beautiful, easeful consciousness of the heroin's effect, in the moment before the naloxone brought me back. But even though I was logy, a little slow, it felt like the right day to open up the place, mark the end of the craziness, and say goodbye to Marina.

Ironically enough, the only person I couldn't invite was the man who'd saved my life. Too many cops in the house for Mickey.

Burton found a rare snapshot of Marina with a smile and set it up on one end of the bar next to a glass bowl of white roses. I hadn't known they were her favorite flower, which felt like a failure of my friendship with her. We spoke a few words, shared a couple memories, but Burton and I were the only people in the place who'd known her well, so we kept the program, such as it was, short and sweet.

I changed the music from the salsa she'd loved to a lighter jazzier set more suitable for a Sunday afternoon at the end of summer. Burton, Liam MacDonald, and a gorgeous female cop Burton only introduced as Francesca sat at a four-top near the stage. I watched them, amused, as they jockeyed to see who got to sit with their back to the wall.

I gathered Francesca had something to do with what happened at the Blue Sash, but not the heroin ring run by Mickey's lieutenant. The details weren't all clear, and no one had bothered to explain in depth. Right now, Burton seemed more interested in hanging out with his cop buddies.

He told me that the cooking school had been operating as a money laundry for Mickey. Pierre Macaron had panicked when Marina started asking questions about the extra "scholarship" money. Fearing that word of his side gig as a heroin distributor would get back to Mickey, he'd injected her with an overdose, though she'd known nothing about the heroin. He came after Syndi because he thought Marina had confided in her, and he'd come after me because Syndi might have told me and I could tell Burton. His bravado in running a heroin business under Mickey's nose evaporated at the first sign of threat.

If he hadn't panicked, none of this would have happened. And he had more to worry about, I suspected, than the grinding of the legal system. Mickey would be able to reach inside the jail system, if he wanted to.

Syndi emerged from the kitchen and stood next to me. She'd put on some weight in the last week and her skin color was healthier.

"I know I told you before," she said, "but thanks for believing me. Not canning me. Lot of bosses would have just let the problem go."

I still wasn't sure Mickey hadn't had an ulterior motive, sending his daughter to work here, but I wasn't doing anything worth his keeping track of. Not any more.

"Not your fault, Syndi. Macaron thought Marina might have talked to you. That made you a threat."

"Even so."

I watched the three cops converse, animated and celebratory, and felt slightly sad, a sense of loss. I wasn't going to get involved with Burton's escapades any more. The price was too high. Not to mention the fact I wasn't terribly helpful anyway—my involvement was on the order of bumbling around until I ran into something, or standing in one place until something ran into me. I'd lost too much, the bar at least once, and the love of a woman I'd expected to spend a long time with.

I viewed the floor with a certain sadness, as if something had changed radically. I was out of the sleuthing business, at which I'd been, at best, the rankest of amateurs.

MacDonald got up to leave. I got the sense he'd only come as a courtesy to Burton. I hoped Burton and I would stay friends after my decision, but I could see how much easier he found it to relax among people who shared his work and his view of the world.

"I'm glad you're here," I said. "It's time we got this place back on its feet in a proper fashion. And you're going to be a part of that."

Syndi turned her head, not before I saw her eyes tear up.

I reached to the back bar, picked up the sobriety coin, and handed it to her.

"Hold onto this," I said. "I know you'll earn it."

59

Burton curtailed his alcohol intake, now that MacDonald had left him with Francesca. They'd hashed out what remained of the cooking-school caper, as she was calling it, and decided Edouard Batarrh would have been a better choice to run the money laundering for Mickey than Pierre. His reputation was as muscle and oversight, but apparently he'd only worked for the school as a pastry chef, trying to refocus his career choices. They both agreed he wouldn't have panicked and killed anyone, however. And he denied all culpability in torturing and killing Antoinette, despite the bullet MacDonald had had to put in his leg.

"Swear to God," Burton said. "It isn't that I enjoy these Alfred Hitchcock deals. Though they do offer a change from the morons and junkies shooting each other."

Francesca rotated the rocks glass in her long hands. She was a bourbon drinker, though not much of a heavy hitter. She was only on her second, although to be fair, it was two o'clock on a Sunday afternoon.

"You think this Frank Vinson character will make another run at Mickey?"

Burton snorted.

"Turns out that was Mickey's paranoia talking."

He'd gotten a short note, purporting to be from Vinson, that thanked him for not shooting him when he had the chance, and explaining his presence in Boston as "an affair of the heart."

"I'm not certain," he said. "But I think Vinson was chasing a woman."

"The thing I like about the Fraud Squad," she said. "It doesn't get all that bloody. My cases are complicated, but mostly people aren't getting killed or beaten up."

"Sounds boring," he joked.

He was thinking her bright looks, the way she was listening and leaning in to him meant she was flirting with him again. He glanced at the photo of Marina and felt no guilt. She had been leaving him for a good long time before he'd left her.

She swirled the remaining whiskey over the melted ice.

"I wouldn't mind working together again, Daniel. If the opportunity arises."

Definitely flirting.

"It usually means someone's dead."

"You take requests?"

He laughed, though she might have been half-serious. It was an interesting question.

"I'm putting together a team for a project," she said. "I could use an investigator with a certain, shall we say, independence of spirit."

So. Professionally flirting, then? Or not at all. But he wouldn't say no to hanging around with her some more.

"If the bureaucracy allows," he said. "I'd be up for it."

"Oh, it will." She finished her drink. "Mickey Barksdale never caught on that Macaron was abusing the money laundry for his own ends. To run his heroin business."

Mickey? Hell. Was she planning to go after Mickey?

"You might be an even bigger help on this one than you know," she said.

Her look was level and serious, as if she could read what he was thinking. And she already knew that when she took the Blue Sash books apart she was going to find some kind of fraud. The expression on her face was as much a challenge as an opportunity.

"So," she said. "You in?"

He smiled, seeing a chance to resolve his own issues with Mickey and maybe do some other good. For one thing, Antoinette Bordaine's death was still open.

"Absolutely," he said. "When do we start?"